SHERLOCK HOLMES
The Stuff of Nightmares

SHERLOCK HOLMES

The Stuff of Nightmares

JAMES LOVEGROVE

TITAN BOOKS

Sherlock Holmes: The Stuff of Nightmares
Print edition ISBN: 9781781165416
E-book edition ISBN: 9781781165423

Published by Titan Books
A division of Titan Publishing Group Ltd
144 Southwark Street, London SE1 0UP

First edition: August 2013
10 9 8 7 6 5 4 3 2 1

A CIP catalogue record for this title is available from the British Library.

Printed and bound in the USA.

SHERLOCK HOLMES
The Stuff of Nightmares

FOREWORD

Concerning the events of late 1890, much has been written, most of it by people wiser and more qualified than I. Historians tell of a period of turmoil in Great Britain when, albeit briefly, the very cohesion of civilised society seemed threatened. They also tell how the machinations of seditionaries from a nation adjacent to our own were foiled by the offices of the good men of Scotland Yard.

Such is the consensus, and I would not wish to gainsay it in any way – at least not openly. This, alas, is another of those occasions when a case investigated and resolved by my great friend Sherlock Holmes must remain a secret from all. I commit an account of it to paper solely for my own satisfaction, by way of a personal souvenir, an old man's memento, not for public consumption. As I wrote in the story entitled "The Final Problem", there were only three cases of which I retain any record for the year 1890, and two of those I published as "The Red-Headed League" and "The Copper Beeches". This is the third, and it has remained solely in note form until now.

The reasons for this are threefold. To start with, some of the content would have been unpalatable to my readership at the time, and would be even to a modern audience, for all that we live in a more permissive age than ever we used to.

Also, there is the matter of relations between Great Britain and a near neighbour which I would not wish to disturb by raking up old enmities and divisions.

The third and most crucial reason, however, lies in my reluctance to risk exposing the true identity of a certain mysterious character who, at the time, was widely held to be a rumour and who now, from the vantage point of thirty-five years on, is regarded purely as a figment of myth and superstition, an entity who never existed except, perhaps, in the imaginations of purveyors of penny-dreadful fiction.

I speak, of course, of the bizarre, terrifying and remarkable individual known as Baron Cauchemar...

John H. Watson, MD (retd.), 1925

CHAPTER ONE

THE WATERLOO MASSACRE

I had just stepped off the 3.47 from Ramsgate when all hell broke loose.

One moment I was presenting my ticket for inspection and preparing to step onto the concourse at Waterloo Station. The next, there was an almighty detonation that reminded me of nothing so much as a salvo of artillery fire, a great percussive roar that seemed to tear the very fabric of the air asunder.

I was knocked clean off my feet, and briefly lost consciousness. When I came to, I was aware of a profound ringing in my ears and a sharp smell of burning in my nostrils.

Before me lay a ghastly sight. The orderly, everyday scene of a few minutes before had been utterly transformed. Where there had been people milling about, railway travellers exhibiting the usual mix of urgency and nonchalance, there was now carnage. The injured tottered to and fro, pressing a hand to some wound or other in order to stem the flow of blood. Cries of distress pierced the air, although in my half-deafened state I could only just hear them. I glimpsed a sailor-suited child gripping a toy bear, peering about himself forlornly for an accompanying adult who was either lost or worse. A bookstall owner sat, stunned, his wares cast all around him in shreds like so much confetti.

Everything was wreathed in smoke. Débris lay scattered on the board flooring of the concourse – chunks of masonry, shards of glass. Bodies lay scattered, too. Some bore no greater sign of harm than a few tattered edges on their clothing, yet their stillness spoke of nothing but death. Others were so mutilated that they scarcely resembled human beings any longer, looking more like something one might find in a butcher's shop.

I could scarcely comprehend what had happened. In a small, distant part of my mind, a voice was telling me: *bomb*. Uppermost in my thoughts, however, was the imperative that I must help people. Was I not a doctor, once a surgeon with the Army Medical Department? Had I not come to the aid of countless wounded soldiers at Ahmed Kel, Arzu, Charasiab, and at Maiwand too, until that jezail bullet put me on the casualty list myself?

My army medical training asserted itself. Even as my head cleared and the ringing in my ears began to abate, I sprang into action.

Of the hour or so that followed, I have little clear recollection. It passed in a haze of frantic activity. I attended to whomever was in distress, making an assessment of the extent of their injuries and spending as much or as little time with them as I felt was required – the process of triage so familiar to me from the battlefield hospital. I tore up strips of clothing to press into service as makeshift bandages. I ascertained which fragments of ejecta from the explosion could be safely extricated from the flesh they penetrated and which were so large or lodged so deep that they were better left in place until such time as a trained surgeon could deal with them under operating theatre conditions. I offered reassurance to those not too badly hurt and gave what scant consolation I could to those who, alas, were slipping into that state which lies beyond the power of any mortal to assist them. I also, I am pleased to say, managed to reunite the sobbing child with his nanny, to the great joy of them both.

I remember one doughty old widow who pestered me time and again to examine her, despite my protestations that she had suffered no worse than a few superficial scratches. I also remember – and it will haunt me to my dying day – a mother cradling an infant in her arms, insistent that the babe was alive and well when all the evidence was to the contrary.

It was a terrible experience, one which even a veteran of the Second Afghan War such as myself found harrowing and nightmarish. All these people had been quietly, innocently going about their business, heading home from work, waiting to greet a newly arrived friend or relative, preparing to embark on a journey, none of them having the least inkling that, in a split second, their lives would be reduced to chaos and horror. Whatever feelings of hope, trepidation or expectation they might have had, had been obliterated in an instant by an act of wanton, unconscionable destruction.

I did not pause to wonder, at the time, who had committed the atrocity. I had no doubt that it was a deliberate act of terrorism, for there had been two similar incidents in London during the previous fortnight, neither bomb blast as devastating as this one but both intended to cause considerable damage and sow fear and discord among the populace. I did not let that concern me. I simply focused on the matter at hand: easing pain and saving as many lives as I could.

When the police arrived on the scene, I directed them towards the victims in direst need of proper medical attention, and soon enough, hackney cabs, private carriages, and even a grocer's wagon, had been commandeered to ferry the injured to hospital.

Once the situation seemed to be under control and the concourse was free of all but corpses, I was able to halt and take stock. The surge of adrenaline that had borne me through the past couple of hours receded, and I found myself starting to tremble. Nausea nearly overwhelmed me. My hands, coated in the blood of others, shook uncontrollably. I had not been in such close proximity to so much slaughter in years and, unsurprisingly, I had not become inured to it in the interim. It was as horrific to me now as it had been a decade ago on the subcontinent.

Two thoughts brought me some slight comfort. One was that my Mary had not been there to witness this appalling massacre or, worse, be a casualty of it. She was some seventy miles east, in the town I had just travelled up from.

My wife was, as it happened, recovering from a miscarriage, her third since we were wed two years earlier. I have not referred to our childbearing misfortunes anywhere in my published writings, as I deem it too private a subject for public consumption and anyway of no real interest to my readers. Here, though, in this account which is likely to be seen by no eyes but mine, I can at least mention how Mary and I, in spite of our best efforts, failed to produce offspring. It is a source of great regret to me, even now, that I have no heirs, no children and grandchildren to lighten the burden of old age. My only hope for posterity, such as it is, lies in the written works that I leave behind.

Mary had taken this third setback particularly hard, so I had prescribed a stay with a cousin of hers who owned a cottage on the Kent coast. There she might find calm and relaxation and recover her mental equilibrium. Her condition had undoubtedly improved, and it had been mooted that she would accompany me on my return to London that very day, but I had seen how wan her features still were and how her eyes continued to lack their usual lustre, and had pronounced her not yet ready to resume city life with all its demands and vicissitudes. I thanked providence that I had made the decision I had.

The other comforting thought was that the perpetrators of

this outrage would face the full might of the law.

I knew this for a fact, because I happened to have a dear friend who had dedicated his life and his vast intellect to the pursuit of justice and who would, if charged with the task, stop at naught to see the malefactors apprehended and arraigned.

Thinking of Sherlock Holmes, I resolved to pay a call on him there and then. Outside the station I hailed a cab and presently was on my way to 221B Baker Street.

CHAPTER TWO

THE DISFIGURED DELIVERY BOY

After the carriage had deposited me at my destination and pulled away, I paused to peer up at the house where Holmes and I had once, until quite recently, shared rooms. The autumnal twilight lent a golden glow to the plaster façade of the ground floor and the bare brickwork of the upper storeys. I felt a brief pang of nostalgia for the period when the two of us had lived here together and for the adventures that had always been a knock on the door away. Anybody might turn up at the residence of the world's first and foremost consulting detective, at any hour, and most likely the result of their visit would be Holmes and I haring off on some wild, extraordinary, often dangerous investigation.

I was now a happily married man, approaching forty and with a thriving general practice. I had every reason to be content with my lot and not to wish to jeopardise it, or myself, in any way. Yet I could not help but miss those younger, helter-skelter bachelor days when, with scarcely a warning, my friend and I might find ourselves confronted with a lethally venomous swamp adder or a vexing mystery arising from something no more apparently innocuous than a few orange pips in an envelope. There had seemed so much *possibility* in the world back then, and for all that I continued to assist Holmes on numerous cases, I doubted life would ever be quite so thrillingly unpredictable again.

As I stood on the pavement, lost in these maudlin musings, the front door of 221B opened before me, and out stepped a telegram delivery boy.

I say "boy" but he stood a good six feet tall and, by his broad shoulders and well-proportioned, generally sturdy physique, I took him to be in his early twenties at least, if not older.

What struck me about him, however, apart from his being a grown-up when most in his profession were too young even to shave, was that he was hideously disfigured. I can put it no less plainly than that. His face bore extensive scarring, particularly on the right-hand side. Waxy-looking tissue distended both corners of his mouth and drew down the edge of one eye, giving him an air of perpetual grievance and mistrust. A chunk of his hair was absent at the temple, just below the band of his peaked cap, and his right ear was all but nonexistent, just a few nubs of cartilage fringing a puckered hole like the rim of a volcanic crater.

Through my work, I was accustomed to the many distortions and mutilations which birth and accident can visit upon the human anatomy. Nonetheless I could not avoid staring at this poor creature as he came down the front steps towards me. Manners ought to have prompted me to avert my eyes, but doubtless I was still in shock from the bombing and its aftermath, so much so that my normal sense of decorum temporarily deserted me.

The telegram delivery boy met my gaze and held it. He must have been used to receiving unwelcome, searching looks from strangers. His eyes, in contrast to the physiognomical ruin that surrounded them, were among the sharpest and clearest I have ever seen. They seemed to dance like starlight amid stormclouds.

I was conscious of being assessed by them, appraised, judged, with a keenness I had beheld in only one other pair of eyes before – and their owner was surely sitting upstairs at this very moment, ruminating on whatever message the delivery boy had brought.

Unless…

Could it be that this individual was none other than Holmes himself, decked out in one of his many disguises?

No. The eyes were the wrong colour, a piercing blue rather than Holmes's flinty, perceptive grey. Altering the hue of his irises was beyond even my friend's great powers of self-camouflage.

The telegram delivery boy took in my somewhat dishevelled state, the dried blood that still caked my hands, the dazedness that I must yet have been exhibiting. Then he smiled and saluted.

"Good day to you, sir," he said.

"Good day to you," I replied mechanically, with a tip of my felt bowler.

More would have been exchanged, but at that moment a first-storey window casement rattled up and Holmes himself leaned out, once and for all quashing any notion I might have had that the delivery boy was actually he.

"Ah, Watson, there you are," my friend barked. "I thought I heard a familiar voice. What are you dawdling for? Hurry on up. There's work to be done!"

Accordingly I hastened indoors and, firing off a swift salutation to Mrs Hudson in her parlour, mounted the stairs.

"Good Lord, man, look at you," said Holmes as he ushered me into the sitting-room. "What a sight. Been in the wars, have we? Or," he added somewhat more soberly, "a bomb explosion at Waterloo Station by any chance?"

"Then you already know about that?" I said.

"I heard the detonation and was able to deduce its location based on the volume of the sound and the direction it came from, namely south-east, just across the river. The likeliest venue, the place where a terrorist bomb would cause the most disruption and loss of life, would be a frequented and crowded spot, such as a railway station at the peak hour of busyness. Waterloo lies more or less due south-east of here. That seemed to fit the criteria. My supposition was corroborated not long afterwards, as word began to spread and I overheard someone in the street gossiping loudly about the incident. Final confirmation arrived just moments ago in the form of a telegram from my brother Mycroft." He shook his head sorrowfully. "A bad business, my friend, a very bad business indeed. And how terrible that you had the misfortune to be caught up in the blast."

"I hardly need ask how you know I was there."

"It is perfectly plain. Even if you were not so clearly distressed and your hands and clothing did not bear the marks that they do, it would have been apparent to me where you had been this afternoon. You are dressed for travel, and there's a copy of *Bradshaw* just protruding from the pocket of your topcoat, its yellow wrapper binding unmistakable. I am aware that you have been making day trips recently to visit your wife in Ramsgate, the line from which terminates at Waterloo. She is improving, by the way?"

I nodded. I had not vouchsafed to Holmes the real reason for Mary's sojourn on the coast, stating merely that she had been unwell and that the bracing sea air would aid her recuperation. I suspect he had a pretty shrewd idea of the truth but he had the good grace not to let on.

"Excellent," said he. "So the deduction was child's play itself. I must say I'm glad that you managed to escape unscathed."

"Unscathed?" I said, lowering myself into an armchair. "Physically, maybe."

"A brandy," Holmes declared. "And perhaps some soap and a basin of hot water, so that you may clean yourself up. Mrs Hudson!"

A snifter of brandy went some way to restoring my equilibrium, and it was a relief to wash off the blood and all that it signified.

"I did what I could for the victims," I told Holmes, drying my hands, "but it felt like far too little."

"I'm quite certain you acquitted yourself with honour," said Holmes.

"Who do you think is behind this beastly bombing campaign? Is it Fenians, as some of the papers say? Anarchists? Opponents of the monarchy?"

"Hmmm." Holmes had not really paid attention to my questioning. With fingers pressed to lips, he was contemplating some other matter. "Tell me, Watson, what did you make of our recent guest?"

"Guest? You mean the delivery boy?"

"Indeed."

"I do not see how he can be of more consequence than the bombings."

"Humour me."

"Well, if you insist," said I. I was well accustomed to my friend's sometimes impenetrable thought processes and the way the locus of his interest could shift sharply and unexpectedly from one matter to another. "Do you wish me to apply your own deductive methods?"

"Absolutely."

"Then, first of all, I think it queer that he was permitted to enter the house. Could Mrs Hudson have not signed for the telegram at the door, as is customary?"

"I told you the message was from Mycroft," said Holmes. "It was an important one, and the delivery boy insisted that it must be placed directly in the hands of the named recipient."

"Odd," I said.

"Singular," said Holmes, "but I can see the reasoning, and

he was adamant about it. In the end, Mrs Hudson had no choice but to relent and allow him in, even though she is under strict instruction not to disturb me unless it is to bring up a client. What else about him did you notice?"

"I don't know if 'notice' is the word, but one's eye couldn't avoid being drawn to that face of his. Terribly badly burned. A house fire perhaps?"

"You are guessing."

"My powers of observation are not the equal of yours," I replied with some asperity. "We all know that. No one's are. In the absence of any further evidence, all I can suggest is that the man was unfortunate enough to have had his face destroyed by fire. The nature and extent of the scar tissue allows for no other conclusion. That he is an adult in a job usually reserved for boys leads me to assume –"

"Never assume!" Holmes rebuked me.

"Leads me to infer, then, that he has been unable to find any other form of gainful employment; no doubt as a consequence of his looks."

"In that respect, I am sure you are on the right track, Watson. Nobody, looking at him, could think otherwise than that his repugnant appearance has barred him from most lines of work and obliged him to accept a low-paid, menial position of the type usually offered to someone far junior."

"I get the impression that you know better."

"No, no," said my companion airily. "Not necessarily."

"But there's more to him than meets the eye."

"Sometimes a man is exactly what he seems, no more, no less." Whatever Holmes had hoped to gain by taxing me about the deliverer of the telegram, he had evidently pursued the issue to his satisfaction, for he changed the subject – or rather, reverted to the topic I had originally broached. "It is, of course, about the bombings that Mycroft wishes to see me."

"The telegram was a summons, I take it."

"Very much so. An urgent one."

"Then what are we waiting for?" said I, rising. "We must leave for the Diogenes Club at once." I consulted the pocket-watch which had been bequeathed me by my not long deceased and sadly rather wayward eldest brother. "It is past a quarter to five and still just shy of twenty to eight, so if we hurry, we will undoubtedly catch him there."

"And I would be delighted for you to accompany me, Watson. On condition that you are quite recovered from your ordeal…"

In truth, I was still not feeling fully myself. However, a call to arms could not go unheeded, especially one that related to a disaster which had ended so many lives and nearly accounted for my own as well. The sooner we got onto the culprits' trail, the nearer we would be to bringing them to book.

As we headed downstairs, I said, "Is the game afoot, Holmes?"

My friend grinned wolfishly over his shoulder.

"In so many ways, Watson. In so very many ways."

CHAPTER THREE

A STUDY IN CONTRASTS

A hansom took us to Pall Mall, and on the way we saw around us a London in ferment. The third and deadliest yet of the bomb attacks had made the headlines of the late editions of the papers. On every other street corner people gathered to hear someone read the relevant article aloud, and cries of shock and groans of dismay greeted almost every sentence. Several times there were loud and angry denunciations of the Irish and their desire for independence and home rule, since Fenians seemed the likeliest perpetrators of these barbaric acts. They had had some form in that department since the Rising in 1867 and the Dynamite Campaign of the early 'eighties. I regretted my fellow countrymen's readiness to condemn an entire nation for the deeds of a single political faction, and moreover without proof or verification. Nonetheless I harboured the same suspicions and felt the same burning need to find someone to blame, perhaps even more strongly than the average person did owing to my first-hand experience of the effects of the Waterloo Station bomb blast.

Once we were inside the Diogenes Club, however, it was as

though such concerns simply did not exist. The denizens of that august institution sat ensconced in armchairs, smoking, drinking, perusing books and periodicals, or gazing softly into the middle distance, seemingly without a care in the world. The club's thick walls and cherished traditions appeared to have an insulating effect, cutting its members off from all external troubles.

Of course, even if these gentlemen had wished to discuss the current situation, they would have been forbidden from doing so by the club's principal and strictest rule. All conversation – even the smallest of small talk – was banned on the premises, on pain of permanent exclusion. The only place where one might utter a word was the Stranger's Room, whither Holmes and I were ushered by a suitably muted attendant.

Holmes's brother awaited us there, and the pair fell to talking immediately, without preamble or greeting, as was their wont. I never failed to be amazed by the difference between them – the corpulent and well-connected Mycroft, the wiry and antisocial Sherlock. It seemed almost inconceivable that two such dissimilar creatures could have sprung from the same set of loins. The sole feature this study in contrasts shared was a prodigious, voracious intelligence.

"First a restaurant on Cheapside, then the bandstand at Regent's Park," said Mycroft Holmes. "Now this. It is quite baffling. I cannot fathom any pattern to the attacks. They have taken place at differing hours of the day, in a variety of locations, with no common target other than civilians, bystanders. There is no apparent logic, no obvious motive other than to kill and maim blindly."

"Sometimes that alone is enough," said the junior of the two Holmeses. "Madmen need no rationale for their deeds beyond the perverted satisfaction of seeing others hurt."

"You think this is the work of madmen, Sherlock?"

"It is one theory. The alternative is that it is the work of sane, highly calculating individuals who wish to be *seen* to be mad. The apparent randomness of the bombings is, in that sense, a pattern of its own. We are meant to think there is no order behind it, and the locations have been carefully selected to reinforce that impression."

"Fiendish," said Mycroft. "So our foes want us to underestimate them."

"Maybe. What is clear is that the attacks are escalating in audacity and severity. The number of dead at the Cheapside restaurant was three, was it not? And at Regent's Park a dozen. And today...?"

"The death toll stands at thirty-one, with a further six not likely to survive the night, according to my sources."

I felt a stab of sorrow and regret, wondering how many of those six I had ministered to at the station. Possibly all of them.

"There is a special session of parliament scheduled for later this evening," Mycroft Holmes continued. "The bombings will be urgently debated. It's fair to say, however, that not much will be achieved. With scant evidence available, the Prime Minister can only make vague threats against nameless culprits and promise some form of retribution – platitudes to reassure the masses. There will be plenty of indignation and hot air in the House but precious little concrete policy."

"And Her Majesty?" said Holmes. Mycroft – it can be revealed here, although it was never a matter of official record – was a frequent habitué of Buckingham Palace and Windsor Castle. Those were almost the only two places he would deign to visit, beyond his rooms on Pall Mall and the Diogenes. I have it on good authority that he was even known by our monarch as her "second Albert", but one daren't speculate on the full implications of that.

"Affronted, alarmed, deeply concerned for the plight of her subjects," Mycroft said. "What else would one expect? Her abiding fear is that, if the bombings continue, the result will be widespread civil unrest."

"She has good cause to believe that. Watson and I witnessed considerable public agitation on the way here. Scared people are apt to take the law into their own hands and lash out at anyone they believe guilty."

"Or," I interjected, "they become a mob and turn on their leaders."

"Quite so," said Holmes. "I presume Special Branch are leaving no stone unturned."

"Melville's men are combing through the wreckage at Waterloo for clues even as we speak," said Mycroft. "The bomb was planted in the gentlemen's lavatories, of all places."

"That at least tells us something about the bomber. He is male."

"Though no gentleman," said Mycroft with a curl of the lip. "Special Branch are also preparing to roust out potential suspects all across the capital. There hasn't been a mobilisation of their forces like this since the Jubilee Plot back in 'eighty-seven. Known anarchists and Irish nationalists should sleep uneasy in their beds tonight, in anticipation of the 3.00am knock and the holding cell below Scotland Yard."

"Then everything would appear to be in hand," said his brother. "I can't understand why you wished to consult me, Mycroft. My presence here seems superfluous in the extreme."

I was startled by the brisk dismissiveness with which Holmes spoke, as though the unfolding crisis was of no significance to him.

Mycroft was similarly taken aback. For several seconds the older Holmes blinked at his seven-years-younger sibling.

Then he said, "I had thought, Sherlock, that you would be keen to see the bombers caught and a state of calm restored, and that this was a goal to which you would be willing to apply yourself. I realise now that I may have been mistaken. Is it a question of money? I'm sure I can raid the Treasury coffers, if it is. What's the going rate for the services of the great sage of Baker Street?"

"You misunderstand," said Holmes, untroubled by his brother's broadside of sarcasm and scorn. "This is not the type of case I normally investigate. Far from it. The police have ample resources and manpower to deal with it."

"Holmes, really!" I ejaculated, unable to contain myself. "I can scarcely credit what I'm hearing. Surely you can't stand idly by while mass murderers rampage unchecked and the cohesion of our society is imperilled. This is not like you at all."

"Your friend is right," Mycroft chimed in. "How dare you shirk your patriotic duty, Sherlock. Granted, there is nothing glamorous here as there usually is in your cases. Nobody has been murdered inside a locked room. There are no exotic, deadly animals involved, no strange faces at windows, no Mitteleuropean monarchs or contested legacies. All the same, I would have thought that mere love of queen and country would persuade you to devote your energies to this problem, for all that it is outside your customary remit." He made an effort to look humble and importunate. It did not come naturally to him. "I would regard it as a personal favour if you agreed to help, dear boy."

"I never said that I wouldn't help," Holmes replied. "But the bombings themselves seem to me to be of secondary importance."

"I beg your pardon? Secondary to what?"

"There is another phenomenon that has featured in the newspapers of late. It may not have made the front pages or consumed as many column inches, but it is a great deal more peculiar and, I am almost certain, has relevance to the matter under discussion."

Mycroft Holmes cocked a bushy eyebrow. "Why do I have the feeling I'm not going to like what I'm about to hear?"

"Put it down to your general choleric disposition," said his brother. "Or else dyspepsia from the devilled kidneys you had for lunch."

"The devilled –? Oh, Sherlock, there is a time and place for these little parlour games you so enjoy, and this is not it."

"Hardly a parlour game, brother. I was trying discreetly to draw your attention to the morsel of food adhering to your left lapel. Conceivably I could have been less subtle about it, but manners – and a concern for what others might think of you – would not permit me to overlook it altogether."

Mycroft looked down at his ample front, located the offending fragment of his midday meal, and whisked it away with his handkerchief and a loud harrumph.

"But as we're on the subject of your haberdashery," Sherlock Holmes continued, "I see that your tailor has at last handed in his notice."

Mycroft set his face in an expression that was both resigned and exasperated.

"Let me guess. The stitching on my trousers."

Holmes nodded. "The waistband has been let out a couple of inches – again – but the quality of the workmanship isn't up to the usual standard. You remain loyal to your outfitters, Messrs Reade and Whittle of Jermyn Street, because you have been their customer for over fifteen years and it would not be like you to change now, you being such a creature of habit. The elderly Mr Popplewell at that establishment was a particular genius with needle and thread, and any alterations he made to your clothing were always nigh on invisible. That it was apparent that your trousers had been altered at all indicated to me that Popplewell was not involved. At his advanced age, the likeliest explanation was that he has retired. Death was also a possibility, but I plumped for the less morbid of the two options. Besides, a master craftsman like him would have merited a mention in the *Times* obituary column, of which I am an avid reader, and I have seen none."

The older Holmes heaved a testy sigh. "Yes, yes, all very ingenious, and I know how your deductive talents impress the police and the rest of the lower orders. But you forget that you are talking to a man every inch your mental equal, if not more so, and I am just not in the mood for such footling diversions today. Pray enlighten me about this 'other phenomenon' that you rank above the continued wellbeing of Britain and its imperial dependencies – even though I have a suspicion I already know what it is."

"Baron Cauchemar," said Holmes.

"Ha-ha!" His brother slapped his meaty hands together. "Yes. I thought as much. Once again your predilection for the bizarre and outré shows itself. Not for Sherlock Holmes something so mundane as a hunt for terrorists. Oh no. He would rather pursue a phantom, a will-o'-the-wisp, a fictitious figure to whose existence only the worst kind of sensationalist journalism gives credence."

"Reports of Baron Cauchemar's deeds are consistent and well corroborated. Sightings of him may have been few, but the eyewitnesses are nearly always reliable and every person describes him in the same way. He has even been spotted by two members of the constabulary, and their testimony cannot be called into question, can it?"

"Pah! You mean to say you actually think this figment of the imagination is *real*? A prancing jack-in-a-box, popping up hither and yon in the East End, scaring burglars and impeding robberies in progress? Really, Sherlock, I can accept Watson here falling for such shilling-shocker claptrap, but *you*?"

I made to protest at the insult that had been levelled against me, but my friend got there first.

"Mycroft, Watson is as astute a judge of the facts as any man. He may embellish and romanticise his accounts of my exploits somewhat, in order to make them more pleasing as literary entertainment, but he has an eye for detail and a nose for the truth, and I will not have you impugning his character or his acumen."

Mycroft, abashed, turned to me and grumbled an apology, something about his having spoken out of turn, the pressure he was under, great weight on his shoulders, no offence meant.

I myself was flattered beyond measure by Holmes's praise. He was not usually so unstinting with his compliments, least of all where my intellectual prowess or my writing skills were concerned. There were times in his company, and more so in the company of him and his brother together, that I was made to feel as though I were a member of an inferior species, a reasonably gifted ape perhaps. It was nice to be reminded that my companion thought more highly of me than that.

"But seriously, Sherlock," Mycroft said, "this absurd Baron Cauchemar rumour, there's no more substance to it than there was to Spring-heeled Jack. In fact, I would maintain that the former is an adjunct of the latter, a modern updating of a fifty-year-old myth, the only difference being that Cauchemar foils crimes whereas Spring-heeled Jack, with his propensity for assaulting strangers and molesting women, perpetrated them."

"It is a crucial difference, one that outweighs any superficial similarities between the two."

"Baron Cauchemar is a story that residents of a dismal, overcrowded corner of London have dreamed up in order to bring a touch of colour and excitement to their otherwise drab, squalid lives," Mycroft insisted. "He is a fantasy, as insubstantial as this table is solid." He thumped the top of the oak dining table to underscore his point. "They say he can leap twenty feet in the air. They say he can break down a brick wall with his hands. They say he can stun a man with a jolt of electricity or knock him out with a puff of gas expelled from his hand. I believe not one iota of it. The slums and rookeries of this city breed all manner of superstition and old wives' tales: giant rats in the sewers, baby-abducting ghouls, flying boats, ghostly coachmen, sinister Chinamen with the power to bend your will to theirs via sheer animal magnetism, and whatnot. I'm almost ashamed to call you my brother if you're going to start putting store by any of that nonsense."

"There is a compelling case for thinking that Baron Cauchemar is more than mere fancy, Mycroft," said Holmes. "I am also of the view that his emergence into the public eye in the past few weeks is not unconnected with the bombings."

"Oh, is that so?"

"Yes indeed," said Holmes stoutly. "And, to that end, Baron Cauchemar is the avenue of investigation I intend to pursue."

"And you're not prepared to accept that it's pure happenstance, this fairytale creature appearing at the same time as a fresh wave of insurrectionist bombings hits the capital? At the very least coincidence?"

"In as much as I'm innately suspicious of coincidences, no. To my mind, it seems more likely than not that the one set of extraordinary occurrences should in some way be related to the other. And if I am wrong, and if the existence of Baron Cauchemar is impossible, as you insist, then at least I will have eliminated that impossibility from my enquiries, leaving me one step closer to the truth, however improbable."

Mycroft's chin sank into the fold of blubber that bulged out over his shirt collar.

"If that is your choice, Sherlock, so be it," he said in a sullen growl, fixing his watery grey eyes on his brother. "Go and chase your silly chimera. I will be in touch again in a couple of days' time to see what progress you have made – which will be none, I'll wager. Then, perhaps, you will change your mind and make the sensible decision to work directly for me after all."

"We shall see," said Holmes. "Come, Watson! We've stayed long enough."

And so we left the silent Diogenes Club and an equally silent, and fuming, Mycroft.

Outside in the street, removed from the club's stifling confines, I once again remonstrated with my friend. "Holmes, should you not at the very least visit Waterloo Station? It is most unlike you to turn down the opportunity to inspect a crime scene. The terrorists might well have left clues."

"Did I say I was not going to look there?"

"You did not say that you were. Come on, a little of your time. Set aside this Baron Cauchemar business for just one moment."

"I'm almost certain it would be pointless. Special Branch will have already trampled all over the place in their hobnailed boots, leaving little useful evidence for someone with a keener eye to detect."

"I would be in your debt if you would go," I said. "You weren't there. It was terrible. Those people – innocents – ripped to bits. And don't forget how close I came to being one of the victims. Anything that can be done to bring us that bit nearer to finding the persons responsible…"

I admit I was playing upon his sympathies. Some might even call it a kind of blackmail. Yet I felt I had a very personal stake in the matter.

"Very well," said Holmes. "Since you insist. I'll warrant *something* may have survived Special Branch's clodhopping vandalism."

He turned his feet in the direction of Waterloo with what seemed to be a show of great reluctance, yet I had the sneaking suspicion it had been his intention to survey the scene of the bombing all along, even without my cajoling. He just hadn't wanted Mycroft to know this, not wishing to appear meekly subservient to his brother's wishes. Whatever sibling rivalries had characterised the youthful years of the two Holmeses remained in force even in adulthood. I don't believe there is a younger brother alive who would willingly be at his older brother's beck and call, and Holmes, for all his genius and his detachment from the tidal pull of base emotions, was no exception to this rule.

CHAPTER FOUR

THE AROMA OF OVERRIPE BANANAS

Arriving at the station, we found a throng of onlookers clustered around the entrance, gawping and prurient. As with any disaster, it never took long for the news to spread and for spectators to come from far and wide, eager for a glimpse of other people's tragedy.

Holmes headed inside, I following with some reluctance. My memories of the bombing were still fresh and raw. I could scarcely bring myself to re-enter the building, fearing irrationally that a second bomb might have been laid, to finish what the first had started.

Holmes made himself known to the Special Branch officer who was supervising. The man, Grimsdyke, was built like a gorilla and had perfected a forbidding glower that would have intimidated a rampaging sepoy. Holmes nonetheless was able to convince him of our bona fides, dropping the name of our sometime ally in the CID, Inspector Lestrade. Grimsdyke admitted he knew of Holmes's reputation.

"Something of a loose cannon, I'm told," he said, "but frankly we need all the firepower we can get."

Grudgingly he granted my friend permission to conduct an examination of the bomb wreckage.

I watched Holmes go through his usual familiar routine at a crime scene: scurrying hither and thither, occasionally going down on all fours to study something on the ground, peering through a magnifying glass at some infinitesimal and seemingly inconsequential detail. His movements lithe and nimble, he resembled a bloodhound questing this way and that to find a scent. He spent a considerable amount of time at the huge gouge in the western wall which betokened where the gentlemen's lavatory lay, the epicentre of the blast. The hole itself and the rubble which surrounded it were of particular interest to him. He also interviewed various members of railway staff who were present.

By and by he straightened up, offered his hand to Grimsdyke, and rejoined me at the main entrance, where I had stayed all the while.

"What did you discover?" I asked as we stepped back out into the lengthening shadows of evening. I was glad to be out of there.

"A few things of interest," he replied. "The bomb was placed in the last of the row of stalls, that much is plain, lodged behind the cistern. I can also say without doubt that the explosive used was dynamite. Nitroglycerin has a distinctively sweet aroma, not unlike that of overripe bananas. The wood pulp that it is soaked in, to give it form and stability, also leaves behind a marked odour after detonation, much like bonfire smoke."

"Dynamite. Which would seem to confirm that the same agency was behind this attack as the previous two."

"It would be surprising if it were otherwise. The useful thing about dynamite, from our point of view, is that it is difficult to get hold of. Legally, at least. Unless one is engaged in the kind of work which requires it of necessity, such as quarrying or mining, it may be purchased only on the black market from disreputable sources. That may prove helpful in our enquiries."

"Anything else?"

"Nothing that adds greatly to the sum of our knowledge. None of the railway employees I spoke to has any recollection of a person behaving erratically or suspiciously in the vicinity prior to the bombing. All stated that it was a busy time of day and that countless people were going to and fro. Our terrorists would appear to be able to pass as ordinary citizens and act in a cool-headed manner under pressure."

"One would wish that they could not."

"Yes, if only every villain would skulk around all swivel-eyed and cackling, it would make life much easier."

The note of sarcasm in my friend's voice irked me. "Well, I appreciate your agreeing to come here, even if it was only to indulge my whim. I trust the time wasn't wholly wasted."

"It's never a waste of time pursuing a potential trail of evidence, even if it appears to lead nowhere distinct. A dead end at least has the function of telling one which way not to go and confirming what the right track might be."

"You mean, in this instance, Baron Cauchemar."

"I do."

"But what I don't understand is, this creature, even if he exists, appears to be the foe of wrongdoers. He prevents crime rather than commits it. Why would you prefer to concentrate on him when there are clear and present evils to be combated?" I gestured back at the station.

"He fascinates me," said Holmes. "And, as I said to Mycroft, I don't believe that his manifesting now in our city is unrelated to the bombings. There is some connection, which I am determined to fathom. Solving the mystery of Baron Cauchemar might well even provide the key to unlocking the identity of the terrorists."

"So what now?"

"Now? I have thinking to do, my friend, and it is best done

at home, with the aid of three pipes' worth of shag tobacco and a few violin pieces. Some of Mendelssohn's *Lieder* would fit the bill, and perhaps Beethoven's *Kreutzer Sonata*. I shall call for you again tomorrow. I trust you will be free."

"I have no other plans," I said.

And even if I had, I would have cancelled them.

CHAPTER FIVE

GROUT THE IRREGULAR

Holmes sent for me towards evening the next day. His messenger was a scrubby little boy, name of Grout, one of Holmes's troop of semi-feral street children, the Baker Street Irregulars. Grout wore a cloth cap several sizes too large for him, which was prevented from slipping down over his eyes by virtue of a jutting pair of jug ears. His face had not known the touch of soap and water in ages, being more smudge than skin, but he had a lively, engaging manner, a birdlike alertness about him.

"Mr 'Olmes says you need to dress down," Grout informed me. "He 'as a job for you what requires you to be able to 'mingle with the undesirables', whatever that's supposed to mean."

"And where am I to carry out this job?"

"You've got me to show you that," said the boy. "Oh, and you ought to bring your service revolver with you, Mr Watson, just in case."

I donned the shabbiest garments in my wardrobe, some tattered, moth-eaten items which Mary would have put out for the rag-and-bone man had I not found them useful for doing the gardening in. In the mirror, I cut a dishevelled, scarecrow-like figure. I mussed up my hair and reckoned that I might, just might, pass for someone more disreputable than myself.

Grout's eyes grew huge as he saw me fetch my gun from its case and check that it was in good working order and fully loaded.

"Cor! Is that a Mark Three Adams, sir?"

"It is. You know your weapons."

"Standard issue for British Army officer class. Six-shot, six-and-a-half-inch barrel, takes a hollow-based roundnosed lead bullet with a thirteen-grain black-powder charge."

Now it was my turn to widen my eyes.

"You really *do* know your weapons," I said, stowing the revolver in a pocket.

"It's, er… a 'obby of mine."

"I see. And not, perchance, a line of business you might dabble in from time to time?" Many of the Baker Street Irregulars were involved in illicit activities, from petty larceny to gun running. Their proximity to the criminal underworld was one of the reasons they were so valuable to Holmes.

"Oh no, Mr Watson," Grout exclaimed, all innocence. "Not me, sir. I'm as honest as the day is long."

"It's autumn," said I, wryly. "The nights are drawing in and the days are shortening."

"I 'ave no idea what you're getting at, sir. But time *is* a-wasting. Perhaps we should go."

"Very well. Lead the way."

A thick fog had rolled in off the Thames estuary, flooding the London Basin and bringing an atmosphere of preternatural stillness and calm to the capital. It was dusk, but already it felt like long past sunset. Grout and I moved through the shrouded city, and sometimes the only sound we heard was our own footfalls and the only signs of human life we saw were our own flickering, etiolated shadows. The urchin knew exactly where he was going, never having to pause to check street signs or take his bearings. He seemed to navigate through the fog by some uncanny sixth sense.

I gathered that we were heading east, but my main preoccupation was sticking close to my guide and not losing sight of him. I feared that if we parted ways, I might become hopelessly marooned in this pea-souper and end up wandering in circles all night long.

"Is Holmes meeting us at our destination?" I asked.

Grout shrugged. "'E didn't say. 'E just told me to get you there and make sure you know who you're supposed to be tailing."

"So I'm to follow someone."

"That's the gist of it, sir."

A little further on, I decided to satisfy another curiosity of mine.

"Tell me, Grout, have you heard of this Baron Cauchemar creature?"

The boy gave a cautious, furtive nod. His voice lowered, taking on a note of anxiety.

"I 'aven't seen 'im myself, like, but there's plenty of folks round my way as 'as. Including my own uncle Bart."

"Really?"

"Cross my 'eart. Uncle Bart's a, well, not to beat about the bush, a cracksman."

"A safe breaker?"

"And one of the best in the land," said Grout with pride. "There ain't a peter made what Bart can't open, and usually in a minute flat. Bart was casing a 'ouse, a fortnight ago, nice place up near Blackheath. Rich bloke owns it, who's often out of town on work. Bart 'ad it on good authority there was a nice big square-bodied inside, a Tann's List Three, jammed with jewellery and readies. 'E was just about to break in, nice and easy, jemmy up the window, slip inside... Only that's when 'e saw 'im."

"Baron Cauchemar."

"Yeah. Baron Coshmar. Coming up the road, 'e was, all kind of bouncing along on these enormous legs. Eyes aglare. Face like a demon's. The Bloody Black Baron himself, out on patrol."

"Your uncle got a good look at him?"

"Well, as Bart tells it, 'e dived into the nearest 'edge and 'id there, on account of being utterly petrified by this *thing* what was striding towards 'im in leaps and bounds. And I could 'ear it in 'is voice, as 'e was recounting the story, that 'e was proper scared, and it takes a lot to scare a 'ard nut like my uncle. But 'e peers out through the leaves anyway, and Baron Coshmar is striding right by, and 'e's eight-foot tall if 'e's an inch, and 'e's all black and gleaming like some kind of beetle, and 'e's making this noise, this 'issing, kind of *psssh-pah*, *psssh-pah*, as 'e goes. And 'is face is sort of this way..." Grout formed his features into an exaggerated leering expression, mouth gaping, eyes agog like marbles. "Shiny and blazing mad. 'Like something out of 'ell,' Bart said. 'Like Satan 'imself come to earth.' And Bart's not one to make things up. Least, not always. Sometimes when 'e's in 'is cups 'e'll spin a yarn or two, but this time 'e was sober as a judge. Which is a funny expression, when you think about it. Some of the beaks I've been up in front of, they've not struck me as sober at all. Especially when it's been after lunch."

I masked a smile. "Did Bart have any further interaction with him?"

"Not on your life. Soon as that monster was out of sight, Bart jumped out from the 'edge and fled. Wasn't conducting any more business that night, no way. One close shave was enough for 'im. The Bloody Black Baron don't like crooks, you see. Everyone in the East End knows that. 'E catches you in the act, red-'anded – *in flagrante delicto*, like – you're going to regret it."

I was not surprised that an ill-educated street urchin like Grout would know a complicated Latin phrase like *in flagrante delicto*. He had doubtless heard it, and others of its ilk, issuing from the lips of members of the bar and the judiciary in the course of a trial which he was attending as a spectator or, more likely, as a defendant. For youngsters like him, a courtroom was often their only classroom, certainly their only exposure to higher culture.

"How so?" I said.

"'E's not killed anyone, so far as I know, not yet. But 'e's left men badly beaten up, broken jaw, busted leg, that sort of thing. Kind of like as a warning. 'Don't do that again.' This gas 'e gets you with, it snuffs you out like a blown candle, and when you wake up you've got a crippling 'eadache and you feel sick for days after. And getting electric shocked by 'im – that just blooming well 'urts."

There was no doubt at all in Grout's mind that Baron Cauchemar was real. He was not some apparition, some ogre out of a bedtime story; he was an entity who genuinely stalked the East End streets, meting out impromptu justice. And on the strength of Grout's vivid account, or rather his uncle's, I was beginning to think there was a kernel of truth in the reports of this outlandish phantasm.

I was also beginning to think – indeed, had suspected all along – that tonight's mysterious outing must be related to Cauchemar in some way. Holmes seemed obsessed with this strange vigilante, to the exclusion of all else. I had learned from experience that my friend was seldom wrong when it came to penetrating to the heart of a puzzle. Moreover, his actions were often cryptic, even downright opaque, until such time as they were explained to me, whereupon with hindsight they became perfectly clear and sensible. I had faith that there was method to this apparent madness of chasing Cauchemar rather than the terrorists. Yet I had doubts too. I would not be human if I did not.

All said and done, I was glad that Holmes had advised me to bring my revolver. If by any chance I was to confront the Bloody Black Baron tonight, I would rather do it armed than not.

Dark had fully fallen by the time we neared journey's end. The gas lamps had been lit, but the fog dimmed their spheres of illumination and made the distances between them seem further and gloomier than ever. I apprehended that we were not far from the docks – Shadwell, if I didn't miss my guess – and Grout was steering me towards a particularly insalubrious part of this already insalubrious area.

We wound up outside a pub just off Ratcliffe Highway, the kind of den favoured by sailors, stevedores, longshoremen, and the doxies who consorted with them. Its name I do not happen to recall, although I believe it might have been The Bottomless Tankard.

"In there," Grout said, gesturing. "You're looking for a bloke called Abednego 'One Arm' Torrance. Shouldn't be too 'ard to spot, being as 'e's got… Well, the nickname's the clue, ain't it?"

"And what am I to do once I've found this Torrance fellow?" I asked. "Simply keep a close eye on him?"

"Ear-wig on 'im. Go wherever 'e goes. Don't let 'im out of your sight. Mr 'Olmes is after whatever you can find out about 'im, and if 'e leads you to the site of some sort of felony – which, knowing 'is reputation, is likely – so much the better."

"Fine," I said, sounding braver than I felt. "That's all Holmes wants, is it? Shouldn't be a problem. Here you are, my lad." I fished in my pocket for a half-crown, which I gave to Grout. It vanished up his sleeve and, next moment, the little rapscallion himself was gone, melting into the fog. It was as though I had just watched two conjuring tricks being performed, first a coin disappearing, then a boy.

I steeled myself and stepped through the pub door.

CHAPTER SIX

ASIAN LILIES

It was a dimly lit establishment, brimming with rowdy patrons and the smells of beer and bodies. The sawdust on the floor looked as though it had soaked up as much spilled blood as spilled drink. A piano with several keys missing was being played by a man with several teeth missing, and he was accompanying a robustly built young woman as she sang a sea shanty about a pirate captain and a mermaid. The lyrics were so spectacularly coarse, and the woman's voice so remarkably shrill and discordant, that I could scarcely bear to listen; yet her audience were lapping up the performance, not least because she was happy to illustrate the song's narrative with appropriate lewd actions.

I kept my head low and did my level best to blend in. On my way to the bar a stooped, elderly Chinese coolie butted shoulders with me. He bowed and bobbed, offering me a garbled apology, and shuffled on. Immediately I checked my pockets – it was that sort of place. Happily both my pocketbook and my gun were still where they should be.

It took me a while to catch the barkeep's attention. Perhaps he sensed I was an interloper, or perhaps making customers wait was a way of asserting his importance. I ordered a pint of porter which not only proved to be watered down but tasted as though most of its malt had turned to vinegar. Sipping this unappetising concoction, I cast around for an individual fitting the description of Abednego "One Arm" Torrance, and soon enough spied the only person on the premises who could be him.

He was a hulking creature, florid of complexion and muscular, with a shaggy crop of black hair and a beard to match. His left arm was missing from the shoulder down, but his right, as if to compensate, was twice as large as any ordinary man's. He was using it, in fact, to arm-wrestle with a merchant navy rating. The two of them vied at a table, teeth bared, sweat gleaming on their foreheads, while around them a swarm of supporters roared and bayed encouragement, meanwhile laying bets on the outcome of the contest.

Torrance won. With a sudden, savage surge of effort he forced his opponent's knuckles hard into one of the puddles of beer on the tabletop. It seemed that up until then he had been toying with the fellow, letting him think he stood a chance. The seaman leapt angrily to his feet, cradling his aching arm, and accused Torrance of cheating. "You macer! You speeler! Playing me the crooked cross..." Torrance rose and, casually, almost absentmindedly, socked him on the jaw. The seaman, who was of no mean proportions himself, keeled over, out cold. This nearly precipitated a mass brawl among the onlookers, but somehow, in spite of a great deal of posturing and chest-beating, the tinderbox moment passed and calm heads prevailed.

As Torrance and a couple of cronies settled in a corner of the snug to drink, I sidled close until I was within earshot. For a while the three discussed nothing that seemed germane to the case or indeed that warrants repeating here. Neither the bombings nor

Baron Cauchemar cropped up in their conversation.

Then Torrance beckoned the other two to lean in. His voice dropped, and I bent forward to catch what he had to say.

"Sup up your pints, lads. That consignment of Asian lilies is waiting to be offloaded, and it's a perfect night for it, what with this fog and all. No chance of us getting spotted and having to answer some awkward questions. If we can get them to the client by nine, who knows, maybe they'll be ready to be plucked tonight. Maybe we'll even get first pick, by way of a thank-you."

The larger of his two comrades, a bald-domed, lantern-jawed brute, chortled heartily at this. The smaller, who had something of the weasel about him, peeled back his lips to expose thin brown teeth; it was as much sneer as grin.

Asian lilies? I did not understand the reference. But the sinister glee in Torrance's voice fair chilled me, and I was almost certain that whatever he was referring to, it was not flowers. Holmes, I was sure, would be able to make sense of it when I reported back to him.

In short order, the three ruffians left, and I, in accordance with Holmes's instructions, tagged along. I allowed them to get far enough ahead that they became mere pale silhouettes in the fog. The gap between us was, in the event, a little under thirty yards, and I wished it could be greater, for my own peace of mind and sense of security. However, to drop back further would have been to risk the fog veiling my quarry from view completely. Close as I was to Torrance and his thuggish friends – too close for comfort, really – I had to trust that my barely being able to see them meant they were barely able to see me in return.

They threaded a circuitous route through the docklands, passing along narrow, zigzagging alleyways and low-covered passages and tramping up and down various flights of slimy stone steps. On occasion the swirls of fog thickened and I did lose sight of them and had to hurry to catch up. Fortunately they kept up a raucous banter as they went, so that I was able to track them by ear when vision failed.

The smell of the river grew ever stronger, that noisome mix of brackish water and ancient mud. Finally we arrived at a wharf. I could hear the Thames lapping against wooden pilings like some enormous hound slurping from its bowl. Ahead, through the fog, loomed a three-masted tea clipper, berthed at a pier. Sails furled, it heaved gently back and forth in the current, testing its moorings.

The three men climbed the gangplank and headed below decks immediately. I took refuge behind a stack of barrels on the quayside and waited. I was not going to follow them on board the ship. There was every chance I might find myself cornered there, trapped without an easy escape route. On dry land, at least I had options. Besides, it was a fair bet that Torrance and his accomplices were here not to set sail but to retrieve something, that "consignment of Asian lilies".

Sure enough, not ten minutes later Torrance reappeared, along with another man whose dress and bearing marked him out as the clipper's captain. The pair of them stood on the foredeck awhile, chatting and smoking cigars. I could not discern what they said, but at one point money changed hands, Torrance paying the seadog some sort of commission. Finally, Torrance gave a piercing whistle and his two cronies emerged from below.

With them came a group of women, Chinese natives, perhaps a dozen all told, in silk dresses that had more or less been reduced to filthy rags. The women moved with a broken, hobbling gait, their heads bent low. They looked half-starved and utterly desolate, as though their souls were as malnourished as their bellies. They offered little resistance as the bald brute and the skinny weasel ushered them along at gunpoint, forcing them to file down the gangplank.

I had been right. Not flowers.

Torrance was a people trafficker.

And I had no doubt in my mind whither these unfortunates were destined. They had been smuggled all the way over from the Orient, spending the long weeks of the journey cooped up in a cramped, airless hold down by the clipper's bilges, a false compartment hidden from the scrutiny of cargo inspectors. Now they were to be sold to some house of ill repute or put to work as slaves, either way subjected to the most hideous abuse and degradation.

My blood boiled. It was all I could do to keep from springing from my hiding place and accosting Torrance there and then. I knew this would avail me naught, however. He and his thugs outnumbered me three to one, and were in all probability armed just as I was. Attacking them would be suicide and would not help the Chinese women one bit.

I stayed put, watching in impotent frustration as Torrance and his accomplices trooped past me with their wretched human merchandise.

One of the women, the last in line, tripped on a loose cobblestone and collapsed to her knees just beside me. Her gaze caught mine and a look of confused surprise crossed her face. I saw that she was young, barely a girl. I noted, too, that her pupils were heavily dilated, and surmised that she and the others had been drugged, probably with opium, to keep them docile during the voyage.

Nevertheless she looked as though she was about to say something, perhaps plead with me to help her. I shook my head vigorously, craving her silence. Revealing my whereabouts to Torrance would benefit neither her nor me. With my eyes alone I tried to convey that I would assuredly assist her somehow, just not here and not right now. She seemed to comprehend, much to my relief.

Then the girl was snatched to her feet by Torrance, who hoisted up her frail form with his one arm as easily as if she were made of feathers.

"No kneeling yet, my little yellow angel," Torrance said to her, gloatingly. "There'll be plenty of opportunity for that later. Let's get you to the Abbess's first. You know..." He examined her more closely, turning her head this way and that like a museum curator studying a new exhibit. She winced at the pressure of his fingers on her jaw. "You really are quite a pretty thing, for one of your kind. I know a certain Froggy toff who'll take great delight in acquainting himself with you. Likes 'em young, he does, and fresh, with the dew still on 'em."

The girl found some courage, perhaps emboldened by knowledge of my presence. She spat directly in Torrance's eye, and I had to suppress a cheer.

Torrance was briefly enraged, but then his grin reasserted itself. He let go of the girl and calmly wiped the spittle off on his sleeve.

"I'd belt you one for that, my dear, if the Abbess didn't insist on her girls being unblemished," he said. "Oh yes, our Gallic chum is going to *love* you all right. A feisty, fiery young filly – right up his boulevard, you are."

I filed the reference to a Frenchman in my memory, alongside the name the Abbess. These were details that Holmes would want to tot up in that abacus brain of his later.

Torrance addressed a few further licentious comments to the girl. Though presumably she had no English, his tone and manner required no translation. He was giving her a verbal foretaste of the actual degradation that would soon be her lot. Her revulsion was plain to see.

"Come then," Torrance said finally. "A few minutes' walking, then the Abbess will get you and all these other lovelies scrubbed up and presentable, ready to earn your keep."

He grabbed the girl by the shoulder.

She shot a last, imploring glance in my direction.

Torrance, damn him, spotted this. He followed the line of her gaze, and at the end of it found me.

"Hello," he said menacingly. "What's this? A Peeping Tom? Up with you, mate. Let's have a clearer look at you."

I had no choice but to rise from my crouching position. At the same time I fumbled for my revolver, cursing myself for not having taken the precaution of drawing it sooner.

Before I could liberate the gun from my pocket, Torrance's hand shot out, grabbing me by the throat.

The phrase "vice-like grip" doesn't even begin to describe it. It felt as though immense industrial pincers had clamped themselves around my neck and were slowly, inexorably crushing. I forgot about reaching for my revolver and struggled instead to unpick the massive paw that was throttling me. That was my priority. Yet I might as well have been trying to dislodge the hand of a stone statue.

"I don't like Peeping Toms," Torrance said. "I don't like anyone sneaking around and trying to learn my business. I tend to put a stop to people who do that."

I gasped for air, but none entered my lungs. My neck was in great pain, but greater still was the dread, the panic engendered by being unable to inhale. That which I had hitherto taken for granted – simple respiration – was now denied me, and my entire body convulsed in desperate horror at its absence. All I could see was Torrance's ugly, leering face, his alcohol-pinkened eyes, his rough, ruddy cheeks. This lumpen, hirsute Neanderthal was murdering me, and I was powerless to prevent him.

In those moments, which I believed to be my final ones on this earth, my thoughts turned to Mary, as they should. I regretted that I would never again see my wife's dear face or tell her how much I loved her. I have to admit that Sherlock Holmes crossed my mind as well. I had let him down. I had failed in the task he had charged me with. I hoped my friend would understand that I had done my utmost, and that he would, at the very least, avenge my death.

Dimly I heard a hissing, wheezing noise. I assumed it must be emanating from my own constricted windpipe, the sound of a man frantically trying to gulp in a few molecules of air in order to prolong his life that tiny bit further. It was either that or the blood rushing in my ears as my heart attempted to feed my oxygen-deprived brain.

Psssh-pah, *psssh-pah*.

I then divined that the sound originated outside me. Torrance could hear it too, and his face registered perplexity and not a little alarm.

His hold on my throat loosened ever so slightly, enough to allow me to draw the smallest sip of breath.

"Sinnott? Creevy? What the hell's that?"

"Don't know," said his bald accomplice. "Sounds a bit like a steam locomotive."

"Only there's no railway round here," averred the weaselly one. "Nor any underground track."

"You don't think..." Torrance began, and then his face fell as a terrible realisation dawned. He let go of me entirely and spun round, peering into the fog.

The *psssh-pah*, *psssh-pah* grew louder, accompanied by a matching beat of resounding thuds, something weighty and metallic striking the ground repeatedly.

"Oh crikey, lads," Torrance said. "Look lively. It's him. It's blooming well *him*. The Bloody Black Baron himself!"

He drew a pistol, and Sinnott and Creevy levelled theirs. The

Chinese women cowered together in a huddle, staring about them in dull, uncomprehending fright. I, for my part, sat in a crumpled heap on the wharf, heaving fog into my lungs and blinking dazedly. At the most basic level of consciousness I was aware of what was happening. I was, however, powerless to act, still recovering from my near-asphyxiation.

Psssh-pah! Psssh-pah!

Lights glowed in the fog, two searching eye-like orbs of brilliance.

A glimmering outline resolved into a tall, roughly man-shaped form.

A creature out of a nightmare had lumbered into view. It glared down at us with a face the likes of which would not have been out of place in a painting by Hieronymus Bosch. Its body was both humanoid and insectile, consisting of long segmented limbs and a jointed torso.

Even in my befuddled, half-witted state, I knew that I was looking at none other than Baron Cauchemar.

CHAPTER SEVEN

THE BLOOD OF A MACHINE

Coming to a standstill, Baron Cauchemar surveyed us from a height of at least eight feet. Grout's uncle had not exaggerated his size at all. His great shining head swivelled, his lambent gaze taking in Torrance and cronies, the Chinese women, and me. He seemed to be assessing the assembled company, sorting friend from foe. The glide of his head from side to side was unnaturally smooth, and I discerned a faint whine that went with it, as of oiled machine parts in action.

For a time none of the humans on the quayside moved, too awed and intimidated to do anything but gape at the abomination before us. Then one of the women let out an involuntary gasp of fright, which seemed to break the spell.

Torrance cried, "We've all got barkers, lads. Let him have it!" and he began loosing off shots from his pistol. "This is for all the mates of mine you've nobbled, you miserable, misbegotten bludger!" he roared. "You won't get me like you got them!"

Sinnott and Creevy added their gunfire to his, creating a veritable blizzard of bullets, all of them aimed point-blank at the great shadowy bulk before us.

The impact of the shots staggered Baron Cauchemar. Each struck with sufficient force to make him recoil somewhat. For all that, the bullets rebounded off him without causing any apparent harm. I heard the ricochets whizzing off in all directions. One even smacked into the barrels behind which I had not so long ago been sheltered.

Quickly the guns' cylinders were spent. The air reeked of cordite.

Baron Cauchemar remained standing.

With an oath, Torrance ordered his cronies to attack in person. Both men hesitated.

"Do as I say, damn you," Torrance bellowed, "or so help me I'll stove your brains in myself!"

Thus spurred, the larger of the two thugs, whom I took to be Sinnott, launched himself forwards with a howling war cry. He drove into the baron headlong, grappling with him like a wrestler. To judge by Sinnott's physique he most likely *was* a wrestler.

He caught Bloody Black Baron off-guard and managed to push him back a couple of paces, but then Cauchemar regained his footing and retaliated. The lower portions of his legs telescoped like pistons and extended to their full length again, and, with a loud *psssh-pah*, *psssh-pah*, he thrust Sinnott backwards. The bald brute could not resist or counteract in any way. He was driven wholesale across the wharf until he collided with the wheel of a dray. Wooden wheel spokes shattered with a dreadful splintering *crack*, as did Sinnott's ribcage. With a groan, the thug slumped to the ground.

Creevy leapt on Baron Cauchemar from behind, brandishing a leather blackjack. He coshed the giant creature repeatedly on the head, which served only to annoy him. Cauchemar reached round and hauled Creevy off his back. He suspended him in the air, seemingly with no effort at all, one hand gripping his shirtfront, and I heard a sharp crackle and saw tendrils of bright blue brilliance pass between his palm and the thug's chest, flickering like lightning.

For a moment Creevy writhed, his entire body jerking with helpless spasms. His mouth worked but no sound came out.

Then his head sagged and Cauchemar tossed him to the cobbles, where he lay as insensible as his colleague Sinnott. A wisp of smoke rose from his chest.

The Bloody Black Baron pivoted on the spot, evidently looking for the third crook, the ringleader, Torrance. He, crafty devil, was nowhere to be seen. He must have sought refuge somewhere out of sight while his two cronies were taking a licking.

So Cauchemar then turned his attention on me.

Those glowing eyes of his fixed on me, and I was, as they say, rooted to the spot. The creature had no reason to differentiate me from Torrance and his accomplices. To all intents and purposes I looked like just another people trafficker and, to him, merited the same harsh handling. I braced myself in anticipation of the attack that was sure to come.

"For goodness sake, Watson! Don't just lie there, man. On your feet!"

The oh-so-familiar voice of Sherlock Holmes, coming to me through the mist, had a galvanising effect. I rose, just in time to see a Chinese coolie sprint in out of nowhere – the selfsame coolie who had bumped into me at the pub. He was not stooped any more. He stood straight and tall and ran with a sinewy grace. Now that he was not acting a role, I would have recognised the posture and deportment of my friend anywhere.

"Are you all right?" Holmes said, helping me up.

"Alive," I croaked. My voice had been left reedy and hoarse thanks to Torrance's strangling fist.

"I am more than glad to hear it. Curse me for not getting here sooner. I arrived in time to see Torrance manhandling you, but before I could leap into the fray, another appeared on the scene and saved me the trouble."

He spun to face Cauchemar, who still loomed over us.

"You," he said, addressing the giant in a loud, clear voice, with greater nerve than I ever could have mustered. "Baron Cauchemar I presume. This man is not your enemy. He is no associate of Abednego Torrance. Neither am I. You must know that. We two are on the side of the forces of law and order, and so are you, if your actions here tonight and elsewhere are any indication."

Cauchemar was momentarily still, like some piece of hideous monumental statuary that had been fashioned with the sole aim of deterring and intimidating. I feared he might yet make a move against us, not crediting Holmes's claim that he and I were unconnected with Torrance or his ugly commerce in any way.

Then, from across the wharf, came gunshots. I glimpsed Torrance, some dozens of yards away, leaning out from behind a handcart. He had reloaded and was shooting indiscriminately, caring not whether he hit Cauchemar or us, so long as he hit someone.

One round came perilously close to embedding itself in Holmes. It tore through the wide loose sleeve of his tunic, missing his forearm by a fraction of an inch.

"Quick!" my friend cried to me. "Your gun! Give it to me!"

I fumbled out my revolver. Holmes was certainly right to ask me for it, for I was still too dazed and disorientated even to think about using it myself, let alone shoot straight.

Holmes snatched the gun from me and returned Torrance's fire. None of his shots found their mark, but they did at least force Torrance to take shelter momentarily. When the hammer clicked empty, I snatched a handful of extra bullets from my pocket and Holmes began feeding them into the cylinder.

Baron Cauchemar turned and lumbered towards where Torrance lay. Holmes's gunfire seemed to have finally convinced the creature that we were not his enemies.

Torrance, having also taken the opportunity to reload, resumed firing. I did not see how he expected to penetrate Cauchemar's hide when he had so signally failed to do so before. A couple of rounds pinged and whined off the baron's seemingly impenetrable shell.

But then, with Cauchemar less than spitting distance away, one of Torrance's bullets struck home, virtually at point-blank range, and there was a sharp grating noise and a spurt of liquid. The baron tottered, one leg crumpling under him. For an instant I thought he might fall.

"Ha!" cried Torrance. "Not so invulnerable after all."

Cauchemar recovered his balance and reached for the handcart. He picked it up and tossed it aside as though it weighed nothing.

Torrance, now exposed, took to his heels, fleeing into the fog.

Cauchemar loped after him. It seemed he could not move as fast as he had before. Torrance's shot had done serious damage. The drumbeat of his footfalls, not so rhythmic any more, faded.

The pace of my fear-quickened heartbeat likewise began to subside.

"Holmes," I said, suffused with relief. "You're a sight for sore eyes. Even in that garish rigmarole."

"This disguise, you mean? Garish it may be, old chap, but it fooled you, as my masquerades invariably do."

"That is true," I allowed. "So you were following me, even as I followed Torrance?"

"Merely making doubly sure that our prey did not elude us. The proverbial 'belt and braces' approach."

Holmes doffed his conical straw hat and approached the group of frightened women. He bowed and addressed a few words to them in their own tongue, haltingly. It sounded to me as though he was offering them reassurance, a promise of help.

Then he returned to my side, peeling off his drooping grey moustache and the slivers of foam rubber which he had attached to his eyelids to mimic epicanthic folds.

"Are you recovered?" he enquired. "Up to a chase?"

I nodded.

"Then we must hurry. Torrance and Baron Cauchemar are both getting away. Although, with his leg lamed, I doubt the latter will move fast or get far."

"How on earth do you propose to track them?" I asked. "Especially in this wretched fog."

"Ah, but even if Torrance has left no obvious trail, Cauchemar has."

Holmes went over and knelt by a dark, glistening puddle of liquid.

"Is that blood?" I said.

He drew a finger through it and held a sample up to his nose to sniff.

"In a manner of speaking," he said. "The blood of a machine. Oil. If enough of it keeps spilling out, it should prove easy enough to follow."

"And what of these women? We can't just abandon them."

Before he could answer, we heard running footsteps. Holmes swung round with the revolver, taking aim. He lowered the gun the instant he perceived that the new arrival was none other than a police constable, easily identified as such by the shape of the conical helmet perched atop his head.

"Quick, Watson," he said. "We must abscond before he sees us."

We darted into the fog, padding as softly as the cobbles would allow. The constable went by without spotting us. Discovering the huddle of Chinese women, he immediately began questioning them in his sternest official tones.

"What's all this then? I heard gunshots. Who are you ladies? What are you doing here?"

Naturally his interrogation got no response – none that he could comprehend, at any rate.

Holmes and I hurried onward. Behind us, the constable started blowing his whistle to summon aid from any colleagues within earshot. Its shrill peeps were soon far behind us, getting fainter.

"A stroke of luck, him coming along," Holmes said. "He and his fellow officers can attend to the women, and the presence of police should deter Torrance, if that villain doubles back to reclaim his 'goods', which I doubt."

"Shouldn't we at least have stopped and explained to the chap what was going on?"

"No time right now. Come on. We must keep on the trail while it is still fresh. Something yet can be salvaged from this night's setbacks!"

CHAPTER EIGHT

The Realm of Rats

The spatters of oil were few and far between but formed a distinct, unmistakable spoor nonetheless, which we followed easily for half a mile.

Until, that is, the trail terminated abruptly. We were in a cul-de-sac, silent warehouses towering to either side of us. Holmes inspected the doors and windows of the building for signs of forced entry. He found none.

He rejoined me in the middle of the road, frowning.

"A dead end," he said. "Yet our friend the baron can't simply have vanished into thin air. It's not feasible."

"I disagree," I said. "You saw him yourself. He's a monster of a thing, capable of who knows what. Why should the normal laws of physics apply to him?"

"Because the laws of physics apply to *everything*, Watson," Holmes said in sharp rebuke. "Don't make the mistake of thinking that Baron Cauchemar is in any way a being of magical or supernatural origin. That might be what he wishes people to believe, but trust me, he is not. He is as human as you or I – just augmented somewhat."

"Augmented? You mean to say he's –"

"Confound it. Of course!" Holmes slapped his forehead. "What a dunce I was not to think of it straight away. The sewers."

There was, dead centre of the thoroughfare, a manhole. Holmes knelt and studied the cover.

"Look there. Those scratches around the edge. Two sets, almost exactly opposite one another."

"As though put there by fearsome talons."

"Watson!" Holmes shook his head in a parody of despair. "Here, help me lift it."

He bent and began to grapple with the heavy iron cover. I joined him, and together, at some cost to our backs and fingernails, we succeeded in dislodging it. The smell of human waste drifted up from the aperture to greet us, along with the faint susurration of running water.

"We're going down there, aren't we?" I sighed.

"Needs must, my dear doctor."

Holmes produced a nickel-plated pocket-lantern from the folds of his silk pyjamas and lit the candle within. The flame, magnified by mirrors, shed a penetrating beam of light through the lantern's glass front.

"How convenient that you brought that with you," I remarked.

"I'm never knowingly under prepared," Holmes replied with the merest hint of a smile.

We descended the clammy iron rungs of the ladder that was bolted to the side of the shaft, and soon we found ourselves ankle deep in a stream of foul-smelling and disconcertingly warm fluid.

"I don't suppose you thought to bring a couple of pairs of galoshes as well," I said.

"Not *that* well prepared, alas. But if the worst we come away with tonight is ruined shoes, we should count ourselves lucky."

Actually, the boots I had on were an old, worn-out pair, in

keeping with the rest of my outfit. I would not mourn their loss that greatly.

Holmes led the way along the vaulted tunnel of the sewer, his pocket-lantern's beam piercing the mephitic darkness. Rats scurried away in alarm from our advance. It was their realm, but they were accustomed to having it to themselves and were unused to intruders. Sir Joseph Bazalgette, who had devised this entire subterranean drainage system just thirty years earlier, could scarcely have guessed that he was creating the perfect environment for rodents such as these to flourish in. The rats thrived off Londoners' effluvium and detritus, their population larger now than at any time in the city's history. Above ground, the capital may have become a cleaner and less noxious place to live, thanks to Sir Joseph and his engineers, but below ground it was more infested than ever with vermin. A paradox of the modern age. For every advance of progress, a drawback.

"Holmes," I said. "These tunnels stretch a hundred miles and more. We've entered a veritable labyrinth. How can we hope to find Cauchemar? He could be anywhere." I didn't add that I had no great desire to meet the baron again; I would not have Holmes thinking me a coward.

"I fear you may be right, Watson. However, there is always a chance that – Ah-ha."

"What is it?"

We had come to a bend in the tunnel. Holmes held the pocket-lantern close to the wall, low down. "Do you see?"

I peered. "It seems to be… a scrape of some kind."

"A straight-edged groove gouged in the brickwork," said Holmes. "Fresh, too." He fingered the mark. "Observe how the brick powder comes away readily to the touch. This was made in the last few minutes. And look, here's another." He moved the lantern. "Running parallel to the first, but a good three feet higher up. And a further one, directly above us. It is as though the edges of something large and metallic has bumped against the wall, something travelling at speed."

"Whatever can it signify?"

"Too early to tell," said Holmes. "But it suggests to me that not only did the baron come this way, he continued his journey with a celerity that we cannot hope to match on foot. No, he is long gone, my friend. Further searching down here will yield little more."

I was not unhappy that he had said that. The stench was starting to get to me. I was dizzy, almost lightheaded with it.

"So we turn back?" I said, not attempting to feign disappointment.

"We do."

As we retraced our footsteps to the ladder, I noticed that Holmes appeared cheerful, more so than the situation seemed to merit. I remarked on this.

"We have made some headway this evening, Watson," said he. "My gambit to draw Baron Cauchemar into the open, using the disagreeable Abednego Torrance as bait, paid off."

"But how did you know he would go for Torrance?"

"I have been lurking around the East End all day, in disguise, eavesdropping. Nobody pays much attention to a coolie, and most assume he 'no speakee English', so people are unusually candid in the presence of one. Once I got wind of Torrance and his shipment of women, it seemed exactly the sort of crime Cauchemar would wish to put a stop to. You know how I like to go on about 'the balance of probabilities'. I applied it in this instance, and it bore fruit."

"Inspired."

"There's no denying that I'm disappointed that Torrance got away from us, as he did from Cauchemar too. The baron was clearly quite badly damaged by Torrance's bullet, so Torrance was easily able to outpace him and elude him. Cauchemar must have then decided to repair to the sewers and make good his own escape."

"All of which leaves us little better off."

"Come, come. Don't be downhearted. We are still alive, that is something, and we are undoubtedly wiser than before. More importantly, we have saved those Chinese ladies from an appalling fate. Speaking of whom, let us return to the docks, where in all likelihood a rather confused constable is still trying to get some sense out of them. I will help him out with my admittedly somewhat sketchy Mandarin. After that, we both deserve a good night's rest. Then, tomorrow, we shall reconvene and consider our next move."

CHAPTER NINE

A Living Ironclad

Owing to the demands of my practice, I did not make it to Baker Street until well after noon the next day. A familiar visitor preceded me there: G. Lestrade of Scotland Yard. The sallow little CID inspector had taken a chair beside the hearth, near the Persian slipper on the mantel in which Holmes kept his tobacco, and was tucking into some buttered crumpets. I asked Mrs Hudson to prepare a plate of the same for myself, and a pot of hot tea, as I had forgone lunch in my eagerness to come over from Paddington and was famished.

"I gather you and Mr Holmes had a close encounter with a bogeyman last night," Lestrade said, licking butter off his fingers.

"If you mean Baron Cauchemar, quite so," I said, with a not altogether simulated shudder. "It is an experience I would not care to repeat in a hurry."

"There's many of my lads who think he's no bad thing. Real or not –"

"Oh, he's real all right."

"Real or not," Lestrade repeated, "the so-called Bloody Black

Baron has been responsible for a marked drop in crime in the East End and environs. A lot of crooks just aren't going out at night any more. Too worried they'll bump into him and come off worse. I only wish I'd thought of the idea myself – put about a rumour that there's a fiend at large who's giving ne'er-do-wells a good drubbing. There's none so superstitious as criminals. It doesn't take much to put the wind up them. Result: safer streets for law-abiding citizens to walk, and we coppers can put our feet up. A perfect world."

"I can assure you, Inspector," said Holmes, "as Watson says, Baron Cauchemar is no rumour. His corporeal existence is beyond question."

"Well, if a perspicacious and noteworthy gent such as yourself says that that is the case, who am I to argue?" said Lestrade. "What is it, then? A gang of armed civilians? Some of the tough eggs this baron's given what-for, and the way he seems to crop up in a dozen different places in the course of a single night, it surely can't be a lone vigilante."

"I believe that's exactly what he is. A singularly resourceful individual who has turned himself into – well, the best description is a 'living ironclad.'"

Lestrade shook his head in wonderment. His hair was slicked down with so much Macassar, it shimmered like a chestnut as the light moved across it. "You must be joking. He's... armoured? Like some sort of latterday knight?"

"Indeed so. But there is more to it than that. More to *him*. I daresay I have only just begun to plumb the mysteries of Baron Cauchemar. But it is not he that you have come here to discuss, Inspector."

"No," said Lestrade. "It's those Oriental lasses you lumbered my colleagues with last night. Or, specifically, the note you left with them, addressed to me."

"You have acted on my instructions, then?"

"I've managed to find the time, Mr Holmes, although frankly

I'm not sure how. In case you haven't noticed, the Yard has its hands full at present. Not only are there these damnable bombings to investigate, but there's unrest all over the city. Protests on almost every corner. Folk demanding action, wanting to see some culprits held to account. We police are stretched to breaking point."

"Which means I appreciate your efforts all the more."

"Yes, well," said Lestrade gruffly. "So, first off, we've put the Chinawomen up in a boarding house for the time being, while we work out what to do with them."

"What will become of them?" I asked.

"It largely depends on what they themselves want. I've made enquiries among the Chinese immigrant community in Limehouse. There are jobs available for the women if they wish to remain on these shores – laundry work, skivvying in restaurants and suchlike. Getting them back to their native land may prove more problematic, but a few of the wealthier Orientals are organising a whip-round with a view to paying for their return passage. They won't be travelling first-class but the conditions will still be a damn sight better than on the journey here."

"And Abednego Torrance?" said Holmes. "What of him? Any sign?"

"I've put the word out, but so far, no sightings. If the miscreant has any sense, he'll be lying low until things blow over. As for his charming accomplices Bill 'The Bull' Sinnott and Jasper Creevy…"

"Both not exactly strangers to the police, I take it."

"Their faces are not unfamiliar, nor are their case files entirely bare. They are, as we speak, recovering in hospital, manacled to the frames of their beds – not that they're going anywhere in a hurry, the state they were left in. Neither is well enough to assist us in our enquiries just yet, but from experience I can tell you that they're likely to remain tight-lipped no matter what. The hardened sort of crook always does. Them and their 'code of honour'."

"That is a shame, although I suspect they do not know anything that could help us materially anyway. They are hired hands, mere stooges. There remains one last matter. Watson overheard Torrance mention a certain 'Abbess'. Is the name at all familiar to you?"

"As it happens, it is," said Lestrade. "The lady – and I use the term advisedly – is well known to us at the Yard. One of London's most notorious madams. We've raided her brothel on many an occasion. Trouble is, we close down one of her emporia, send her and all her trollops packing, and a week later she's upped stakes and opened another somewhere else. She's a persistent one, and no mistake."

"Perhaps she would not be so persistent if there wasn't such a demand for her wares," Holmes observed. "And if the courts did not treat her so leniently."

"True, Mr Holmes. Regrettably, she has friends in high places. Some of her clients are men who hold great sway with the Met Commissioner. Charges against her seldom stick. I doubt she's seen the inside of the Old Bailey more than twice in all the years she's been plying her trade."

"Would it be possible for me to speak to her?"

"I can't stop you," the policeman said with a casual shrug. "I daresay I can even furnish you with her current address, if that'd help. She doesn't keep regular, sociable hours, mind."

Holmes smiled thinly. "She and I have that in common, at least."

"She's more like an owl, or a bat. You go to see her now, you'll probably find her just rising from her slumbers."

"Then I pray we shall give her not too rude an awakening."

CHAPTER TEN

The Froggy Toff

All I could think was: Thank God Mary can't see me right now.

For I was in the parlour of a brothel just off Moorgate, seated opposite its madam and two of her harlots. Holmes was with me, but this did little to mitigate my discomfort.

The room was decorated to look opulent, yet the brocade upholstery on the furnishings was old and worn in places and the flock wallpaper was peeling at the corners. Likewise the entire building, a tall terraced tenement house on a reasonably decent street, gave off an air of respectability until you noticed the occasional cracked and unrepaired windowpane and the patches of crumbling brickwork that begged for re-rendering.

The Abbess herself was a flaxen-haired woman no longer in the bloom of youth but still presentable, her beauty mellowing into handsomeness. She was fleshy, one might even say voluptuous, the hourglass curvaceousness of her figure in no way disguised by the cut of her nightdress, especially its plunging décolletage. We had indeed, as Lestrade predicted, caught her just as she was beginning her "day".

The presence of the two harlots seemed superfluous, yet the
Abbess had insisted they accompany her during the meeting.
They spent the whole time pouting provocatively at Holmes
and me and offering us sly, come-hither looks. Neither of them
was unattractive, nor was either of them fully dressed, wearing
nothing but corsetry, stockings and bloomers. I found their
undergarments and their coquettish behaviour deeply distracting,
which was no doubt the point – an attempt to put us off our stroke.
I felt as though the collar of my shirt had been over-starched and
was constricting my throat. Holmes, by contrast, seemed able to
ignore them and direct his focus solely on the Abbess. His powers
of self-control bordered at times on the superhuman.

"My dear lady…" he said.

The Abbess let loose a laugh that was ingenuous yet seasoned,
some way between a giggle and a cackle. "Ooh, hark at him. 'My
dear lady'! Proper gent you must be, Mr Holmes. Easy on the eye,
too, if you like your lovers on the lean side, which I happen to.
Please tell me you're unattached. I've been looking to settle down
and make an honest woman of myself, and you might be just the
husband material for me."

Her two companions found this highly amusing, and one of
them directed a flirtatious smile at me and said, "His friend has a
kind of rugged charm about him and all."

I held up my left hand, proudly displaying my wedding band.
"I am most happily married."

"That doesn't bother me if it doesn't bother you, dearie," said
the lass, and she and her friend dissolved into fits of sniggering.

"How would you rather I addressed you, then?" Holmes
asked the Abbess, not in the least bit sidetracked by this saucy
banter. "I certainly shan't call you 'mother superior'. Perhaps Marie
Robertson would be better? Or how about Margaret Rowbotham?
Madeleine Ramsey? Maggie Reilly? Millie Ryker? Matilda Robb?"

"Been checking up on me, eh, Mr Holmes?" The Abbess's accent affected a wispy refinement but underneath lay a husk of pure, ineradicable Cockney.

"I've done my homework." In fact it was Lestrade who had supplied the litany of aliases, declaring that the Abbess had had more of them in her time than hot dinners.

"I should be flattered that you're so inquisitive," she said. "Your list barely scrapes the surface, though. Even I am not sure any more which name's the one I was christened with, so just 'the Abbess' would be simplest. It suits me fine. It's a common nickname for someone in my position, but I also like to think I look out for the welfare of the girls in my care, much as a real abbess tends to the needs of her nuns."

"The comparison is hardly apt," I spluttered. "A place like this could never be confused with a convent."

"Don't be so sure, Dr Watson. I've known many a client who likes a girl to be dressed up in habit and wimple before he ravishes her. Some of them have even been clergymen."

"I shall pretend I never heard that."

"The only difference, as I see it, is that a convent trades solely in the spiritual whereas my establishment trades solely in the physical," the Abbess said. "Mind you, even that is open to debate, given some of the tales I've heard about what goes on in convents after lights out."

"We are straying somewhat from the purpose of our visit," said a pained Holmes.

"A man who likes to get quickly to the point. I hope you are not so quick in other respects. That would be very disappointing."

Again, the harlots found this hugely amusing.

"Abbess," said Holmes, "you and I both know that you were supposed to be in receipt of an influx of new recruits last night."

"I have no idea what you're talking about," the woman said airily.

"We have eyewitness testimony that would link you clearly to the smuggling-in of a number of girls from China."

"You can't prove anything."

"Do you deny it?"

"Most strenuously." The Abbess's façade of joviality slipped somewhat, revealing a glimpse of a steely nature beneath, like a stiletto dagger being part-way withdrawn from a velvet sheath. "There is nothing to connect me to any such girls."

"Nothing directly," Holmes admitted, "but the circumstantial evidence is strong. Strong enough that the police would take little persuading to pay a call and turn this place upside down."

"For all the good it would do them. All I'd do is pay a few fines, wink at the right people, and be back in business in next to no time."

"Yet I would imagine you'd prefer to avoid the related upheaval and the temporary loss of earnings."

"So that's how it is, is it?" said the Abbess. "And here was I thinking you a gentleman. What's your price? I could offer you the night of your life, if that's what you're after. On the house. Your friend too. Together? One of you watching? We cater for all tastes here."

"*All* tastes," said one of the two harlots, and to my horror she turned and caressed her friend's cheek, then planted a kiss full on her lips. The other girl responded as if this were the most pleasurable thing in the world, uttering a soft guttural moan.

Holmes merely looked wry. "Information is all I require. Names. A list of the names of some of your regulars."

"Which ones? I have hundreds. You'll have to narrow it down."

"Foreign ones. Ones with titles. Frenchmen specifically."

"And supposing I had such a list, what would you do with it?"

"Simply run an eye over it. I'm searching for one name in particular. Once I have that, I can discard and forget the rest."

"Hmmm." The Abbess looked pensive. "And you give me your word that that's all? You get a name, and I get no hassle from the bluebottles?"

"None that will come as a result of anything I have done. I give you my solemn promise on that."

She studied my friend. "Over the years I have come to be a good judge of character, Mr Holmes, especially of men's characters. I've seen them all, at their best and their worst. I know the ins and outs of them, in more ways than one. You strike me as honourable. I'm inclined to take you at your word. Pearl?"

One of the courtesans stood, like a soldier called to attention.

"Fetch me the book."

"Which book, Abbess?"

"You know the one. The one we keep hidden."

The girl disappeared, returning a minute later with a small journal wrapped in oilcloth.

"I would suggest that behind a loose brick inside a chimney breast in the kitchen is not the securest place for such an item," Holmes said. "You might want to consider putting it somewhere else where there is less danger of it being so strongly heated that it catches alight."

The Abbess was startled. "How did you –?"

"I observed the faint soot marks now adorning Pearl's hand and forearm, which were not there before and which are of a particularly greasy kind such as are left by a cooking fire. They extend almost to her elbow, indicating that she has had to reach inside an aperture to some depth. That and the brick dust adhering to the book's oilcloth covering led me to my conclusion."

The Abbess regarded my friend with newfound appreciation. "We do not actually use the kitchen for cooking. The soot is old, dating from the previous owners. This used to be a family house. But I can see that I shall have to be unusually wily around you, sir."

She brandished the journal. "Here it is, my full client list. Actual names, or if those aren't known, the false names they choose to give. I keep it in case… Well, a lady has to have something up her sleeve, should she find herself in real trouble. A contingency plan."

She handed the journal, with a show of considerable reluctance, to Holmes.

"They're arranged according to type. Age. Financial circumstances. Marital status. The foreigners section is about halfway through. I don't really distinguish between nationalities. I lump them all together. You could say they're all Greek to me!"

Holmes flicked through the pages until he arrived at the section she spoke of. I peered over his shoulder, and immediately my eyebrows rose and my jaw fell. There were noted diplomats named there, a couple of ambassadors, a royal courtier, not to mention several prominent aristocrats, and even a prince from one of those forested and castled little countries that sit in the hinterland between Germany and Russia. On any given page there was enough material to keep the Fleet Street scandal sheets busy for a year.

"These symbols," Holmes said. He pointed to the sets of peculiar little hieroglyphs which attended each name: crosses, spirals, strange algebraic squiggles. "They are… predilections?"

"That is correct," said the Abbess. "Every man who comes here has his quirks and peccadilloes, his likes and fancies. I make a note of them. That way I can keep track of which girl to match to which client, and also, if the circumstances ever became so dire, threaten to reveal the full sordid truth to a wife, an employer, even a newspaper. It's my weapon, my last line of defence if friendly persuasion fails."

Holmes ran a finger down the list until it stopped at one. "Here," he said. "This could be he, the man we're after."

He showed the name to the Abbess. Her face soured a little.

"His name has these two symbols appended to it," Holmes

said, pointing to a V and a shape like a black teardrop. "What do they stand for?"

"That," said the Abbess, indicating the teardrop, "is a drop of blood. It means he tends to get a bit rough sometimes. The girls don't mind that so much, as long as they know in advance and they're sufficiently well compensated for it."

"And the V?" I said. "Does it stand for 'virgin'?"

"Not necessarily. I derived the symbol from… Well, imagine it represents a part of the anatomy where on a mature lady there would be hair but on a young girl there would be none."

All at once I felt queasy.

Holmes pursed his lips grimly. "That confirms it," he said. "We have our man." He returned the book to the Abbess and stood to leave. "I thank you for your assistance, Abbess."

"You're welcome, Mr Holmes. You didn't get his name from me, of course."

"Of course."

"And my offer still stands. If ever you and your friend want a night you'll never forget, here's the place to come. My treat."

"I doubt we shall avail ourselves of your hospitality again," said Holmes briskly, and he swept out of the parlour, as did I.

Outside I inhaled a few deep breaths of acrid London air, which was somehow sweeter than the cloyingly over-perfumed interior of the brothel.

"By Jove," I said. "I feel quite unclean. If my wife were ever to find out…"

"I shan't tell her if you won't," said Holmes.

"That list, though. It beggars belief."

I am not a naïve man. In my way I am quite worldly, and my experiences with Holmes have brought me into contact with some of the worst individuals this world has to offer, the most corrupt, the most venal. Still, I found it hard to believe that personages of rank and renown would frequent an establishment like the Abbess's. Did they not fear for their prestige and status, were their private indulgences ever to be made public? How could they represent the interests of overseas powers and yet risk bringing so much shame not only on themselves but their fellow-countrymen? What about the sensibilities and reputation of their wives, their families? Who would be willing to jeopardise all they had purely to slake their lusts? It baffled me.

Holmes was his usual inscrutable self, his face betraying little of the sentiments which I am sure he was feeling and which were doubtless akin to mine.

"The list, shocking though it is," he said, "was, of course, the reason we put ourselves through that. I was looking for the French nobleman whom you overheard Torrance mention in such an oblique and casual fashion."

"Ah yes, the 'Froggy toff'."

"There were a number of Frenchmen named. However, the Abbess's code identified this particular one as being fond of barely pubescent girls, and did you not tell me that Torrance said something about the nobleman liking girls who were 'fresh, with the dew still on them'? Putting the two things together yielded only one possible candidate."

"And the Frenchman and Baron Cauchemar are connected somehow?"

"What makes you say that, old chap?"

"You seem mad-keen on pursuing Cauchemar, almost to the point where nothing else matters, not even the bombings. I can only assume this is another manifestation of that monomania."

"Monomania? I would not put it so strongly myself."

"That is how it might appear to a dispassionate observer."

Holmes chuckled wryly. "What would I do without you, Watson? You remind me constantly that the workings of a mind like mine must seem incomprehensible to a mind like yours. It is like a tortoise trying to fathom the speed of a cheetah."

"Oh," I said, not flattered.

"But you're right all the same. About this being about Cauchemar. It is, to some extent. There is the Torrance link, of course. Hearsay but no less valuable for that. There is also the superficial-seeming fact that *cauchemar* is a French word."

"Meaning...?"

"'Nightmare'. Apt, *n'est-ce pas*? We must bear in mind, too, that the Abbess's French client has a title, and our ironclad vigilante has bestowed the rank of baron upon himself. Each, individually, a slender association, but together, cumulatively, I find them persuasive. At the very least, they are enough to make me think that you and I should pay a house call on a certain French peer who currently resides in London: the Vicomte de Villegrand."

CHAPTER ELEVEN

AT THE VILLA DE VILLEGRAND

We journeyed by cab from Moorgate to a grand Gothic villa up in Hampstead, a stone's throw from the Heath. The house was well-kept, the front garden tidy and orderly, the wisteria that overhung the porch trimmed.

Even now, in the broad light of day, outside this fine and desirable residence, I could not wholly dismiss the events of the previous night from my thoughts. I was oppressed by the memory of our encounter with Baron Cauchemar and found it hard to shake the feeling that, in spite of Holmes's insistence to the contrary, we had been in the presence of something not wholly of this earth.

I had learned, with Sherlock Holmes, to be wary of expressing notions that were not entirely in keeping with his ultra-rational world view. Only the year before, during our hair-raising escapade at Baskerville Hall and on the surrounding moors, it had been amply demonstrated to me that something which seemed supernatural, even hellish, could be explained away as a product of human ingenuity combined with human suggestibility.

And so now, while a part of me continued to maintain that Cauchemar was nightmarish in more than name alone, that he was at least in part paranormal, that he even carried a whiff of infernal brimstone about him, I knew better than to raise this possibility again with Holmes. He would have none of it. He would pooh-pooh the very idea and ridicule me, and I feared his scorn almost as much as I feared another meeting with the Bloody Black Baron.

Holmes's voice summoned me out of my brooding.

"Watson," he said as we strode up the front path, "whatever happens in the next few minutes, do not intervene and do not protest. Just follow my lead and trust my judgement. Is that understood?"

I nodded assent.

In answer to our knock, the door was opened by a manservant whose lugubrious demeanour belied his relative youthfulness. He enquired, in a thick French accent, who we were and what our business was.

Holmes handed over his card, and the manservant invited us in to wait in the hallway while he went to see "whether *monsieur le vicomte* is receiving the visitors today".

The villa's interior was decorated tastefully but expensively and exhibited a cleanliness that matched the neatness of its exterior. It was just the sort of house I would have loved to call my own, although at that time I never in my wildest dreams would have been able to afford it. A GP's salary by itself, irregular and unreliable as it was, was far too meagre to cover the mortgage, and my accounts of my adventures with Holmes, though popular, had yet to make me my fortune.

Yet somehow, for all the pleasantness of the surroundings, my unease would still not abate. Perhaps it was the fact of knowing that the master of this household frequented the Abbess's brothel – and no doubt other places like it – where he took his delight with girls who were not even yet fully adult. Children of such a young age participating in the world's oldest profession were not uncommon, but I myself could not fathom how any man could desire them as he might a grown woman. It seemed perversion of the rankest kind.

The manservant returned and wordlessly ushered us through to a drawing room at the rear.

Here sat a man in his mid-thirties, with hair artfully combed and curled and a moustache upon which great care and attention had been lavished, its tips teased into points with the aid of liberal quantities of beeswax pomade. A neat, straight scar traversed the left-hand side of his face, from cheekbone to jaw, but in spite of that, and a pendulous nose and somewhat too full lips, he was handsome, one might even say rakishly so.

Giving a low, straight-backed bow, he introduced himself as Thibault, the Vicomte de Villegrand.

"And," said he, "I have the pleasure of meeting the incomparable Sherlock Holmes himself? In person? Why, this is an honour. Your renown has reached us even in France. Your methods, your prowess – formidable." He turned to me. "You, of course, must be Dr Watson, his faithful chronicler. I salute you too, *monsieur le docteur*. Without you, the world would know nothing of this mighty Englishman and his achievements. You have done us all a tremendous service, sharing your accounts of Monsieur Holmes's cases, and relating them with such skill too. Together, the pair of you represent all that is great about Great Britain. You are shining beacons of your nation."

It would be hard not to be unmoved by such praise. However, there was something a little unctuous about it. It was excessive and, I could not help but feel, insincere. And of course, knowing what I knew about him, I was hardly inclined to warm to the man.

"Please, take a seat," said de Villegrand. "Make yourselves at home. Benoît!"

The gloomy-looking manservant stiffened. "À *votre service.*"

"Tell Aurélie to bring us refreshments. Some sherry, I think. That is a very English aperitif to take of an afternoon, *non?*"

While we waited for our drinks to arrive, de Villegrand regaled us with positive opinions of our country, of which he had many. He rhapsodised about Britain's literary heritage from Shakespeare to Dickens, her empire ("on which 'the sun never sets', isn't that what they say?"), her vitality, her prosperity, and last but not least her queen, whose long and exemplary reign, he said, almost made him regret that his own people had done away with their monarchy and embraced republicanism. When he began to wax lyrical about the British climate, that was when I began to think that, in some obscure Gallic manner, he was actually mocking us. I have never met a Frenchman, before or since, who had anything good to say about the weather in this island kingdom. I have never, for that matter, met a native Briton who did anything but moan about the rain, wind and fog that beset our homeland.

Holmes must have felt likewise, for he said, "Surely you cannot be serious, your lordship, to suggest that a summer's day in London could be the equal of a summer's day in Paris?"

"Surely I can, Monsieur Holmes," came the reply. "Have you ever been in Paris in August? It is unbearable. The heat makes one's clothes stick to one's skin in a most uncongenial manner, and it is so oppressive that one can barely walk down a street without feeling faint. And the stench. *Mon Dieu!* It is not as bad nowadays as it was in my youth, not since Haussmann set to work revitalising the city, but even so, sometimes on hot days the smell from the slums floats over the bourgeois areas and everywhere the air stinks like a farmyard. No, there is much to be said for a temperate climate. And good sewers."

Holmes pounced on the remark. "You admire our sewer system too?" The question, though casual-sounding, carried weight. He was probing for a reaction.

Did Holmes think that de Villegrand and Baron Cauchemar were one and the same? It was hard to believe, yet that was the line of enquiry he appeared to be exploring. Accordingly, I took a closer look at the vicomte, reappraising him. He was tall, well built, and seemingly in excellent physical condition. For all that he dressed with a certain flamboyance and was clearly not immune to the sin of vanity, he was not someone, in my view, to be taken lightly or trifled with. There was a dark slyness in those eyes of his, and his forehead, though not a match for Holmes's in size, was still broad and high, suggesting that behind the effusive bonhomie lay a considerable brain.

"Paris, of course, had sewers long before London," he said, "and they are extensive and supremely effective. Yours, though, are a marvel of modern sanitation all the same."

"How tactfully put," said Holmes.

"But of course. I am, after all, a diplomat. A cultural attaché, to be exact, affiliated with the French embassy. And what is a cultural attaché's function but to appreciate the accomplishments of his host nation, while at the same time trumpeting the accomplishments of his own? Ah, here is Benoît again, with Aurélie."

The manservant had re-entered, accompanied by a maid carrying a salver on which sat a crystal decanter and glasses. The maid was young and exceedingly comely, and de Villegrand's gaze did not stray from her once while she was in the room. Neither did Benoît's, who followed her every movement closely. There was no need for Benoît to look on while she performed her duties of pouring out the sherry and distributing it to her master and his guests, but he watched her like a hawk anyway.

Aurélie herself kept her eyes demurely lowered, scarcely glancing at anyone. Nor did she utter so much as a single syllable, even when, in a moment of inattention, she tipped my glass and poured a few drops of sherry onto my lap. Her reaction then was to blush profusely and bow her head in abject shame, much like a dog that knows it is in disgrace. I reassured her, in my rudimentary French, that she had done nothing wrong, accidents happened, it was *pas de problème, mademoiselle*, and I dabbed away the dampness with my handkerchief. Aurélie seemed little comforted, however, and left the room in distress, Benoît guiding her by the arm and speaking softly to her in their mother tongue.

"I must apologise, Doctor," de Villegrand said. "Aurélie is not normally so clumsy."

"It is quite all right. No harm done. Quiet girl, though."

"Yes. But do not be perturbed by her silence, nor for that matter Benoît's protectiveness. He is her older brother, you see, and Aurélie is… How to put it? Simple. Painfully introverted. A congenital condition. She seldom speaks and is shy to a degree that would seem like rudeness to the uninitiated. Yet she does what she is told to do, that is her saving grace. Give Aurélie an instruction and she will perform it to the letter, usually without error. She is like an automaton in that way, her actions controllable and predictable. The corollary of that is to break from her routine or to err is a source of great distress, as you have seen."

I noted how he dehumanised the girl by comparing her to a machine. Perhaps that was how he felt about all women – indeed all people.

"She and Benoît are the daughter and son of my father's estate manager," de Villegrand continued, "so I, one might say, inherited them and have assumed responsibility for them. My father did not leave me much else, beyond a title. He was, sad to relate, a man of many bad habits, principally drinking and gambling, and when he died, the land and château which should have been mine were instead sold to pay off his considerable debts to his many creditors. I grew up in expectation of a life of moneyed leisure, but *hélas*!

It was not to be." He shrugged his shoulders in that way unique to his race, an eloquent expression of regret and resignation. "I am, however, quite content in my role as a member of the *corps diplomatique*, representing France to her sister nation across the Channel. It is a worthy and dignified position. Now, esteemed guests, if you would kindly join me in a toast…"

De Villegrand raised his glass, and Holmes and I reciprocated.

"To the remarkable Monsieur Holmes and his companion the redoubtable Dr Watson, and to the good relations which I hope and pray will continue to prevail between our two great countries and their dependencies in perpetuity. *Vive l'Entente Cordiale!*"

The sherry was a particularly good Amontillado, and I drained my ration of it in a few quick sips. Holmes, by contrast, barely touched his.

"Tell me, Dr Watson," the vicomte said, "are we to be treated to any more of your fine books soon? I enjoyed *A Study In Scarlet* and *The Sign Of Four* very much, and am most eager to read more of Monsieur Holmes's exploits."

"I am preparing a dozen or so manuscripts even now," I replied. "These will be in short-story form, not novel-length. That seems to suit the narratives better, on the whole. I am inclined to move on from *Beeton's* and *Lippincott's*. I have heard word that a new monthly magazine from George Newnes Limited, name of *The Strand*, is to begin publication in December. I plan to submit my latest efforts to the editor of that."

"I will be sure to purchase an edition if I see your name on the cover. It is fascinating to learn about Mr Holmes's methods and powers of analysis, which surpass even those of the great Eugène Vidocq, founder of our own Sûreté."

"I am flattered to be mentioned in the same breath as one of the forefathers of modern criminology," said Holmes. "However," he added brusquely, his tone that of someone whose patience was fast dwindling, "forgive me, but we did not come here to make small talk."

De Villegrand gave no sign of offence at my friend's peremptoriness. "No, I suspected this was not a purely social call, much though I would like it to have been. You are, it is obvious, engaged on a case. Perhaps you seek my help in some way. Or am I by some chance implicated in a crime? I sincerely hope not the latter. I am, believe me, an honourable man."

"Yes, honour matters to you. That much is evident from the scar on your cheek. Inflicted in a duel, if I'm not mistaken. It has the straightness of a sword cut. A sabre, to judge by the width and depth of the wound."

De Villegrand touched the scar reflexively, and his face coloured a little.

"Someone had the temerity to accuse me, in front of witnesses, of a shameful deed. I do not take slurs on my name lightly. He lived to regret his mistake."

"Then I trust that I shall too," Holmes said. "Live to regret mine, I mean."

The Frenchman's face reddened further.

"How so? Have you come to bandy about baseless accusations also?"

"That would be unwise."

"It would."

"Were they baseless," Holmes added. "This room is not a public forum. There is no one here but we three. An informal gathering. So it would not, technically, be a slur on your name if I mentioned that you have visited, on more than one occasion, a house of ill repute run by a woman widely known as the Abbess."

De Villegrand shot to his feet. "That is a lie. A most outrageous fabrication."

"You deny it?"

"Vehemently. With every breath in my body."

"Then perhaps you deny, too, a predilection for the younger female – girls that are little more than children."

The vicomte's head purpled from the neck up. It was difficult to tell if this was from indignation or embarrassment or both.

"Monsieur, you provoke me," he thundered. "You insult me in my own home. What you are saying is a gross calumny. I demand a retraction and an apology, or there will be consequences."

"You will have neither, my short-tempered friend," said Holmes calmly.

"Then I will have satisfaction some other way. Monsieur Holmes, do you fight?"

"I am not unskilled in pugilism and other forms of hand-to-hand combat."

"*Très bien*! Then I challenge you, right now, to fight me. We shall step outside and settle this like men." Already de Villegrand had whisked off his velvet smoking jacket and was rolling up his shirtsleeves; the matter, to him, a foregone conclusion. He had invited Holmes to engage in fisticuffs; so they would.

Holmes rose, and I shot him a look, as if to say, "Are you mad? What are you doing?"

He batted my concerns aside, saying to de Villegrand, "It's good we have Watson to hand, his medical expertise will prove invaluable should one or other of us suffer injury."

"One of us will," said the vicomte, throwing open the glass-panelled doors that gave on to a large, wrought-iron conservatory, which in turn gave on to the back garden. "And rest assured, Monsieur Holmes, it will not be *moi*."

He exited. We followed. In the conservatory, he paused to pat the heads of a pair of stuffed animals which stood sentinel either side of the doorway. One was a grey wolf, the other a wild boar.

"My trophies," he told us. "I shot them myself in the Forest of Tronçais, when I was still in my teens. I take them with me wherever I go. They are my talismans."

The message was clear. The vicomte wanted us to know that he was a hunter, unafraid of danger, not squeamish about bloodshed.

And both wolf and boar were intimidating, I cannot lie. The taxidermist had done a skilful job with them. Fangs and tusks bared, haunches hunched, they looked as though they were ready to charge at us at any moment and tear us to pieces.

Holmes must have spied the apprehension on my face, for he leaned close and said, "Fear not, Watson. If they magically come to life, I'll protect you."

"It's not the stuffed creatures I'm worried about. It's what they represent."

"I see. It is a good thing, then, that *le vicomte* is not carrying a gun. And," he added, "that I am not a dumb animal."

CHAPTER TWELVE

SAVATE VERSUS *BARITSU*

We stood on the patch of lawn that was shortly to become a gladiatorial arena. De Villegrand set to limbering up, working out his shoulders and performing little jumps on the spot. Holmes doffed his jacket and gave it to me to hold. Then, as the vicomte had done, he unbuttoned his shirtsleeves and rolled them up.

"Holmes," I whispered, in a final attempt to talk him out of it, "this is not necessary. What's to be gained? Apologise to de Villegrand. Call the fight off. Sparring with him is hardly the way to establish his guilt or innocence."

"No," said my companion, "but it is a reliable yardstick by which to take the measure of the man."

"Someone who is so swift to challenge another to combat would not do so if he were not confident of his abilities in that field."

"I am no slouch myself when it comes to the use of the fists, Watson. I boxed at university, remember, and have picked up various associated skills since. Our bout promises to be interesting as well as instructive."

"If you say so," I sighed, accepting that he would not be dissuaded.

I stepped to one side, leaving Holmes and de Villegrand to square off against each other. I noticed a couple of faces peering out through a downstairs window of the villa. It was Benoît and Aurélie. Something told me that this was not the first time they had watched their employer enter into a physical altercation with another man. Benoît looked on quite avidly, his hangdog features for once animated.

"I should have you know, Monsieur Holmes," said de Villegrand, "I am an exponent of the martial art known as *savate*. You have heard of it?"

Holmes nodded. "*La boxe française* is not unfamiliar to me."

De Villegrand unleashed a couple of ferocious kicks in Holmes's direction. They were showpieces, for display purposes only. Holmes, I am pleased to say, did not flinch, for all that de Villegrand's shoe soles came within an inch of his nose.

"*Savate* uses the feet primarily," the vicomte said. "It was developed on the streets of Marseille, by sailors."

"A somewhat lowly origin. I'm surprised a man like yourself would care to be associated with anything quite so *déclassé*."

"Ah, but that is the precise reason why I have studied it. No one in the circles in which I move would expect it of me. They prefer the more refined pugilistic sciences. That gives me the advantage."

Two further kicks came Holmes's way, not feints this time but the real thing. The first swung at his head, de Villegrand spinning full circle as he delivered it. Holmes ducked sideways out of its path. The second followed swiftly, the vicomte crouching low and sweeping at Holmes's ankle with his instep. This one Holmes barely managed to anticipate and avoid.

"You're fast," Holmes said.

"As are you, monsieur. But I will land a blow on you soon enough."

There ensued a flurry of attacks from de Villegrand. He was like some whirling dervish, his legs flying in all directions, his body twisting and revolving. Holmes, for his part, met the assault with a series of blocking moves, deflecting the vicomte's feet with a forearm or a shin. It was all I could do simply to follow the action with my eyes. The two of them had become intertwined blurs of motion.

Then, perhaps inevitably, de Villegrand made good on his threat. He got past Holmes's guard and planted a firm, solid heel in my friend's midriff. Holmes staggered backwards, the wind driven out of him. A subsequent kick caught him on the jaw and, to my horror, he fell.

He was on his feet again in a trice, but I could tell that he had been stunned and was groggy. He shook his head in order to clear it and wiped a trickle of blood from the corner of his mouth.

De Villegrand, after so impressive a display of sustained athleticism, was not even out of breath.

"I am loath," he said, "to inflict further harm on you, monsieur, lest I damage that amazing brain of yours. Shall we call it quits and say that honour has been served?"

Mentally I urged Holmes to acquiesce to this suggestion.

"Why, my lord?" said Holmes. "We're only just getting started."

De Villegrand grinned savagely. "Then *en garde* again. Prepare yourself."

Up came Holmes's fists, as de Villegrand embarked on another dynamic volley of kicks. His legs lashed out at every level – aiming at the head, the abdomen, the thigh, the ankle – and sometimes they shot forwards like pistons and sometimes they hooked round from the side in an effort to knock my companion off his feet.

Holmes darted nimbly this way and that, staving off the attacks. He was defending himself more than adequately, but I found it puzzling, not to mention frustrating, that he would not actively retaliate. De Villegrand was making all the running, and Holmes seemed content to let him. I could not fathom why Holmes wasn't trying to turn the tables and become the aggressor.

Once more de Villegrand managed to make contact with one of those spinning kicks of his, and Holmes was toppled. He hit the ground hard, narrowly missing the trunk of an acer which was then in its autumnal finery of crimson and gold.

De Villegrand paused, at last needing to catch his breath. Holmes, meanwhile, lay prostrate, and I was convinced I heard him emit a groan.

"Really!" I exclaimed. "Enough is enough. You've proved your point, de Villegrand. I am throwing in the towel on Holmes's behalf."

"You will do no such thing, Watson," said my friend hoarsely, pushing himself onto his side. "The vicomte has been lucky, that's all. A few of his blows have got through. It's nothing."

"Lucky?" growled de Villegrand. "You're the one who is lucky, Monsieur Holmes. Lucky I haven't knocked your block off, as you English say."

He lunged at Holmes, making as if to stamp on him where he lay, but Holmes was quick, quicker than either I or de Villegrand might have expected. He sprang aside, panther-like, and the vicomte, in his blind rage, charged headlong into the acer. As the Frenchman recovered from his collision with the tree, Holmes was upon him, punching him several times about the torso. With a roar, de Villegrand launched a backward kick which my friend was forced to leap away from.

Holmes looked almost as fresh now as when the fight had started, and I perceived that his moments spent in distress on the grass had in fact been a sham, a pretence designed to make de Villegrand overconfident and entice him into precipitate action. This, then, was a fight as much on the mental plane as the physical, a battle of wits as well as fists.

Holmes circled his opponent. His hands were raised, half-cupped, and describing small serpentine arcs in the air.

"I, too, am a student of a martial art," he said. "It is called *baritsu*, and it is little known outside Japan. It synthesises numerous different fighting styles, from wrestling to ju-jitsu. I would be very surprised if you were at all cognisant of it."

I feel entitled to insert a digression here on the subject of *baritsu*. No one can censure me for halting the narrative briefly, since no one but me is ever likely to read it.

Four years on from the events I am relating, Holmes would call upon all his skills as a practitioner of the art of *baritsu* during his grim, life-or-death struggle with Professor Moriarty atop the Reichenbach Falls. However, several of my readers have felt moved to point out that *baritsu* itself only became popular in England at the turn of the century, too late for Holmes to have mastered it for his confrontation with Moriarty, let alone for this tussle with de Villegrand.

In this instance, though, as in so many others, Holmes was ahead of his time. He adopted *baritsu* long before any of his contemporaries, simply so that he could have an edge over his foes. He was forever enriching his arsenal of knowledge with new and advanced techniques, the better to fulfil his vocation.

My readers' confusion may arise because a variant form of *baritsu*, known as *bartitsu*, enjoyed a brief vogue at the tail end of the nineteenth century. It was devised by a certain Edward William Barton-Wright, who learned *baritsu* while working as an engineer in the Far East in the mid-1890s and then brought it over to England, where he opened a club dedicated to its promotion and promulgation and even staged a few exhibition matches. He added the extra "t" to the name in order to make it chime with his surname and thus put his personal stamp on it. *Bartitsu* was an impure version of *baritsu*, according to Holmes, who was deeply scathing of it, calling it "a clumsy reproduction of an Old Master, worthy only to hang in a boudoir, not a gallery".

De Villegrand, certainly, was unaware of the existence of *baritsu*, and scoffed loudly at its mention.

"You are bluffing, monsieur," he said to Holmes. "You hope to intimidate me with some absurd made-up martial art, to bamboozle me. But I am not so easily misled."

"It's no bluff, your lordship," Holmes responded. "*Baritsu* even includes elements of *savate*. Allow me to demonstrate."

All at once, Holmes was executing a range of kicks similar to those de Villegrand had deployed. His lacked the blunt force of the Frenchman's but more than compensated for that with their pinpoint accuracy and their almost balletic grace. De Villegrand protected himself with reciprocal kicks and some open-handed slaps, but he was undeniably rattled by the turn of events. He understood that, until now, Holmes had been merely toying with him, lulling him into a false sense of security. It was a blow to his considerable pride.

Holmes manoeuvred himself in close, at which point he switched to a different fighting style, one more akin to judo. He grasped de Villegrand's clothing and flipped him neatly onto his back. As de Villegrand attempted to rise, Holmes grabbed him, lofted him up, doubled him over his thigh, and downed him again. *Savate* afforded the vicomte little in the way of riposte to this kind of manhandling. His kicks were rendered almost ineffectual when delivered from a prone or supine position. Repeatedly he was dumped onto the lawn by Holmes. Repeatedly he strove to regain his balance or the initiative, and failed.

At last Holmes let go of him and stepped back. De Villegrand was on all fours, panting stertorously, looking both disgruntled and nonplussed.

"I could continue to humiliate you," Holmes said, "but I do not believe in labouring the point. You acquitted yourself admirably, my lord. I shall trouble you no further today. *Vive l'Entente Cordiale* indeed."

With that parting shot, Holmes beckoned me to return him his jacket, and we both made our way back towards the conservatory. Behind us de Villegrand growled something deeply uncomplimentary in his native tongue, which I shall not reproduce here. He did not, however, pursue us. He remained where he was, a sorry sight, the picture of arrogance brought low.

As we passed indoors, I glanced at the window where the two servants were standing, spectators to the contest. Aurélie's expression was more or less unreadable. On her brother's face, however, I caught a distinct look of triumph, as though he were rejoicing at his employer's humbling. The look vanished as he caught my gaze, his erstwhile blank lugubriousness reasserting itself, but I had seen it plainly, and resolved to remark upon it to Holmes.

CHAPTER THIRTEEN

BRAWL ON PRIMROSE HILL

Holmes eschewed catching a cab to Baker Street, declaring a wish to travel on foot instead, so that he might cogitate.

He seemed in no mood to talk, so I left him to his thoughts and instead imbibed impressions of the city around us. London remained in a febrile mood. I discerned on the faces of shopkeepers and passers-by clear signs of worry and strain. Some masked it better than others. Only children remained oblivious, gaily playing on doorsteps with their dolls and tin soldiers, for all the world without a care – which is how it should be.

The headlines that the newspaper sellers yelled from their pitches were all about the bombings. "Scotland Yard Stumped!" "Still No Arrests Yet!" "Where Will Terrorists Strike Next?" They were doing a roaring trade. I had heard tell that some of the broadsheets had more than doubled their circulation. At least someone was profiting from the general misery.

On Primrose Hill we happened upon one of those protests that Inspector Lestrade had talked about. An angry multitude marched, brandishing placards and decrying the authorities' apparent inaction. As we watched, members of the constabulary arrived in order to waylay the protestors and make them disperse, as they were holding up the traffic and preventing other citizens from going about their business peacefully.

The confrontation rapidly degenerated into a slanging match. Someone threw a punch – it might have been protestor, it might have been policeman – and a brawl broke out. The police resorted to their truncheons, while the protestors used the wooden stakes of their placards for the same purpose. It was all highly reprehensible and regrettable, and left several on each side with bloody noses and aching crowns but, thank heaven, nothing worse than that.

Holmes and I skirted the mêlée and carried on along side streets. I noticed that my friend was walking somewhat stiffly, favouring his left flank. De Villegrand had hurt him worse than he had let on at the villa.

"Holmes," I said, "you must allow me to take a look at you when we get home."

"Kind of you, Watson, but I beg you not to worry. It's nothing. A few mild contusions. Nothing a bath of Epsom salts and bed rest won't cure."

"That de Villegrand. He's the very Devil. I can only hope that, having been comprehensively trounced by you, he will think twice before throwing down the gauntlet again with anyone else."

"He doesn't strike me as a man who learns his lessons," said Holmes. "But at least he now knows there is someone who isn't cowed by him, who will stand up to his bullying ways. Who knows? Perhaps as a result of the chastening he has received, he will be inclined to curb his depraved appetites, at least for a time. We can but hope."

"Is he Baron Cauchemar, do you think?"

Holmes barked a laugh. "What makes you say that?"

"I thought... Well, dash it all, you mentioned sewers while you were talking to him. I assumed..."

"You assumed de Villegrand is the one who puts on an extraordinary suit of armour of an evening and goes out foiling crime in the East End."

"Yes," I said. "And uses the sewers to move about undetected." And, I nearly added, has struck a deal with Beelzebub to grant him abilities beyond those of a mere mortal.

"Oh, Watson," said my friend pityingly. "You and your assumptions. How long have we known each other? Nigh on a decade. In all that time, have you not divined that logic lies at the heart of my methods? Logic and logic alone. If facts cannot be made to fit a theory, one must not bend the theory to fit the facts; one must reassess the theory itself. Assumptions! Let us look at this case so far and review what we know. We know that someone adopting the sobriquet Baron Cauchemar has taken it upon himself to roam the East End, attacking felons. We know that he has some sort of mechanised carapace which he wears to protect himself and, also, to hide his identity. We know that he has offensive weapons which stun and temporarily disable but do not kill. Now tell me, honestly, do any of those seem like something the Vicomte de Villegrand might do?"

"He is an aggressive man."

"That he is, and all too easy to rouse to anger. But the Bloody Black Baron, disconcerting appearance notwithstanding, acts from motives of altruism. He is an opponent of sin, while the vicomte is an *ex*ponent of sin. Cauchemar is a force for good, while beneath de Villegrand's polished, genial exterior there lies, I believe, a cruel and ruthless soul."

"Could it be a front?" I offered. "A ruse, to put people off the scent? No one would suspect him of being Cauchemar if he feigns a touchpaper temper and the habits of a libertine."

"A very perspicacious remark, my good fellow. And it is precisely that that I wished to put to the test by fighting him. As soon as I saw his duelling scar I realised that de Villegrand was not the sort to take insults lying down. However true what I said to him was, his instinct would be to automatically deny it, and with vehemence. I judged that he was a martial artist from the way he held himself, even in repose. There is a certain poise, an inner stillness, which is the unmistakable mark of a trained combatant. All in all, it seemed to me that I could stir him into a fit of high dudgeon with just a few judiciously chosen words and, through violence, get him to reveal his true character. In that I succeeded. There are no liars 'in the ring'. What you are, who you are, comes across loud and clear with every punch and kick."

"His house was grand, though," I said. "Must have cost a pretty penny, even in an unfashionable area like Hampstead. And yet he told us he is penni*less*."

"That is an anomaly, I grant you. Even on an attaché's salary, I doubt he could afford such a residence, unless the French embassy is liable for his overheads."

"Possibly his father did leave him some portion of inheritance after all, just not the full amount he was hoping for. Often when the rich say they have no money, what they mean is they have little by their own standards, whereas by the standards of most of us they have a great deal."

Holmes acknowledged my point with a bow.

"And he can afford to keep servants," I went on. "Only two, granted, but if he were truly without funds even that would be impossible."

"They were a peculiar pair, Benoît and Aurélie, would you not agree? I am quite firmly of the view that Benoît loathes his master."

"A definite look of glee came over his face when you laid de Villegrand flat."

"You saw that too? And he does not trust his sister to be alone in a room with the vicomte."

"Had I a sister, I would feel the same," I said. "De Villegrand, then, is nothing more than the swaggering, vice-ridden dandy he appears to be?"

"Up to a point," said Holmes. "He has depths still hidden to me. He is not, though, Baron Cauchemar. That much I can safely avow. Bear in mind this. Abednego Torrance, by his own admission, is an associate of de Villegrand's, yet Cauchemar attacked Torrance."

"Allies fall out," I suggested. "No honour among thieves, and all that."

"Furthermore, a viscount outranks a baron. De Villegrand is hardly the type to demote himself, even when taking an alias."

"But the two of them have a connection. That is already established."

Holmes nodded. "How close that connection is remains to be seen and its nature must be ascertained. There is something I haven't told you, Watson."

"There so often is," I sighed. My friend liked to play his cards very close to his chest. It was one of his more exasperating attributes.

"I must confess that Torrance was no randomly chosen piece of bait last night. During my investigations yesterday, while passing myself off as a nondescript, unremarkable coolie, I ascertained that he traffics not only in people. He is an habitual smuggler of all manner of goods. Opium is one. He has connections throughout Limehouse, in countless opium dens. Arms and weapons of all kinds are another of his fortes. He moves them around in bulk." Holmes paused slyly, then added, "Explosives, too."

"Explosives," I said. "As in dynamite?"

"Quite so. My interest in Torrance, then, was twofold. Not only was I using him to lure Cauchemar into the open so that I could see him for myself, but I also hoped I might be able to derive some information from Torrance, something that might lead us to the bombers."

"So this isn't all about Cauchemar?"

"Not entirely. If Torrance is the one supplying the terrorists with their dynamite, then it would have been useful interrogating him. Even if he isn't, he might well know who is. I was unlucky, though. Events spun out of control and Torrance slipped through our fingers. It is a mistake I shall not repeat."

"Cauchemar, de Villegrand, Torrance, the bombing campaign – it's all one and the same thing? Is that what you're telling me?"

"They are all pieces of a single jigsaw," said a grim Sherlock Holmes. "But, for the life of me, I cannot yet fit them together to my satisfaction. And time is running out. I do not feel that I have long left in which to assemble them correctly and solve the puzzle. That near-riot we saw just moments ago indicates that London is poised on a knife edge, and not only London but potentially the entire country. If matters come to a head before I can unravel the mystery, then I fear greatly for the future."

His sombre words were belied by the glint in his eye. Holmes was never happier than when presented with a seemingly intractable problem. The greater the challenge to his deductive skills, the more he relished it.

In a sense I was glad, for in the absence of intellectual stimulation lay danger for my friend. Holmes, with nothing weighty to engage his restless mind, was wont to slip into enervation and torpor, and the needle and the seven-per-cent solution of cocaine were then seldom far from reach, with the concomitant deleterious effects on his health.

At the same time, however, I was filled with foreboding.

After all, if Sherlock Holmes himself was stymied and muttering ominously about the nation's safety and security, then there was cause to be alarmed.

CHAPTER FOURTEEN

The Calm Before the Storm

A lull prevailed during the next two days. Holmes told me he wished to be left to his own devices until further notice. He had enquiries to develop, he said, strategies to formulate, checks to make, and in none of these endeavours was my assistance required.

I acceded to his request and busied myself treating patients in my surgery and doing my rounds. I even squeezed in another visit to see my wife. Waterloo had reopened for business, and the train services were running more or less as normal. The initial shock to the railway system was over, but its after-effects still reverberated.

Down in Ramsgate, I was keen to assure Mary that the situation in London was not as dire as the papers were making out and that the crisis would soon pass, as crises did.

She, I could tell, was not wholly convinced by my placations but she put on a brave face to match my own.

"I just know you and Mr Holmes are in the thick of it," she said.

"Hardly!" I blustered. "The very idea."

"I'm no fool, John." She interlaced her fingers with mine. "I know that Holmes would never allow a cancer of this magnitude to fester unchecked, and I know that you would never allow him to perform surgery on it unsupported."

Spoken like a true wife of a medic!

"That is one of the reasons why I love you," she went on. "You have such courage and such a strong sense of moral imperative. And you are implicitly loyal to your friend. I recognised those qualities in you the moment I first laid eyes on you, during that beastly affair with my late father and those pearls that were sent to me in the post and the dreadful murder at Pondicherry Lodge. I was instantly attracted to you not just because you're a fine figure of a man but because you are thoroughly decent and upstanding too. These things mean much to a woman, more than a firm jaw or a stout masculine chest. But…"

"But…?"

"I want you to take special care. Please. You and Mr Holmes are wont to get into such awful scrapes. The criminals you come up against are an appalling lot, so devoid of mercy. I could not bear it if, having lost so much already, I were to lose you as well."

The tenderness of her smile and the soft glistening of her tears all but melted my heart. It was an almost insurmountable effort to get back on the train and return to London. I felt heavy with care, and my funk deepened when I reached Waterloo and observed once again the damage caused to the building's fabric by the bomb.

Repairs were already under way, however, scaffolding in place, navvies assiduously stacking bricks and mixing mortar, and this sight lifted my spirits somewhat. Order, I saw, could be restored. Injuries could be patched up and healed. Normal life would resume eventually.

It was, as I say, a lull.

On the third day, it ended.

A storm broke.

CHAPTER FIFTEEN

The Fourth Bomb

I mean a literal storm as well as a metaphorical one. Ink-black clouds moved in over the capital and sent down a drenching rain, attended by bolts of lightning that seared the retinas and thunderclaps that rattled windows, dislodged roof slates and left you temporarily deafened in their wake. And in the midst of this tempest of almost Biblical proportions, the terrorists detonated yet another bomb, and panic erupted everywhere.

The bomb was planted at the boathouse in St James's Park. Had the weather been less inclement and the park as full of perambulating pedestrians as was usual, I dread to think what the death toll might have been. In the event, only one person perished, a groundskeeper, although several dozen ducks were found floating upside down in the lake, killed stone dead by shock.

What mattered about this explosion was not the relatively minimal loss of life it caused, but its location. The park lies almost equidistant between Buckingham Palace and Westminster. In other words, the bombers had struck very close to the two main seats of government in the land. The blast even cracked windowpanes at the royal seat. Her Majesty, by great good fortune, was not harmed, nor any others in her household. All the same, there was no mistaking the bombers' message: no one is safe from us, not even the mightiest among you.

Examination of *Hansard* for that day reveals the moment at which the detonation interrupted proceedings in the Commons. Discussion of an amendment to a somewhat dreary bill on the registration and inspection of domestic water boilers was abruptly cut short, the record stating that "A loud noise being heard in the immediate environs, the Speaker counselled that the Honourable Members should repair to a place of safety until further notice". By the time the session reconvened it had been established that the "loud noise" had in fact been a bomb, whereupon a motion was tabled calling for an emergency debate and was carried unanimously.

What follows makes for sobering and disheartening reading. I am afraid that the men elected to the highest offices in the land spent the next hour and a half bellowing insults at one another across the Dispatch Box, none of them exhibiting anything approaching dignity or statesmanship. The tone of *Hansard* is invariably dry and factual, yet one can still, perusing these exchanges, detect the note of braying desperation in the parliamentarians' voices. Had the stenographer been entitled to include exclamation marks in his transcription, I suspect they would have been littered liberally throughout.

Rarely have I seen a more conspicuous example of leaders failing to lead. The phrase "headless chickens" springs to mind. Accusations of incompetence and inertia were hurled willy-nilly back and forth across the chamber, and the level of vituperation and sanctimony from all parties was breathtaking. The upshot was that nothing was achieved beyond the airing of political grudges and some quite uncouth name-calling.

And if those who were supposed to be among the wisest in

our country were acting like louts and yahoos, how could the general public be expected to behave any better?

That night will be remembered as one of the most shameful in British history. In all the major cities of England, Scotland and Wales, but particularly in London, mobs went on the rampage. The pelting rain and crashing thunder did not deter them. If anything it served to excite them to greater violence, as though Mother Nature was giving their activities her blessing by wreaking climatic havoc of her own.

Mostly it was the Irish who were on the receiving end of the mobs' wrath. Businesses run by Irishmen, or simply bearing an Irish-sounding name, were attacked and ransacked. A butcher's just round the corner from my house in Paddington was one such.

Mary had been buying our meat from Mr O'Flannery ever since we moved to the area, and by her account he had never been anything but courteous, obliging and honest. He was, for that matter, a Londoner born and bred, though his parents hailed from Dublin. This mattered naught to the frightened, enraged men and women who took to the streets armed with crowbars, pokers, rolling pins and other implements. All Irishmen were Fenians as far as they were concerned, and all Fenians terrorist murderers, and so O'Flannery's shop was broken into, the windows smashed, the fixtures and fittings reduced to kindling, and the produce looted. Not content with that, someone then set fire to the premises, and O'Flannery and his family, cowering in their flat above, managed to escape being burned alive by leaping from a second-storey window onto a mattress they threw into the back yard. O'Flannery's wife fractured her ankle but, thankfully, all of them survived.

Countless similar stories unfolded across the capital, and across the country, and it was not only those who were purportedly or genuinely Irish who suffered. In some places Jews were singled out as the likely culprits, and Blacks, and Chinamen; in fact anyone who was deemed not sufficiently "British" for some reason or other. The bombers, it seemed, could be just about anybody – a neighbour, that fellow across the road who seldom left the house, that suspicious-looking chap with the shifty eyes and the hint of a foreign accent, he had radical-leftish sympathies, and wasn't he a vegetarian too? A queer sort. Just the type to be hoarding dynamite in his basement and plotting the overthrow of the government.

The irony is blindingly obvious. The bombers might have some specific political aim, some point to make, but it was clear that their principal agenda was to sow discord and set Briton at odds with Briton. In which case, the mobs were helping them achieve their goal admirably. People were playing right into their hands.

A proper, better response would have been not to react at all, to remain calm and indifferent, to go about one's affairs as though nothing untoward was happening. That, I would submit, is the one way ordinary folk can resist the tactics of extremist seditionaries.

As it was, a herd mentality prevailed, and the bombers were handed a victory. The whole nation was in uproar. Fear meant that few were thinking clearly or rationally. We had taken it for granted that ours was a civilised society built on rock-solid underpinnings, but that had now been cast into question, the foundations seeming more fragile than we had thought. All at once Britain appeared imperilled, and that in itself was the greatest peril facing us, for the perception of danger was spawning the actuality of it.

CHAPTER SIXTEEN

DEATH OF AN ABBESS

The next morning, in the aftermath of that night of countrywide mass hysteria, Holmes and I found ourselves back in Moorgate, in an alley which ran behind a row of tenement buildings. The storm had passed, the rain had ceased, and a pewter-grey sky hung above the city, the sun valiantly attempting to peek through the overcast.

With us was Inspector Lestrade and one of his sergeants, a certain Bryant. At our feet lay a corpse.

The body was that of a flaxen-haired woman known to both Holmes and myself.

The Abbess.

In life, she had been lusty and lascivious. Dead, she was sad and pitiable, as the dead so often are. Rainwater had pooled in the sockets of her eyes, which were now dulled and fish-like. Her rouged lips were fixed in an everlasting cry of dismay. Her sodden dress clung to her ample frame in a clammy embrace. I had not warmed to the woman, but in no way had she deserved this cruel fate, dying alone in the mud of a filthy alley. Few do.

Holmes crouched beside her remains, inspecting them

minutely. He looked tired and drawn, even more gaunt than usual. I recognised the symptoms. He was in one of his manic phases, so utterly consumed by an investigation that he neglected the basic necessities of eating and rest. I doubted he had slept more than a couple of hours since we last parted. He was subsisting on raw nervous energy alone.

"Death would appear to have come from a crushing blow to the upper thoracic," said Holmes, feeling the body carefully. "Would you not concur, doctor?"

I knelt and examined her too. There was a deep concavity in the front of her chest, centred around the manubrium. Broken ribs gave to the touch with a palpable crackle.

"The absence of visible blood suggests a penetrating wound to the heart rather than, say, the lungs," I said. "Fatal traumatic cardiac arrest would have resulted. In other words, she would have died more or less instantly." I offered this as though it were some consolation.

"No other bruising or breakage," said Holmes. "No evidence of defensive wounds, either."

"Meaning she didn't see the attack coming?" said Lestrade.

"Or wasn't expecting it, which is not quite the same thing. I would be able to tell you more, but that wretched storm has obliterated every last scrap of evidence. I can find no footprints, no physical traces, nothing. All washed away by the rain."

"I've been into the knocking shop and interviewed the dollymops," said Sergeant Bryant, nodding to the rear of the nearest house. At various of the windows, distraught female faces could be seen peering out at us from behind curtains and blinds. "They report that the Abbess stepped outside around midnight."

"In the storm?" I said.

"Apparently she had a rendezvous with someone. None of the girls know whom. Some prearranged clandestine meeting."

"When did they first become aware that she had not returned?" Holmes asked.

"Not until first light. It was, by all accounts, a busy night. Plenty of comings and goings."

"What?" I said. "With everything else that was happening?"

"You would be surprised, Dr Watson," said Lestrade. "Trade at a place like the Abbess's isn't affected by social unrest or the vagaries of the weather. Clients will visit come hell or high water. Their urges know no bounds."

"Needless to say, none of the girls saw or heard a thing," said Sergeant Bryant. "What with the storm in full spate, it's hardly surprising. It was only at daybreak that one of them ventured outside and found her."

"If you ask me," said Lestrade, "this is the handiwork of Baron Cauchemar."

"I seldom do ask you, Inspector," said Holmes. "However, on this occasion I'm moved to enquire how you arrive at that conclusion."

"Well, it stands to reason, doesn't it? Cauchemar takes a dim view of anyone who breaks the law of the land. The Abbess is just the latest in a line of his victims. He sneaked up on her and slew her without mercy, in cold blood."

"'Sneaking up' is hardly Cauchemar's thing. But, more to the point, he hasn't killed before."

"There's always a first time. It could be that he never meant to kill the Abbess. She was more physically delicate than he thought, or else he hit her harder than intended. That, or this is something he has been working up to over the past few weeks. Not content with dishing out beatings any more, he has taken it to the next level. It is often the way, in my experience. Killers don't become killers just overnight. They evolve into the role. An apprenticeship in petty violence, graduating to murder, that's how it goes."

"We're slightly outside the baron's East End stamping ground, though."

"He has been too successful for his own good. The pickings have got thinner there of late. He is expanding his territory."

"And this is a being whose existence, three days ago, you cavilled at," said Holmes, rising from his crouch. "Indeed, were happy to dismiss as sheer conjecture."

The barb found no purchase in the CID inspector's thick hide.

"I'm ever willing to shift my viewpoint. You were the one, were you not, who insisted adamantly to me that the Bloody Black Baron *is* real."

"What if this is a killing made to look as though Cauchemar committed it? A put-up job? What would you say then?"

"I would say that the simplest explanation is almost always the truest one. And what's more, Mr Holmes... Mr Holmes? Hullo, Mr Holmes? Can you hear me? Am I talking to myself?"

My friend had become distracted, no longer listening to Lestrade. His attention had been caught by the appearance of an enclosed black brougham which had drawn up at the end of the alley. Its driver sat hunched at the reins, face almost entirely obscured by the brim of his trilby and the upturned collar of his ulster, although I noted a bristling moustache and a fierce, forthright nose. He summoned Holmes over with a slow curl of the forefinger, and my friend complied, setting off towards the carriage.

I made to follow, but the brougham driver barked, "Stand your ground, the lot of you. Just Mr Holmes. No one else."

"Stay put, Watson," said Holmes. "I shan't be long."

"But…"

I couldn't fathom quite why the black brougham so disturbed me, but disturb me it did. There was something sinister in the way all the blinds were drawn down, rendering the interior entirely in shadow. The very fact that the coach had turned up at the scene of a murder, out of the blue, set my nerves on edge. Who could be in it? What did they want with Holmes?

Had I known then what I know now, I would have gone down on my hands and knees and pleaded with Holmes not to clamber inside the brougham, which squatted like some huge malevolent beetle, ready to consume him.

For, as I was shortly to learn, the carriage belonged to none other than Professor James Moriarty.

CHAPTER SEVENTEEN

THE BOOBY-TRAPPED BROUGHAM

The driver leaned round and opened the brougham's door, revealing a rectangle of pure darkness. Holmes stepped in and was swallowed from sight. The door shut, and thus the carriage remained for the next quarter of an hour, stationary, with Holmes and its passenger engaged in who-knew-what within. The horse, a jet-black gelding, stamped its hooves and whinnied a couple of times, the driver smoked a cigar, and Lestrade, Sergeant Bryant and I watched and waited.

I'm minded to say a word or two about Professor Moriarty here. I first made mention of the "Napoleon of crime" – to use Holmes's own striking epithet – in the story entitled "The Final Problem". There I detailed how my friend apparently met his end locked in mortal combat with his arch-enemy. This marked the beginning of Holmes's three years of self-imposed exile from these shores, the period now commonly known as the Great Hiatus which saw him wandering the world's more exotic, far-flung regions and during which he was believed by all and sundry, not least me, to be dead. (Only Mycroft was apprised of the true state of affairs.) I wrote in that tale about a conversation Holmes and I had during which he asked me if I had ever heard of Professor Moriarty and I declared, "Never."

The events in "The Final Problem" occurred in 1891, yet in *The Valley of Fear*, which I published in 1914 but which harks back to the year 1888, Holmes and I chat freely about Moriarty in the very first chapter.

Critics who take huge delight in spotting inconsistencies in these narratives of mine have gloated over this apparent chronological discrepancy. Perhaps I ought to be flattered that they care enough about my works, and about Sherlock Holmes, to devote so much time and effort to finding fault, scrutinising the texts for flaws like chimpanzees grooming for nits.

To these people, I reply: in 1893, when "The Final Problem" first saw print, I was reluctant to admit publicly that I knew anything about Moriarty at all, so sinister were the man and his machinations. My true recollection of that conversation with Holmes, backed up by my notes, is that I of course *had* heard of him, only too well; but I chose to amend the record. At the time, I felt that people were not ready to learn the true extent to which the latter's criminal empire had spread through society, its tentacles insinuating into nearly every walk of life. I quoted Holmes's description of Moriarty as "the organiser of half that is evil and of nearly all that is undetected in this great city" but spared my readership the full, precise details so as not to alarm or disquiet them. Not only that but certain of the examples I could have cited were *sub judice*, still undergoing prosecution and trial, and I did not want to interfere with the workings of the justice system in any way.

Furthermore, and more pertinently, I had no wish to dwell too deeply on my friend's antagonism towards Moriarty, which had been even more intense and protracted than I gave everyone to believe. I was, let us not forget, in mourning when I penned the tale. I believed Holmes to be dead, and Moriarty to have been the agent of his demise, so why should I spare Moriarty any more attention than the minimum necessary?

I am not proud that I committed the small evasion I did, but I felt then that it was warranted and justified, and still do to this day. Let the carpers carp. I am old now, old enough to be blithe about the opinions of others, and one seeming error does not invalidate Holmes's legacy or my worth as his biographer.

At any rate, when Moriarty's brougham showed up, I was already aware of the villain's existence, albeit ignorant that the carriage was his and he the passenger. I was likewise ignorant that the driver was his infamous henchman Sebastian Moran, disgraced colonel of the 1st Bangalore Pioneers, who four years hence would attempt to assassinate Holmes with a German-manufactured airgun. My instinct was that the situation was inherently *wrong*; but it wasn't until it was over that I discovered *how* wrong.

At last, after what seemed an age, the brougham door reopened and Holmes emerged. It gladdened my heart that he was safe and sound. Well, safe at least, for there was a discernible wobble in his stride as he moved away from the carriage. He looked not a little shaken, and this a man gifted with the steeliest of nerves.

The driver whipped the horse and the brougham clattered off. Holmes did not turn round to watch it go, but his shoulders unbent with its departure, as though a weight had been lifted from them. Indeed, the air itself seemed the cleaner for the brougham's absence.

"Watson," Holmes said, "come. I am in dire need of a pick-me-up. Let us repair to a coffee house, if we can find one open at this ungodly hour. Lestrade? I bid you adieu."

"But Mr Holmes, the Abbess…"

"There is nothing I can do for the unfortunate woman right now, Inspector. Her death is not irrelevant to the case I am investigating, but it muddies waters that are already murky, rather than clearing them. Rest assured that, in due course, I will identify the guilty party and present him to you. You have my solemn word on that."

I asked Holmes, as we walked, whom he had met in the carriage and what they had discussed, but he would not answer me until he had a measure of strong black coffee inside him. Happily for us, not far from the brothel there was a coffee house whose proprietor had been prepared to brave the streets after the night's disturbances and open up for custom. Other, neighbouring businesses were doing likewise, although several of the less fortunate proprietors were having to sweep up broken glass into heaps and compile a list of breakages for their insurers.

"Watson," my companion said as he set his empty cup down, "it is not in my nature to indulge in hyperbole. However, I'm willing to vouchsafe that I have just been in the presence of the most egregiously malignant individual ever to walk the planet. You will perhaps be able to deduce to whom I refer."

It was not difficult.

"Professor Moriarty," I intoned.

A silence fell momentarily over the coffee house, as though merely being within proximity of the mention of the name sent an unconscious shiver down the spine of every patron present. It was like one of those silences that fall at dinner parties, when a guest will often remark in grim jest that the angel of death has just passed over.

"The very same," said Holmes. "I knew, even before I got into the brougham, that it was he who lurked within."

"Yet you entered nonetheless. What on earth possessed you, Holmes? You yourself once called him 'one of the first brains of

Europe, with all the powers of darkness at his back." I recalled verbatim this description from my notes for *The Valley of Fear*, which I had recently been compiling, although almost a quarter of a century would elapse before I got round to writing them up in narrative form. "You strolled willingly straight into the lion's den. Good God, man, it could quite easily have been a trap. A fatal one!"

"I entertained that notion. Yet, on the balance of probabilities, I decided I was not in immediate danger. Would Moriarty really abduct me, in plain view of two officers of the law, not to mention your good self? In broad daylight? That is not how he works. His way is far more subtle and insidious. To move against me overtly like that would be to risk exposing himself to the glare of scrutiny. He does not wish his criminal endeavours to be suspected by anyone. He would like to be known simply as a harmless academic who, although forced to resign his chair amid a swirl of dark rumour and whispered allegations of impropriety, continues privately to pursue his researches into binomial theorem and other, more obscure mathematical disciplines. The spider scuttles into the shadows when light is shed on it, and the same is true of Professor Moriarty. He hides, and commits his malefactions from the cover of darkness, utilising a network of proxies and underlings. To approach me directly, in person, as he did this morning, is a rare act from one normally so circumspect and shrewd."

"Well, if he did not plan on killing you, did you at least consider not showing him the same courtesy?" I was only half joking. Slaying Moriarty would have eliminated most of the crime in London at a stroke and spared countless future victims of his nefarious schemes.

"It occurred to me. I am not someone who is liable to commit cold-blooded murder, but I daresay I could have conquered my scruples and managed it on this occasion, and not lost a night's sleep over it afterwards. I was unarmed, but my bare hands would have sufficed. It will come as no surprise when I tell you that Moriarty had anticipated such an eventuality. The brougham, he assured me as soon as I entered, was fitted with a half-dozen booby traps which could silently eliminate a man in an instant.

"'At the flick of one of several secret switches,' he said, 'I can trigger a pneumatic device that will fire a curare-tipped blowdart into your neck. Or a set of hollow spikes will pierce through the upholstery of your seat and inject you hypodermically with a lethal toxin derived from the liver of the pufferfish. Or a porcelain reservoir embedded in the roof above you, containing concentrated nitric acid, will dump its corrosive load onto your head. Many and terrible are the ways this brougham can end your life, should you attempt to lay a hand on me in violence. So kindly refrain from doing so, Mr Holmes. Hold very still, keep your hands where I can see them at all times, and you should survive this encounter.'

"I did not doubt him, either. In my experiences of dealing with his various plots and conspiracies, he is ruthless and quite without conscience or compunction. These were no idle threats he was making.

"'Although it would,' Moriarty went on, 'be a tremendous pity to have to destroy you. I regard you as not only my great adversary but also my intellectual equal, perhaps the only person alive to meet the criteria for that position.'

"'I am honoured,' I said, not without irony.

"'You should be,' he replied, not without sincerity. 'How intriguing it is to be in such immediate physical propinquity with you. Hitherto we have always competed at one remove from each other, have we not? Like chess grandmasters, with London our board, its citizens our pieces. You have inflicted reversals on me, though not as many as I on you.'

"I could have disputed the point, but refrained from doing so.

"'Every time you manage to outwit me, I find the defeat instructive,' Moriarty continued. 'I learn from it and resolve not to make the same mistake twice. You are useful to me, Mr Holmes. You are the anvil on which I forge my strategies, the whetstone on which I sharpen the blade of my wits. This is why you continue to live – for now. It is the only reason I haven't arranged to have you done away with in some "accident" or other. You oppose me, and in opposing, strengthen me.

"'That will not always be the case, mark you,' he added. 'There will come a time, and it may not be too long hence, when you and I clash in one final, all-out battle, our endgame. Then we shall discover who is whose nemesis.'

"'I look forward to it,' I said, 'as one looks forward to any true test of one's mettle.'"

"The tone of the exchange sounds almost cordial," I remarked.

"It is a queer business, my relationship with Moriarty," Holmes said. "I detest the man and all he represents, and yet in some strange way that even I cannot understand I respect him too. He would appear to feel likewise. He is not wrong with his chess analogy. We are playing a game, he and I – an elaborate, deadly game, the outcome of which will inevitably be the loss of my life or his."

My stomach churned at the thought of Sherlock Holmes perishing at Professor Moriarty's hands. I felt a frisson, almost a presentiment of things to come.

"But to the purpose of our conversation," said Holmes.

"Which was?"

"As far as I can tell, principally for Moriarty to gloat. He raised the subject of the present public unrest. I suggested that perhaps the troubles were bad for business, impeding his well-laid plans.

"'On the contrary,' said he with glee. 'Granted, I have had to curtail one or two carefully developed stratagems, postponing their point of fruition. But nothing is happening that will affect my long-term goals too adversely. I have made sure of that.'

"'What a relief that is to hear,' I said dryly.

"'Chaos is, in truth, fertile soil. There is always opportunity when nobody is sure of anything and the general mood is of panic and outcry. I expect to prosper in the coming days. It is likely, after all, that there will be interruptions to the supply of foodstuffs and other essentials, if matters continue as they are. A wise man who makes provision to stockpile such goods may then profit by selling them to people who will pay any price he demands.'

"I cannot tell you, Watson, how smug he looked as he spoke these words. The massive dome of his forehead seemed to throb from within, like some pale pulsing octopus, and his deep-sunken eyes fairly glowed with self-satisfaction. I might gladly have broken his neck on the spot, and would have launched myself at him but for the threat of those booby traps.

"I should have disguised my thoughts more clearly, for Moriarty's fingers strayed towards a false panel set beside him, within easy reach, beneath which must lie the switches he had mentioned.

"'We must endeavour to remain civil,' he warned.

"'I am nothing but,' I replied.

"'What you seem unable to perceive, Mr Holmes, is the true extent of the danger posed to this country. I, on the other hand, do, and should things work out the way I anticipate – and I cannot foresee that they won't – then I shall prosper immensely.'

"His smile – it was not a pretty sight. I am not sure it should even be termed a smile. It was as ghastly as any death's head grin, his thin lips peeling back like a gash splitting flesh, to reveal long yellow teeth. Brrr."

I shivered in sympathy, thanking all the stars that it had been

Holmes in the back of that brougham, not me.

"Might we not wonder if Moriarty has had a hand in the bombings himself?" I said.

"Not his style."

"But if they are to his advantage…"

"Too disruptive," Holmes stated firmly. "Too blatant. The effects are too hard to predict or control. He is happy to exploit the situation, and I warrant that somewhere, at some remove, he is involved. It would be astonishing if, as the pre-eminent criminal mastermind of our times, he were not. But he is not the instigator. The hints he dropped suggest that he is, rather, an abettor and a benefactor, something like a godfather." Holmes succumbed to an enormous yawn. "Another coffee, I feel."

"Shouldn't you be finding time to rest?" I said. "Rather than resorting to stimulants? You look wrung out, man."

"It has been a busy forty-eight hours. But I do not feel that I can take a breather quite yet."

Having given his order to the serving girl, Holmes resumed the thread of his narrative.

"Hoping to goad Moriarty into further revelations, I broached the topic of Baron Cauchemar. 'The bombings may not be bad for your business,' I said, 'but can the same be said for this vigilante roaming the East End?'

"Moriarty nodded as though pained to concede it. 'That… personage has been of considerable inconvenience to me. His shenanigans have curbed several of my more lucrative enterprises and put a number of my operatives out of action. I have even had employees come to me and ask to be excused from duties until further notice. I do not need to tell you how astonishing that is. They fear the Bloody Black Baron more than they do me!'

"'Remarkable,' I said.

"'No matter how I chivvy or browbeat them, they will not be

swayed. They refuse to work for me while Cauchemar continues to stalk the streets. I have had to make an example of one or two of them, but even that has failed to bring the rest into line.'

"'When I and the baron next meet, I shall remember to congratulate him warmly on a job well done.'

"'He is a blight,' Moriarty hissed. 'A scourge. If I ever find him, if I ever have him in my clutches, by God I will make him pay. He will rue the day he ever crossed the path of James Moriarty.'

"He made it clear that our meeting was at an end, but he had one final word of warning for me.

"'In the near future, Mr Holmes,' he said, 'our world is going to alter radically. You, I fear, are going to wind up on the wrong side of some very powerful forces, and I do not rate your chances of survival. Which leads me to think: perhaps now is the time for you to see sense and use your much-vaunted abilities to further your own ends rather than help the common man.' He smothered those last four words in a sneer. The thought of helping anyone other than himself was anathema to him.

"'What are you suggesting?' I said. 'That you and I join forces? Forge an alliance?'

"'We are alike in so many ways, both of us set apart from the herd by our brilliance. What if we were to put aside our enmity, these silly hostilities of ours, and co-operate? My great brain alone has achieved so much. Imagine what it could do in concert with yours. The summits we could scale together! The heights to which we could ascend!'

"'The prospect revolts me. What you call heights, Moriarty, I call depths. I will hear no more of this.'

"'Very well,' said he, pouting, more than a little put out. He honestly thought I would jump at his invitation. 'But in spurning my proffered hand of friendship, you doom yourself, sir.'

"'The atmosphere in this carriage is becoming most

uncongenial to me,' I said. 'I have known cesspits less foetid.'

"For the merest of moments I thought that Moriarty was going to unleash one of the brougham's booby traps on me, out of sheer spite. His face clouded and his eyes were filled with a baleful malice. 'Perhaps,' I said to myself, 'you have overstepped the mark, old boy. You have allowed your emotions to trump your better judgement.'

"But then he smiled once more – ugh – and bade me a courteous farewell. I left with the impression that he had been taunting me, so sure of his position and his predictions that he believes nothing I can do will make any difference. Which, of course, leaves me all the more determined to resolve things."

"Perhaps he was sounding you out, too," I said. "Seeing how far along you are in your investigations."

"That is a very astute observation, Watson."

"To be honest, I don't see that we are very far along at all, other than that we now have a fresh murder on our hands and no suspect."

"Not far along? On the contrary. It should be obvious that I have not been idle this past couple of days. I have been rushing hither and yon, finding myself in any number of unusual venues, gathering crumbs and morsels of intelligence. I also received another peremptory summons from my brother, as threatened. He proved to be in a very sour frame of mind, I must say. He berated me over my apparent lack of progress. I believe he is feeling pressure from several quarters and needed to vent his frustration on someone. I did my best to reassure him that everything is in hand, but Mycroft is hard to mollify when he is in one of his funks. I fear he may be provoked into doing something rash and intemperate."

"Such as neglecting his own health?" I said. "Pushing himself too hard for his own good?"

"But," my friend went on, ignoring my pointed remark, "the good news is that I have, as a consequence of my labours, unearthed a palpable lead. One which we shall act upon tonight and which, if my sources are correct, should herald the re-emergence of at least one old acquaintance."

CHAPTER EIGHTEEN

"Mrs H to the Smiths' Place"

Another telegram from Mycroft arrived at Baker Street that afternoon, this one delivered by a traditionally juvenile courier, who said that a reply was expected.

The telegram read:

Propose that Mrs H be moved north to the Smiths' place. Advise. M

"Who," I asked Holmes, "is this Mrs H?" I wondered whether it might be an oblique reference to our own dear Mrs Hudson, but could not for the life of me think why Mycroft would wish to recommend a change in her whereabouts. Unless he had reason to believe that Holmes and those immediately around him were in grave and imminent danger...

"Can't you guess? Mycroft is being very cryptic and coy. He must fear his message being intercepted. Would it help if I said the H stands for Hanover?"

"Mrs...? Goodness gracious! He means Victoria. And 'the Smiths' place'?"

"The architects who designed and built Balmoral Castle were John Smith and his son William."

"Then it all makes sense," I said. "Your brother believes the Queen will be safer if she is relocated to Aberdeenshire. I can't say I disagree. Balmoral is remote and, I'm led to understand, somewhat fortress-like. The terrorists will be far less able to threaten her there."

"Ah, but Watson, you are not thinking clearly."

I bristled. "I'm not? Our monarch's security is surely paramount. A bomb went off scarcely half a mile from her official London residence yesterday, Holmes. And with the masses up in arms and mayhem on the streets, it isn't wise for her to remain in the capital. Inconceivable as it may seem, the people might turn against her. There are those out there who regard our nation's figurehead as a legitimate target. Remember how she was attacked four times by as many different men during the 'forties, and again, much more recently, by that poet whose work he posted to her for her approval and she rejected. What was his name? Maclean. Some of them took direct pot shots at her!"

"All of her assailants were in various ways insane, and one of them used a rusty flintlock and another a cane, hardly lethal weapons."

"These are insane times. Her Majesty may have brushed off those previous attempts on her life with the words 'It is worth being shot at to see how much one is loved', but right now, things are different. She must go to Balmoral. It is imperative."

"No, Watson. Think how it will look. She will appear to be running away from trouble."

"Not running away – making a tactical retreat."

"It will weaken her authority," Holmes insisted. "It will give the impression that the nation as a whole is a shambles, the ship of state rudderless. She must stay put and ride out the turbulence. I suspect that Her Majesty herself knows this and is adamant about not going, contrary to Mycroft's wishes. My brother is being over cautious, far too protective, and hence losing objectivity. This is what I feared might happen."

"He is cleverer than you. You have told me so yourself. There has always been some sort of unspoken rivalry between you two, but perhaps, just this once, you should accept that he knows best."

"What I have said is that Mycroft possesses a faculty for observation and a facility for detection that are superior even to mine. What I have also said – and this is crucial – is that he does not apply his skills with the same logical exactitude as I do. He is prone to arrive at solutions to problems through leaps of reasoning rather than precise, methodical thoroughness. He is, in essence, lazy. Omniscient, yes, and capable of assessing and pigeonholing reams of data at a glance, but lacking in rigour and foresight. This telegram shows that he himself is uncertain of his course of action. Hence the request for me to 'advise'. And my advice to him will be to desist from having Victoria transported north of the border. Her taking refuge at Balmoral will only fan the flames further."

"Holmes, you would gamble with our Queen's life?" I said, aghast.

"Fools gamble, Watson. I make measured judgements."

"But if you're wrong… The potential cost…"

Holmes sat back in his chair. "In the event that I'm wrong, I daresay that posterity will view me in a very harsh light. But it is a risk I am prepared to take."

He scribbled a note to Mycroft and had Mrs Hudson pass it on to the delivery boy downstairs, along with a shilling.

"And now, my friend, we must focus our energies on this evening. We have an address and the hour at which we need to be there. It promises to be a long, arduous night, so I suggest you take a nap beforehand. The bed in your old room is made up."

"And you? Will you not sleep too? You should."

Holmes tamped tobacco into the bowl of his pipe and applied a match.

"I," he said, "shall do what I do best."

So saying, he slipped into a contemplative pose, gradually wreathing himself in a pall of smoke. He appeared calm, but as I was on the point of leaving the room, a sound caught my attention and made me turn. It was the grinding of teeth.

Holmes's jaw was working even when he wasn't puffing on the pipe, the mandibular muscles tensing and flexing visibly beneath his skin. I refrained from commenting on it, but I knew it could mean only one thing.

He was angry.

My friend was a man to whom emotions were remote and alien. He was apt to regard them distantly and with curiosity, much as an astronomer regards the planets through his telescope. On the rare occasion when one overtook him, it affected him strongly.

What had provoked his ire? Was it the Abbess's murder? The meeting with Moriarty? The telegram from Mycroft?

Possibly it was a combination of the three, and I must confess it made me uneasy to see Sherlock Holmes for once not the master of himself. It left me fearful of an unsuccessful outcome to the investigation.

CHAPTER NINETEEN

GRAVEYARD VIGIL

Midnight saw us in Stepney, in the graveyard of a deconsecrated parish church.

The church, situated between Whitechapel Road and Commercial Road, had fallen into disuse not through any lack of attendance but thanks to subsidence. It had been erected on a patch of unusually soft marshy soil and had begun to sink, becoming unsafe, potentially a fatal hazard to clergy and congregation. Signs had been posted all around, warning passers-by to keep away: the edifice was condemned and scheduled for demolition.

The signs were hardly required. One look at the church itself ought to have sufficed. Deep fissures ran through the stonework, forking like lightning. Chunks of fallen masonry, and even the broken-off head of a gargoyle, littered the precincts. The bell tower was canted alarmingly, its angle with the earth more acute than that of the Leaning Tower of Pisa. The whole building had been shored up with thick timber braces, but still seemed fragile, as though a casual sneeze could bring it all crashing down. I confess I felt nervous being in such close proximity to it. Nervous, too, at the prospect of the "re-emergence of an old acquaintance" that Holmes had promised. Who? Baron Cauchemar? I feared as much.

My anxiety communicated itself to Holmes via my constant shifting of position. I just couldn't get comfortable in our hiding place, crouching behind a brace of large headstones.

"Watson, you fidgeter," my friend hissed. "Do keep still!"

"I am getting to be of an age," I said, "when lying in wait in damp grass at an absurd hour of the night no longer seems appropriate or sensible behaviour."

"Nonsense. Stop complaining. I am marginally your senior, and did I not spend several days in the wilds of Dartmoor just last year, in the bitterest of conditions and the crudest of hovels?"

"You are evidently made of sterner stuff than I."

"As an army surgeon in Afghanistan, you had to camp out in inhospitable mountain regions, assailed by icy winds and in constant fear of sneak attack by the forces of Ayub Khan, for months on end. How can this even compare?"

"That was a long time ago and I was a much younger man. I am married now. I have responsibilities."

"Pshaw! If your marital and professional obligations were really so important to you, you would not be here at all. The truth is you relish the thrill of these adventures of ours, Watson, albeit usually in hindsight, from the vantage point of having survived them. They make you feel young again and alive."

This I could not gainsay, although it irritated me how Holmes had picked his way to the nub of the matter. It irritated me whenever his insights into my character were dead-on. One could hide nothing about oneself from him.

"At least I needn't ask if you have brought your revolver," my friend added. "You keep checking the blasted thing every five minutes. It's another habit that speaks of nerves and insecurity."

"Give me one good reason, Holmes, why I should not feel –"

"Hsst!" Holmes silenced me with a forefinger to my lips. "Hear that? Someone is coming."

I drew back the hammer on my revolver, ready. There were voices, faint in the dark, and then the gleam of a lantern.

Three figures hove into view, entering the graveyard by a side gate. One was bent, pushing a wheelbarrow in which lay two shovels.

The man leading the way, the bearer of the lantern, was immediately recognisable by silhouette alone. That barrel chest, that beard, the absence of a left arm…

Abednego Torrance.

The other two were unfamiliar but, from the glimpses I got of them by the lantern's light, they resembled in dress and bearing the two accomplices whom Torrance had had with him at the docks in Shadwell. Two more burly bravos to aid him in whatever shady practices he was engaged in.

"Right-ho, lads," Torrance said, coming to a halt not thirty yards from where Holmes and I were sequestered. "This is the spot. I had it buried right here, under this rather fetching statue of an angel. See? Looks like a recently dug grave, but it ain't. Grab the shovels and get to work."

"It's not six feet down, is it, boss?" one of the accomplices asked. "Only, that's a long way to dig."

"Of course it ruddy isn't six feet, Gedge. What do you take me for? I'm not stupid. And the soil's not long been turned, so it isn't as if it'll be back-breaking work. I'd do it myself, only a shovel's a tool that demands two hands, and I come up short in that department. Sinnott and Creevy did the job on my behalf last time, but since they are currently indisposed, you two are my new left arms."

"I don't know," said the other accomplice gloomily. "Digging in a graveyard? It seems sort of wrong. Blasphemous, like."

"Shut your hole and get on with it, Kaylock," snarled Torrance. "You're being paid, aren't you? Anyway, this here church has been de-holy-fied. God's been spring-cleaned out of it. So you're not doing anything that'll offend Him, but if you do nothing, that'll offend *me*. Got that?"

Kaylock nodded avidly and got busy with a shovel. Gedge joined him. Torrance, for his part, trained the beam from the lantern on them as they laboured. Meanwhile he remained on the alert, casting a keen gaze around, keeping lookout. I almost admired him for daring to venture out at all tonight, so soon after his last run-in with Cauchemar. Talk about tempting fate. He was clearly a man of some inner fortitude. Or perhaps he reckoned he couldn't be that unlucky twice running.

"Holmes," I whispered, "should we charge them? Element of surprise and all that."

My companion shook his head. "Let us wait and see what they are here to retrieve."

"Here, Torrance," said Gedge. "How come you lost your arm anyway?"

"I've heard all manner of stories," said Kaylock.

"Oh yes?" said Torrance. "Such as?"

"I've heard you were in a shipwreck in the tropics, afloat for days clinging to a section of broken mast, and a tiger shark bit your arm off, although you snatched the arm out of the beast's jaws and beat it to death with it."

"I've heard," said Gedge, "that you were wounded in a knife fight with three lascars in a tavern on the Malabar Coast, so badly you had to have your arm amputated."

Torrance gave a gruff chuckle. "Well now, there's a grain of truth in both of those, but only a grain."

"What happened, then?"

"Fact is, I did get bitten, yes, but not by a shark. It was back in my sailing days. I was crewing with a scientific expedition ship, the SS *Mayumba*, collecting live samples of rare and supposedly extinct animal species from the islands of the South China Sea and the Indian Ocean. Leading the show was this young shaver, George Challenger by name, fresh out of university and looking to make a reputation for himself, as well as gather material that would help earn him his doctorate. You think I'm built big? Challenger was a giant, and devilish smart too, but also crude, opinionated, and not one to give a fig about the feelings of others."

"Sounds like you liked him."

"I did, and he me. Education aside, we had much in common. But to cut a long story short, we were tracking down a rodent in the jungles of Sumatra, a massive thing, a rat the size of a cat. No, bigger. Of a dog. I found it. Or rather, it found me. Sank its teeth into my forearm and wouldn't let go, no matter how I whacked it and pounded it. In the end Challenger had to kill it with his machete, because there was no other way of getting it off me. He was not best pleased about that, I can tell you. He bawled at me for an hour. 'Prize specimen, the fabled Giant Rat of Sumatra, we'll probably never find the likes of it again, thanks to you I've had to chop it in half,' et cetera, et cetera. And that would have been that."

"But?"

"Damn me if the wound didn't become infected. Badly. That vermin had been carrying some nasty germs in its gob, and within hours the bite was inflamed and starting to fester and my arm had swollen up like a football and I was stricken with a fever like you wouldn't believe – the sweats, the shakes, cramping, agony. There was a likelihood of gangrene and even death, so young Challenger stepped up to the mark. I never did learn what he was a student of. All the sciences, as far as I can tell, and one of them was medicine. As the ship's resident sawbones he saw there was only one possible course of treatment, so he got me stinking drunk on rum, rammed a pad of leather in my mouth so I wouldn't bite my own tongue off, and set to work with a hacksaw and a bone file." Torrance winced at the memory. "Saved my ruddy life, he did, but was it pleasant? No, it was not."

"Phew," said Gedge. "Rather you than me."

"That was the end of my career as a seaman. You can't tie a sheet or hoist a sail with only one arm. I had to look to other forms of employment to make ends meet. And that's your bedtime story for the night, lads. Back to work with you."

Gedge and Kaylock had ceased digging while Torrance recounted his tale of woe. Now, they stopped leaning on their shovels and resumed using them.

"Professor Challenger," Holmes mused softly. "I know of him. One of these days I'd like to meet the fellow – see if he's half the objectionable braggart everyone makes him out to be."

After several minutes, the blade of one of the shovels thudded against something hard.

"Think we found it, boss."

"Dig around it, then. Ever so gently, mind."

Gedge and Kaylock scraped and spaded. In short order they had excavated a wooden crate, which they heaved out of the earth by its rope handles. It looked heavy.

"There we are, my beauty," said Torrance. He set down the lantern some distance from the crate, then knelt to prise off the lid.

"Any chance you'll be able to make out what's inside once he gets it open?" I asked Holmes.

He shook his head. "Not from this vantage point. I shall attempt to get closer."

"Be careful."

Holmes crawled forward on his belly, slithering slowly from the cover of one headstone to the next, making incremental progress towards the trio of ruffians.

Abruptly, Torrance jerked his head up.

"What is it?" said Kaylock.

"Hush! Did anyone else hear that?"

Holmes froze on the spot, pressing himself as flat as he could to the grass. I nosed the barrel of my revolver round the edge of the headstone I lay behind, steadying my wrist with my free hand and sighting on Torrance. It would be a tricky shot at this range but not impossible. Should he make a move in Holmes's direction, I would drop him where he stood.

Torrance turned this way and that, ear cocked.

"You don't suppose it's Bar –" Gedge began, but Kaylock interrupted him.

"Don't say it. Don't say his name. It summons him, everyone knows that. He hears it and he comes, like a dog answering a whistle."

"Will you both pipe down!" Torrance snapped. "I'm trying to listen."

Seconds passed, each seeming a minute in length.

"Nothing," Torrance said eventually, and I let out a breath I wasn't even aware I had been holding. "Not like me to be so jumpy," he added. "I forget that tonight I have a guardian angel watching over me."

I took this to be an ironic reference to the monument beside him, the marble angel with its wings furled and head piteously bowed.

Torrance returned to prying open the crate, and Holmes, likewise, continued on his surreptitious serpentine course across the graveyard.

What happened next was of the nature of a phantasmagoria, and had I not been there myself and witnessed it in person, I doubt I would have believed it.

The ground burst open, erupting from below. Turf and soil

flew into the air, raining down in clods in all directions. Headstones toppled and tumbled. It was like a landmine going off. The terrific jolt sent me sprawling onto my back. Holmes, nearer to the point of disturbance than I was, was hurled sideways by the force of it and thudded helplessly into the pedestal of a raised tomb.

From a crater in the earth, a shape arose, sturdy, black and intimidating. A revenant from the nethermost pit.

Baron Cauchemar was back.

CHAPTER TWENTY

THE FALL OF THE HOUSE OF GOD

I was momentarily gripped by fear. All I could do was stare.

There he was, Baron Cauchemar. It was my first completely clear view of him, with no fog to blur and shroud him this time.

I saw those segmented limbs again, that torso made up of various cunningly interlocking metal plates. I saw also, now, how a kind of armature was affixed to the outside of each of his arms and legs, and how this armature, manifestly a means of reinforcement and mobilisation, consisted of rods and cogs that moved in perfect meshing synchrony.

I perceived other aspects of Cauchemar's appearance that I had missed before. His hands were of exaggerated proportions, like huge gauntlets, and from the palm of the left there protruded a pair of spherical brass studs, not unlike electrodes. His back was humped, fitted with the housing for some sort of miniature powering furnace. Flames danced within, visible through small glass portholes, and steam purled out, expelled through louvred vents.

All this made him seem yet more monstrous and inhuman. Indeed, it crossed my mind that the Bloody Black Baron was no man at all, nor anything demonic, but in fact pure machine, a fusion of automaton and steam locomotive, built by some demented toymaker in a huge hellish workshop-cum-foundry and operated by internal workings I could only guess at, a brilliant profusion of cogs and levers.

No sooner had the idea suggested itself than I dismissed it. Holmes was right: this was surely just an extraordinary, steam-propelled suit of armour, a "mechanised carapace" as he put it, with a human wearer inside – a pilot, one might call him.

Holmes!

In my dazed, amazed state, I had neglected to think of my friend, who had been so violently catapulted aside by Cauchemar's spectacular arrival from underground.

I scrambled over to where Holmes lay. He was semi-conscious. I patted his cheek a few times to bring him round. He moaned, eyelids fluttering.

Meanwhile, Cauchemar took a couple of steps towards Torrance, Gedge and Kaylock. They three were in various states of fright, Gedge and Kaylock most of all. Gedge quailed and Kaylock quaked as the baron thumped over to them.

Then – perhaps the most remarkable thing of all – Cauchemar spoke.

"Abednego Torrance. I have come for you."

The words came out in a dull resonant rasp, as though intoned through a long hollow tube.

"This must end. You betray your own country. There will be no more hiding from me. Prepare to atone for your sins."

Torrance responded with a defiant snarl. "I have wounded you once already, and escaped your clutches. I shall again. If there's anyone who's facing a reckoning tonight, it's you, you jackanapes."

Cauchemar appeared taken aback, this not a reaction he was expecting.

Then a shot rang out, the *boom* of a powerful rifle.

Cauchemar reeled. The round had caught him in the back of the head. Knocked off balance, he sank to one knee. The rear of his helmet now bore a deep dent.

A second shot clipped his arm, the bullet whining off to take a gouge out of a headstone. Cauchemar lumbered round, scanning for the source of the gunfire. From the angle of the shots, the sniper had to be firing from the rooftop of a nearby house that overlooked the graveyard, but which rooftop, I could not determine; neither could Cauchemar.

By now Holmes was back in the land of the sentient, more or less.

"Someone is besieging the baron," said he, thickly. "This has been an ambush."

A third shot found its mark dead centre of Cauchemar's face. Astonishingly, the baron keeled over, like a tree felled.

"Heavy-calibre, high-velocity," said Holmes. "The bullets might not penetrate his shell but the force alone is enough to stun him."

"But who?" I said. "Who is this sniper, this 'guardian angel' of Torrance's?"

Holmes did not have leisure to answer, even if he knew.

Torrance tore the lid off the crate, and from inside produced a stick of dynamite. He lit the fuse and tossed it at the supine Cauchemar. Before it even landed, he had fished out another stick and was lighting that one too.

Gedge and Kaylock scurried for cover as the first stick detonated.

Cauchemar managed to regain his senses in the nick of time. He dug his heels into the ground, and his armour's feet shot out, extending hydraulically from his legs. This propelled him several yards across the grass, so that the dynamite, which had been lying right next to him, blew up nothing but earth.

The next stick came fizzing through the air at him, tumbling end over end.

Miraculously, Cauchemar swatted it aside with a sweep of his arm, like a batsman returning a skilfully delivered googly. The dynamite spun towards Gedge and Kaylock, who were huddled together beside the church. They both ducked behind a buttress, which bore the brunt of the blast and saved them from harm.

Baron Cauchemar rallied, leaping to his feet with a clanking of metal and a great rushing hiss of steam. His glowing eyes, I now perceived, were circular lenses set into his mask and illuminated from within. One of the lenses had been cracked by the second gunshot. Through them, a pair of only-too-human eyes peered out, seeking Torrance.

A slew of rifle rounds thudded and whacked into Cauchemar's chest. He staggered backwards under the onslaught, unable to catch his balance. No sooner had he recoiled from one bullet than another smacked into him. The sniper, I concluded, must be using a bolt-action repeater in order to be able to deliver such rapid fire, perhaps a Lee Metford or a Lebel.

Cauchemar was driven against the flank of the church by the volley. This seemed to be what the sniper, clearly a crack marksman, intended, for no further shots came the armoured giant's way.

What did come his way was a bundle of dynamite sticks from Torrance, the lit fuse sizzling with barely an inch left to go.

"Watson!" Holmes cried out. "Look out! This is not going to end well."

The dynamite went off with one of the loudest bangs I have ever heard – louder even than the bomb at Waterloo Station.

Cauchemar was slammed against the church by the explosion, with such force that his body was partially embedded in the stonework.

The inevitable ensued.

That church was already a teetering, enfeebled edifice, barely able to remain upright unaided. The dynamite, and Cauchemar, proved the last straw as far as it was concerned.

A deep, aching rumble reverberated through the venerable building, a cavernous groan as of a leviathan in distress. The fissures which crazed the stonework all over widened and lengthened, joining up, multiplying. Tiles slithered down from the roof, shattering as they hit the ground, a hailstorm of slate. Gargoyles plummeted from the sky like pheasants at a shoot. The church shuddered along its entire length, from narthex to sacristy. Stained-glass windows burst outward in sprays of many-coloured shards.

Gedge and Kaylock were showing a clean pair of heels, haring away from the scene. Torrance was not far behind them.

Holmes and I were likewise on our feet and making good our escape, in a different direction. Holmes, however, had not yet fully recovered from having the wits and the wind knocked out of him, and I was obliged to support him. Hence our progress was not as fast as that of the three ruffians.

The rumbling intensified. I glanced over my shoulder, and what I beheld all but unmanned me.

The bell tower was crumbling, along with the rest of the church.

Holmes looked round too.

Before our very eyes, the entire tower sheared loose and tipped over.

Straight towards us.

"Watson! Move!"

Holmes gave me an almighty shove from behind. I stumbled forwards and fell headlong onto the grass. Behind me came the thunder of countless tons of limestone and mortar succumbing to gravity and plunging to earth. It was as though the fist of God Himself had descended from the heavens to punch the ground.

I thought the cracking and crashing and roaring would never cease. I was quite convinced that, at any second, some chunk of tumbling masonry would land clean on my cranium and that would be the end of me. I covered my head with my arms, for all the good that might do. I heard a man screaming and belatedly realised that it was me.

That I could hear my own voice at all was an indication that the tumult of the church's collapse had died down. I stopped screaming. I lay for a long while, scarce able to believe that I had survived and, what's more, was intact.

Rising to all fours took an almost superhuman effort. My limbs felt nerveless and numb.

The air was clogged with a haze of dust. The moonlight showed that little remained of the church, just a few truncated pillars and the corner of one transept, like the ruins of an ancient Roman temple. All else was merely a field of formless rubble.

Nothing moved. Nothing stirred.

"Holmes?" I said, my voice sounding hopelessly small after the devastating cacophony just past.

"Holmes?" I said again, a little louder and a lot more plaintively.

"Holmes!" I shouted.

No answer. No sign of him.

Holmes was lying somewhere under all that débris.

My friend was dead.

CHAPTER TWENTY-ONE

"THE FATAL STONE NOW CLOSES OVER ME"

Now, I am not going to maintain the pretence here that Holmes really was dead. What would be the point? Of course he was not. I ended the foregoing chapter on a note of dramatic suspense because that is what I have been wont to do in these narratives of mine. Old habits are hard to shake. Even when writing for no audience but myself, I still feel the need to incite a theoretical reader to read on.

In those dreadful minutes after the church in Stepney came down, however, I was quite firmly of the belief that Holmes had perished. There was no earthly way, to my mind, that he could have withstood having a significant portion of an ecclesiastical edifice dropped upon him.

What made my distress yet worse was the knowledge that Holmes, by shoving me forwards, had saved me. He had bought my life at the expense of his own. I did not deem this a fair exchange.

I began combing through the rubble, heaving aside the largest lumps I could manage. I knew it was in vain, but I had to act. I had to do *something*, however futile it might seem.

Lights had come on in various of the nearby houses, and a furore arose. People shouted from their windows, demanding to know what had transpired. I called for help but got no response. Londoners had become fearful: of bombs, of one another. The locals were more than eager to know what had disturbed their sleep but less than eager to sally forth from their homes and find out for themselves.

After several minutes I took a rest, worn out, my arms and back aching. A sense of desolation broke over me. I began to weep. Sherlock Holmes was dead. How to break the news to the world? I could scarcely accept it myself.

Then came the clatter of stones shifting. To my left, where the main body of the church had stood, the surface of the rubble was moving. Someone beneath was trying to claw their way out.

"Holmes!" I exclaimed, transported by a surge of joy and relief.

I hurried over in order to help. Before I got there, however, the rubble burst open and up rose a tall, imposing silhouette.

Baron Cauchemar stood, shaking the last few fragments of masonry from his shoulders. His armour bore several deep scratches and scrapes, which in tandem with the pockmarks left by the sniper's bullets made him look, for the first time in my experience, truly vulnerable.

His head swivelled towards me.

For a moment I thought he was going to go on the offensive, and in my ecstasy of grief, having just had my renewed hopes of Holmes's survival dashed, I honestly did not care if he did. With my best friend and one of the greatest men I had ever known dead, what did it matter if I lived? A world without Holmes was a world depleted, a world benighted, a world hardly worth being in.

"Go on then," I said to Cauchemar. "Get it over with, if you're going to. What's the use? Your armour protected you, while

Sherlock Holmes is crushed. Where is the justice in that?"

It was then that the smallest, faintest of sounds reached my ears. A voice which I had despaired of ever hearing again was calling to me, as though from miles distant.

"Watson," it said. "You buffoon. I am fine. A little stifled, perhaps, but on the whole hale. Possibly you could see your way to unearthing me…?"

"Holmes!" I began to search frantically, Cauchemar all but forgotten. "Where are you? Keep talking."

Holmes went one better and began to sing. I recognised the tune as '*La fatal pietra sovra me si chiuse*' from *Aida*, the aria which Radames launches into just after he has been buried alive in the crypt below the temple of Vulcan. I burst out laughing at the ironic absurdity of this. Trust Holmes to make light of so dark a predicament.

Following his voice, I discerned that he had somehow contrived to take refuge inside a small mausoleum. The entrance, however, was blocked solidly by a heap of broken masonry, several lumps of which were as big as boulders.

I outlined the problem to him. "There isn't a hope of me lifting any of it away. That will require a block and tackle, along with several men. You must hold on. I'll fetch help."

"I fear, Watson, it may not arrive in time. The supply of air in here is limited and diminishing fast. Can you think of something else? Perhaps Torrance's dynamite."

"That is buried too, and I have no idea where."

"Oh dear. Things do look bleak, then."

"Wait! There is something we can try."

I turned. Baron Cauchemar was still standing where he had arisen. He was busy extricating a lump of stone that had become wedged between his armour and a part of the surrounding armature.

"Cauchemar," I said, "listen to me. I don't know who or what you are, or what motivates you, but you have shown yourself to be an enemy of the forces of evil. In that mausoleum lies another enemy of the forces of evil, trapped and in danger of suffocation. You have the power to free him. I beg you to do so."

Cauchemar surveyed me through his eye lenses. Then said, in that weird, vibrating voice of his: "I was wondering when you'd get around to asking, Dr Watson. Step aside."

He crunched across the rubble to the mausoleum and bent to the task of removing the débris that blocked the doorway. With little apparent effort, he single-handedly hefted masses that a dozen men would have struggled with. Cogs whirred and steam hissed as he toiled. I looked on with no little awe, while a part of me kept asking the question: how come he knows my name?

Soon the work was done. The mausoleum door was fully exposed. It was made of copper that had turned turquoise with oxidisation. Holmes must have dived through after pushing me out of harm's way, then slammed the door shut behind him so as to keep the avalanche of chunks of the bell tower from following him inside.

Cauchemar shoved it open again with a thrust of his fist, and out stepped Holmes, dusty and dishevelled but smiling.

"A brief but not unpleasant stay amongst the departed," he said, "though I have no desire to make it a permanent condition until many years hence. Happily none of my fellow 'guests' had been too recently interred, otherwise the accommodation might have been far less congenial." He brushed a cobweb nonchalantly from his sleeve.

"Good Lord, Holmes," I said. "I thought we'd... I mean, you'd... Dash it all, man, I was certain I'd seen the last of you."

"I am not that easy to kill. Note that well, Watson. I am as crafty as a cat and have almost as many lives. Baron Cauchemar." He presented himself to the armoured goliath beside me. "I owe you a debt of gratitude for rescuing me. I would shake your hand, but I fear *my* hand would not survive the experience."

Cauchemar gave something that approximated a bow.

"Glad to be of service, Mr Holmes. Now I must take my leave. I have been somewhat incommoded by the night's events."

"You mean your armour has suffered damage and requires repair."

"That is so. It is not functioning at full capacity, and while there is little likelihood of it seizing up or overheating, I must nevertheless shut down the engine and overhaul the whole as soon as possible."

"Understood. Yet I would wish to engage in further discussion with you at some stage, Baron. We are, at present, both pursuing similar goals, if from slightly different trajectories, and were we to pool our information, I fancy it would –"

Bang!

The sniper!

I had assumed, erroneously, that we were no longer at risk from our unseen marksman. I had imagined that he had fled the scene in conjunction with Torrance, Gedge and Kaylock.

The bullet, this time, was not directed at Cauchemar but at Holmes. Only by some miracle did it fail to find its mark. Possibly the haze of dust that still hung over the rubble-strewn graveyard foiled the assassin's aim. A section of the frieze on the mausoleum wall disintegrated, just adjacent to Holmes's ear. He and I both fell into a crouch and scrambled on hands and knees round to the other side of the stone structure.

"You told me it was going to be a long, arduous night, Holmes," I said as we sheltered behind the mausoleum. "By God, you were right."

"Sometimes I wish I weren't," replied he.

The bullets continued to come our way with monotonous regularity. The sniper had us pinned down. Aside from the mausoleum there was precious little cover immediately around us. If we moved from where we were, our would-be killer would have a clear field of fire. I attempted to deter him with a couple of shots of my own, but I was firing blind and my Mark III Adams did not have nearly the range of his rifle. I might as well have been peppering him with pebbles from a slingshot.

Baron Cauchemar again proved to be our salvation.

"Gentlemen, I can get you out of here."

"That would be most welcome," said Holmes.

Cauchemar enjoined us to go ahead of him. With him interposed between us and the sniper, we were more or less shielded from the gunfire. He herded us, much in the manner of a hen with her chicks, towards the hole he had created in the ground when staging his dramatic entrance. The aperture was partly filled with débris, but not to the extent of this being an obstacle. The sides were reasonably shallow-angled, too. Holmes and I slid down into it, our ears resounding to the gong-like chime of bullets striking Cauchemar's back.

The last section of the descent was sheer. Pitch-blackness beckoned below. There was nothing for it but to throw caution to the winds and jump. Holmes leapt, and I, trusting in his judgement, did the same.

CHAPTER TWENTY-TWO

The *Subterrene*

It was a drop of some ten feet onto flagstones. Ignorant as I was in regard to how far down I was falling, I landed awkwardly, jarring my heel. As I straightened, hissing in pain, Holmes's hand reached out from the darkness and yanked me towards him. A split-second later, Baron Cauchemar thundered down on the very spot where I had been standing, missing me by a whisker. Had he plunged on top of me with his armoured bulk, there is no question which of us would have come off worse.

Holmes groped inside his coat to produce his pocket-lantern, but Cauchemar saved him the bother. A beam of light shot forth from a high-wattage electric bulb implanted beneath a panel in his chest. Its incandescence illuminated a catacomb with a low, vaulted ceiling.

"This way," Cauchemar said, and in the absence of a viable alternative, Holmes and I did as bidden and followed him.

A tunnel had been bored through the catacomb wall, leading down into the earth at a gentle incline. We entered, I still limping somewhat on my sore foot. There was just headroom enough in the tunnel that Cauchemar could pass along it without bending.

"Your doing?" said Holmes to Cauchemar.

"These hands of mine make for efficient spades."

"You are like some large steel-jacketed mole, burrowing."

"It is one of my many attributes. Watch your footing."

The tunnel floor was desperately uneven and treacherous with roots and loose rocks. Luckily, it did not go on for long. Within twenty paces we had arrived at its exit. An obnoxious stench told me all I needed to know about where we now were.

"The sewers," I sighed. "Again."

"You need not concern yourself, Dr Watson," said Cauchemar. "An unpleasant environment it may be but you won't be exposed to it for long. We don't have far to travel."

"That's all very well for you to say, ensconced in all that armour. What I wouldn't give for a pair of fisherman's waders. And a muffler."

"You'll have to forgive Watson, Baron," said Holmes. "He grows crotchetier with each passing year. I shouldn't be surprised if one day soon he retires to Tunbridge Wells and spends the rest of his life penning choleric letters to the editor of the *Daily Telegraph*. What is it about domestic bliss that makes a man so intolerant of inconvenience and hardship? I suppose the clue is in the word 'bliss'. That state makes all others dismal by comparison."

"I say, old chap, that's rather unfair," I declared. "You must not bring Mary into this. If I am less than overjoyed about trudging through human waste, or catching a chill in a graveyard at night, or having some madman with a rifle try to take the top of my head off, that is entirely my own consideration. My marital status has nothing to do with it."

"I am not decrying marriage, Watson, yours or anyone's. On the contrary, marriage is a noble and necessary institution. It is not for me; but in most instances it is the making of a man. It transforms the callow, unruly youth into an upstanding, productive member of society. With that, however, comes a certain, shall we say, softening? The groom becomes the unwitting captive of his bride, and is tamed, like a circus beast. 'I want' becomes 'yes, dear'. The growl of the bachelor diminishes to a miaow. It is as inevitable as it is regrettable."

"My vigour remains undimmed," I protested. "If an element of caution has crept into my personality, that is only to be expected. I no longer live solely to please myself. I am a husband, and shall one day, God willing, be a father." Alas, an expectation forever denied me. "There is more to think about now than just myself."

"And that is a wholly commendable attitude. You seem to take what I am saying as a personal slight."

"Isn't it?"

"No." Holmes grinned slyly. "But it has been a useful distraction. For, look. We have walked some distance, and have arrived where Cauchemar is taking us, and you were so busy bickering with me, you ceased to pay attention to the disagreeable nature of our surroundings."

"Holmes. Why, you… you…"

"Scoundrel?"

"Yes!"

"All in a good cause. Now, what's this?"

The beam of Cauchemar's chest-mounted light fell on the outline of something cylindrical and metallic that filled almost the entirety of the sewer tunnel ahead. It was tapered at the front, similar in its streamlined shape to a rifle cartridge, and was constructed from solid plates held together by rivets. Rows of huge knurled wheels projected at intervals all round its circumference, and a series of viewing portals extended across its front, through which I glimpsed a set of controls and what can only be described as a driving seat.

"Some kind of vehicle," I said.

"The selfsame vehicle which left those grooves we observed in the wall of the sewer at Shadwell," said Holmes. "This is how the baron gets around London unseen and so swiftly. Am I correct, Baron?"

"You are, Mr Holmes." Cauchemar unlatched a large hatch, opening up the nose of the vehicle. "I call it the *Subterrene*. A submarine that travels under the ground rather than under the sea, powered by steam."

"It is like a thing from a Jules Verne novel," I professed. "But then so, in your way, are you, Baron."

"I'll take both those remarks as a compliment. You go aboard first, gentlemen."

We stepped inside the extraordinary machine, finding just enough space for ourselves between the driving seat and the bulkhead behind. Cauchemar joined us, closing the hatch after him. It was a snug fit, all three of us in the confines of that "wheelhouse". The vehicle had apparently not been built with a view to transporting passengers in comfort. It was made for one.

Cauchemar lowered himself into the driving seat, which was sufficiently large and reinforced to accommodate his dimensions and weight. The controls, likewise, were proportionate to the size of his huge, gauntleted hands. He threw a couple of levers and a large knife-switch, and from behind Holmes and me came the hiss of gas burning, the rattle of pipes heating up and the rumble of steam coalescing. An instrument panel lit up. Needles on gauges started to creep round. Indicator bulbs brightened.

"You might want to hold on to something," Cauchemar cautioned, and we did as he suggested. "The *Subterrene* doesn't afford the smoothest of rides."

The vehicle was vibrating all around us like a greyhound in the trap, shuddering with pent-up energy, which Cauchemar released by means of twisting a stopcock valve. All at once we were lurching forwards. Powerful headlamps lit up the curvature of the sewer. Brickwork shot by us at increasing velocity.

The acceleration was so tremendous, it pushed us back against the bulkhead. The *Subterrene* juddered and rocked as it rocketed along. Now and then came a grinding sound from outside as the vehicle wended its way bumpily around a bend, wheels digging into brick.

Whenever we approached a junction, Cauchemar deftly spun a set of calibrated brass knobs which applied a brake to certain of the wheels. The *Subterrene* slewed in the desired direction and entered a new tunnel.

"Remarkable," said Holmes, voice raised above the vehicle's clamour. "To have made such good use of a relative novelty such as the sewer system. And unlike the underground railway there are no tracks to follow. The *Subterrene* may go anywhere, shuttling back and forth, left and right, at liberty."

"I spent six months familiarising myself with the tunnels," said Cauchemar, "and establishing which ones were navigable and which not. They have proved highly convenient. At the same time I was testing the *Subterrene*'s 'sewer-worthiness'. It has more than passed muster."

The vehicle's speed I must say I found disconcerting. We were plunging headlong through those sewers at a rate of knots, faster than any train I had been on, and with seemingly less security and restraint. Baron Cauchemar handled the controls in a manner which ought to have inspired confidence, yet I couldn't help thinking that if we crashed, it was all right for him inside his armoured shell. He was well protected. What about us frail humans sheathed in mere textiles? We would end up hideously broken and mangled. I had once tended to the victims of a ghastly railway accident on the Southampton to Dorchester line, while

I was at the Army Medical School at Netley, us trainees being called in to assist doctors at the local hospital who were in danger of being overwhelmed by the numbers of casualties, so I know whereof I speak.

Finally the *Subterrene* began to decelerate, our ultimate destination near. Cauchemar brought the vehicle to a halt in a side-tunnel that branched off a larger one. We were beside a walkway raised above the flow of effluent. He deactivated the engine, quieting its din, then opened the hatch.

Out we all went, across the walkway and up to a vast, thick door of the kind one might normally see guarding the entrance to a bank vault. Where we were, how far below the surface, in what part of London, I had no idea. There was no way of telling, not one visual clue to help.

Cauchemar spun a locking wheel and the door swung inwards. Holmes and I gamely followed him through into a high-ceilinged, windowless chamber which was filled with equipment, machinery and engineering paraphernalia. There was a lathe, a metalworking forge, and a plan table on which lay several sets of blueprints. There was also a baffling array of gadgets and devices, placed on various workbenches.

Cauchemar bade us make ourselves at home while he removed his armour.

This he accomplished by installing himself within a convoluted cat's cradle of steel joists and beams which neatly fitted around his armoured form, as though he were the final piece that completed a jigsaw. A huge clockwork mechanism groaned into life and began peeling off his black metal carapace bit by bit, using pincers mounted on pistons which operated in a complex sequence.

First the furnace-powered engine was lifted from his back. Then the sections of armour that covered his limbs were dismantled, each falling smartly apart into two pieces. Then off came the torso segment. Last to be removed was the helmet, and with it the rig which piped his voice to the armour's exterior, somewhat in the manner of a gramophone speaker.

Watching this automated dissection was like watching a giant insect being broken down into its components by the hand of some dispassionate entomologist. One could only marvel at the rapidity and intricacy with which it was done. Whoever had designed the apparatus, and for that matter Cauchemar's armour, was an engineer of singular skill and ingenuity, a genius to rival Telford or Brunel.

Had Holmes and I harboured the hope of seeing Cauchemar's face, and thus establishing his true identity, it was to go unfulfilled. For beneath his helmet he wore a padded woollen "under-mask", doubtless to cushion his head as the knights of yore did with their arming caps and helm bonnets. It covered his face entirely save for two holes for the eyes, which made it also reminiscent of the knitted balaclavas which British troops took to wearing in the Crimea to stave off the cold. The rest of him was encased in a similarly padded set of longjohns.

Without doffing this under-mask, Cauchemar spent some time damping down the armour's portable furnace. Holmes availed himself of the opportunity to wander the chamber, inspecting the blueprints on the plan table and also the many barely explicable constructs around us. I accompanied him.

The devices turned out on closer examination to be items of weaponry, for the most part. Many were obviously still in the development phase, works in progress, incomplete. A stubby crossbow-like thing was primed with three brass balls connected to one another by thick wire – I took this to be a method of projecting, at speed, a bolas such as the ones used by South American gauchos to bring down errant cattle. Another similar weapon employed a spring-mounted torsion engine to launch a bundled-up steel-filament net, which presumably unfurled in midair to wrap itself around its target. A third weapon resembled nothing so much as a small multi-barrelled cannon, equipped with clamps that would permit it to be attached to Cauchemar's forearm. In place of cannonballs, mortar shells or any similar kind of shot, there were hessian sacks filled with rock salt and sewn into a tight purse shape.

"The baron," Holmes observed, "seeks to put his enemies out of commission but not to kill them. There is evidently a line he refuses to cross."

"That is true," said Cauchemar, having conducted his business with the furnace. "And Dr Watson, I would be wary of touching that, if I were you."

I had been about to lay hands on an intriguing contraption. It consisted of an elaborate arrangement of vacuum pump and pneumatic tubes, all connected to a glass tank filled with a glutinous white substance.

"It has something of a hair trigger," Cauchemar continued, "and would cause a frightful mess if you got the contents all over yourself." His voice, though now not distorted by the sound-conduction system his armour used, remained muffled by the under-mask. Even if Cauchemar had been a close friend of mine, I might not have recognised him purely from hearing him speak.

"Antipersonnel glue?" said Holmes inquisitively.

"Just so. A fast-acting, quick-drying paste, a formula of my own devising, which if jetted out in sufficient quantities covers its subject from head to toe and sets in an instant, rendering him immobile. I'm still experiencing a few teething problems with it, mainly related to speeding up the system of delivery. As yet, the paste works so efficiently, it tends to gum up the tubes before it can emerge, and the spray from the nozzle is as a result inconsistent and intermittent. But I am convinced I can get the thing to function properly in due course. As with any problem, it's merely a question of time and the application of brainpower."

"A fine sentiment, well put," said Holmes. "You are a man after my own heart."

Cauchemar greeted the accolade with an appreciative nod.

"We are," he said to Holmes, "not so dissimilar, you and I, sir. We both rely on the strength of our minds, above all else, to combat crime. I lack your capacity for logical analysis and deductive reasoning, but what I have in its place is a knack for building things, especially things powered by compact motors using ultra-condensed steam."

"You are also," Holmes said, "of the middle classes, a scion of a modestly well-off family. I would put your age as early thirties, and your accent bespeaks a Home Counties upbringing, Sussex if I don't miss my guess. You have a faint South Coast burr, modulated by education at a public school, one of the minor ones, because a top-tier public school would have thrashed every last trace of regional diction out of you. You came into a healthy-sized legacy in the not-too-distant past, not from your parents, because they were not of means, but from a rich relative, someone who was close kin but not that close. A childless uncle. That is how you have sponsored all this research and manufacture. Yes?"

Cauchemar's bright blue eyes betrayed a flicker of surprise, which confirmed Holmes's deductions.

"It is one thing to read about your uncanny ability to divine a stranger's history from just a handful of personal traits," he said. "It is quite another to see it put into action at first hand."

"The novelty never wears off," I commented. "Although it is preferable when Holmes practises it upon somebody other than oneself."

"Furthermore," said Holmes, "you have travelled, and even resided for some time on the Continent. France, to be precise."

"What gives you cause to say that?"

"Elementary. Your adopted surname. A French word. Granted, you could simply have learned '*cauchemar*' at school or plucked it from a dictionary, but it seems to me a very specific choice, one that has significance for you. Ergo, you must have lived in France and absorbed some of that nation's culture. The Francophone regions of Canada were a possibility, or one of the French- or Belgian-dominated African nations, but France itself seemed, on balance, likeliest. An English *nom de guerre*, perhaps even 'Baron Nightmare', would have made sense if your goal was purely to intimidate the thieves and murderers of the East End, but there is more to your activities than that. I'd add that bestowing a peerage upon your armoured alter ego is no arbitrary act either. Your claim to a 'barony' has a purpose and an ulterior –"

"Please, Mr Holmes. Enough." Cauchemar made a chopping motion. "I do not wish to regret inviting you and Dr Watson into my lair. I would prefer it if, as a professional courtesy to me, you desisted from prying into my background or motives. That is why I am keeping this mask on. I need to remain anonymous if I am to succeed in my aims. My admiration for you is unbounded, but I have my secrets and I would like them to remain such."

"Since Watson and I owe you our lives," Holmes said, "I will respect your request."

But I recognised on my friend's face an expression I knew all too well. Holmes had a hawk-like tenacity when confronted with an enigma. He could not rest until he had plumbed its every depth; and the more someone tried to discourage him from doing so, the more relentless his determination grew.

"Might I at least enquire," he said to Cauchemar, "why you accused Abednego Torrance of being a traitor to his country?"

"Is it not obvious? The man was retrieving a hidden stash of dynamite, clearly with a view to helping perpetrate another bombing atrocity, which, thank God, has at least been prevented."

"You believe he is a terrorist."

"On the face of it he would fit the bill. His surname is of Irish origin. It would be easy to take him for a committed Fenian."

Holmes looked sceptical. "The facts would certainly appear to support that conclusion. Yet it seems out of character for Torrance to espouse a political cause. He is a man who is driven by only one imperative, and that is lining his own pockets."

"As a matter of fact, I agree," said Cauchemar. "Torrance is a freelancer, mercenary in every sense. Not only does he supply the terrorists with their dynamite, they employ him to do their work for them."

"It does strike me," I said, "that Torrance would conduct a bombing campaign if paid to. He would offer his services to any bidder who came along, regardless of what they asked of him."

"He is not overburdened with morality," Holmes agreed. "The fallacy in logic here, though, is assuming in the first place that the bombers are Fenians. There is little conclusive evidence for that. No overt political statements have been made. No Irish nationalists have stepped forward to claim responsibility for the bombings. No one has yet made political capital out of them. The silence from the Home Rule advocates is resounding, and very telling."

"I concur," said Cauchemar. "Your conclusions jibe with my own. My mention of Fenianism was a feint."

Holmes studied the young man with approval, and at last I began to perceive why my friend was so fascinated with this vigilante. They were in many ways alike, both possessed of a powerful brain and a burning desire for justice. Holmes saw a reflection of himself in Cauchemar. He felt an affinity for him. He had found a kindred spirit.

"Do you care to explain that comment?" he said.

"Not really."

"You know more than you are willing to let on."

"I have my reasons."

"You won't divulge?"

"No."

"That in itself is illuminating. What a man withholds from saying can be as instructive as what he actually says. I shall try another tack. How did you learn that tonight's little 'grave-robbing' episode was going to occur?"

"I have my sources." Cauchemar deliberated. "You see, I have the means to tap into – Well, it's simpler if I show you. Walk this way, gentlemen."

CHAPTER TWENTY-THREE

THE LAW IS AN ASSET

Cauchemar led us to an adjoining chamber, not as large but no less cluttered. If what we had been in was an armoury-cum-workshop, what we were now in was a hub, a centre of operations, a campaign headquarters. Maps of London were tacked to the walls, along with diagrams of the sewers and underground railway lines and rivers and all the other subterranean features of the city. Newspapers lay piled high on the floor, and clippings from them were pinned to display boards. The articles were exclusively devoted to crime and criminals, providing names and pictures of the city's most notorious villains and the dates and locations of their misdeeds. There were bookcases on which sat Dr Krafft-Ebing's *Psychopathia Sexualis* and other criminological case studies, alongside bound editions of the *Proceedings Of The Old Bailey* and *The Illustrated Police News*. Cauchemar took his vocation seriously, then, pursuing it with the thoroughness of a scholar.

Overhanging the centre of the room was an agglomeration of wires. Dozens of them were gathered in thick sheaves that ran down from the ceiling, drawing together like strands of a web. All of them fed into the back of a large brass teleprinter, which was chattering away diligently, producing coil upon coil of paper tape.

As Holmes's gaze alighted on this, he let out a small cry of pleasure.

"Oh, this is very clever," he said, gesturing at the teleprinter. "Bravo, Cauchemar, you cunning fellow. You have, if I'm not mistaken, spliced into London's telegraphy network and secretly run a wire off each of the principal cables."

"I have." Cauchemar sounded both proud and bashful. "I am able to eavesdrop on every single message transmitted along the wires. It is an invaluable resource. Any telegram that gets sent, I automatically receive a copy of it, and no one is any the wiser. Sorting through them is another matter, though. Thousands of these communications zip back and forth each day, more than one man could hope to read and digest. To that end, I have made various adaptations to the teleprinter, guided in part by the tabular-computational principles of Babbage's difference engine."

"Elucidate."

"I have installed a mechanism which is set to recognise the letter-patterns of certain words and phrases – I call them 'key words'. Most messages pass through the system unremarked and are not printed. Only those containing pertinent or suggestive terms get singled out for me to study. I can even block them from passing on to their destination, if I wish, although I have done that rarely – in fact only once. The machine is like a prospector in the Klondike, sifting through the stream-bed gravel for nuggets of gold."

"Heavens above," I said. "No wonder you routinely turn up in your armour as crimes are being committed."

"Criminals, even the less sophisticated representatives of that species, are known to organise their schemes and recruit accomplices via telegram," said Holmes. "Scotland Yard also conveys many of its instructions the same way."

"A valuable source of tip-offs," said Cauchemar.

"Who knows, if the police were to adopt a similar method of tapping into telegraphy such as you employ, they might increase their prevention rate a dozenfold. However, there's the ethical dimension to that to consider. When does listening in become prying? It could be construed as an invasion of privacy."

"The police might find a way of putting this technology to use, although I warrant that their intrinsic lack of co-ordination and endless layers of bureaucracy would still hobble them," said Cauchemar. "The beauty of the way I work is that I can strike exactly when and where I choose, without the hindrance of mobilising a posse of officers and arranging arrest warrants and other practical considerations like that. Also, owing to my mode of transportation, no one knows I'm coming; whereas the average police raid is conducted literally with bells and whistles and may as well be heralded by an engraved calling card and an announcement in the Court and Social pages of the *Times*."

Holmes chuckled, amused to find someone whose low opinion of the constabulary's competence matched his own.

"Some might argue," I said, "that what you do falls outside the rule of law, Cauchemar, and thus you are no better than the criminals you hurt and intimidate."

I had meant the remark casually, so as to offer an alternative viewpoint, but Cauchemar found it vexing.

"The law," he snorted. "Let me tell you about the law, Dr Watson. The law does nothing to protect the rights of individuals when they really need it. The law is there to preserve the fiefdoms of the rich and powerful and give them another stick with which to beat the common man. The law is not 'an ass', as the playwright Chapman would have it, but an *asset*, one of benefit only to those who have the wealth and influence to use it. There is no law in places like the East End. There, people have one basic rule they all abide by, and that is 'do unto others before they do unto you.'"

"But, for the majority of us, if laws did not exist there would be out-and-out anarchy," I countered. "We've had a taste of that these past few days, with the bombings and the riots, and I for one would not wish to see it become a lasting state of affairs."

"It's a comforting illusion, Doctor, to think that the law keeps us safe in our beds at night. It does not. Most people are constrained from committing illegal acts not by some inner morality but by fear of unwelcome consequences. The truth, if only they realised it, is that the police and courts are a blunt, inefficient tool and what little justice they uphold is not nearly enough. For every crime that is cleared up and punished, a hundred others go uninvestigated and unsolved. What I have been doing in the East End has amply proved, by example, the law's ineffectuality. I am there where the police fear to tread. I am accomplishing what they cannot hope to. I am instilling a true fear of consequences in a section of the populace who until now have been raping and robbing and cozening and killing with impunity."

Cauchemar had grown quite heated. I must have hit a nerve, to bring forth such an impassioned tirade.

I felt no great urge to mollify him, but in the interests of goodwill I said, "No one could deny that you have made a difference. Just the other day a police inspector of our acquaintance remarked on the substantial drop in the crime rate in that area since you came along."

"It's good to know that someone has noted my efforts," said Cauchemar. "I am striving to bring some decency and order to the beleaguered East End, and to London in general, while at the same time honing my skills and refining my techniques. On that front, if no other, I have reason to be grateful to Abednego Torrance. He by accident discovered a chink in my armour when he shot me a few nights back. There was a vulnerability around the leg pistons which

I use to leap around. The metal was necessarily thinner there, at least in my original design, and hence less resistant to gunfire. I have since rebuilt both pistons in reinforced form, using steel that is quenched rather than tempered and has an increased carbon content. The weak point should now have been eliminated."

"Yes," said Holmes, "but the sniper who assisted Torrance this evening showed that your armour is still not a perfect defence."

"What is?" said Cauchemar with a shrug. "Let us put things into perspective, though. Had I not been wearing it, the three of us would not be talking to each other right now – we would all be pushing up the proverbial daisies. An entire church fell on me, and I suffered no more harm than the odd scratch and bruise. That said, I may have to make a few alterations so that next time someone comes at me with an elephant gun, or whatever it was, the impact of the shots won't be quite so debilitating. Hmmm. Perhaps if there were some way to distribute the force of the bullet across a wider surface area. I could introduce a thin outer layer to absorb and disperse it. But then there's the additional weight to factor in. Upping the power output of the engine would produce a higher compression rate with the steam, and I'm already at the acceptable limit of tolerance there. But what if I simply increase the size of the micro-furnace pack...?"

Cauchemar lost himself in his musings. He wandered over to a table, on which lay what appeared to be a jumble of machine parts, random odds and ends that had migrated across from the neighbouring room.

I glanced at Holmes, whose attention had reverted to the teleprinter. He was frowning at it, rapt. Then his expression cleared.

"Watson," he said in a low tone, so as not to be overheard. "I believe we have met the baron before."

"We have," I said. "A few nights ago at Shadwell. But I suspect that is not what you mean."

"Prior even to that."

"When?"

"When we had a visitor. An unusual-looking one."

I ransacked my memory. So much had happened during the past week that it felt more like a month. "You mean the scarred delivery boy."

"Precisely. The rather adult delivery boy, with the egregiously burned face. I know that I am prone to using disguises. So, it would seem, is Cauchemar. The application of wax and panstick can easily mimic fire-damaged skin tissue; I've done it myself. Not only did this alter his features and justify why a man his age might be employed delivering telegrams, it was all one could notice when looking at him. It was, in the parlance of stage conjurors, misdirection. One marked little about the man other than his disfigurement."

"Did you know at the time that it was not real?"

"I had my suspicions. Certainly something about the fellow seemed 'off', which was why I entreated you to offer your own opinion of him. The makeup fooled even your experienced medical eye, so I deemed that it must be genuine damage rather than fake. Perhaps I should have placed greater faith in my own judgement."

"Well, I'm sorry, old chap. I was not in my right mind at the time. I had just undergone a traumatic experience."

"Oh, I'm not blaming you, Watson. I'm blaming myself. But I see now, with this marvellous machine before me which pirates all the telegraphic communiqués of London and beyond, how Cauchemar must have intercepted Mycroft's missive to me, donned a delivery boy's uniform, applied counterfeit scar tissue to his face, and come to Baker Street with it. This is the occasion he referred to, the 'only once' when he blocked a telegram. Mycroft's original never made it to our local telegraph office. It arrived by Cauchemar's hand instead."

"But for heaven's sake, why?" I declared. "For what reason did he go to all that trouble?"

"That is the question, isn't it?"

"The answer," said Cauchemar, "is straightforward."

He had padded stealthily up behind us while we had been conversing. The chattering of the teleprinter had drowned his footfalls.

"To pay my respects," he said. "To meet, in person, the inimitable Sherlock Holmes. To see for myself the great lion of detection in his den. To confirm the righteousness of my own mission by entering the presence of someone who, like me, combats crime on his own terms, in parallel to the official authorities."

"There are far easier ways of achieving the same result," Holmes said. "You could merely have knocked on my front door. People do, you know, and I receive them in."

"And have you see my true face, my own clothes, my hair, my complexion? Have you log all of those particulars in that extraordinary calculating brain of yours? Expose myself to the full force of your penetrating deductive scrutiny? No thank you. You have discerned enough about me as it is, for all that I am masked and clad in virtually my undergarments. I could not have you learning any more."

"What is it you are keeping behind your back?" Holmes enquired, with a sudden squint.

Cauchemar did indeed have his hands hidden behind him. I had assumed they were just clasped together there, Cauchemar having adopted a rather formal stance.

He brought his hands to the fore, and in them were a pair of small canisters which he must have fetched from the table of assorted spare parts.

He raised these until they were level with Holmes's and my faces.

"I truly regret this, gentlemen," said he. "Were there any other way…"

"Watson!" cried Holmes. "Quick. Cover your –"

But the warning came too late for me, and Holmes himself was a fraction of a second too slow to act.

Cauchemar depressed triggers on the canisters, and two jets of mist sprayed out. The smell of the stuff was sweet, cloyingly so. I recognised it instantly as chloroform, albeit a more pungent variety than I was familiar with.

I was aware of falling, Holmes falling beside me, both of us choking and spluttering. My vision telescoped down to a narrow field. Cauchemar's masked face loomed over me, framed by a wondrous iridescent corona. His voice came as though echoing down a speaking tube.

"My oneirogenic gas is very fast-acting," he said. "The chloroform is augmented with a mixture of distilled ethanol and oil of vitriol, amplifying its effects by several orders of magnitude. You will feel some discomfort when you come to, and I apologise in advance for that. But I can't have you leaving here by any other means. Another journey by *Subterrene* might enable you, Mr Holmes, with your keen mind, to triangulate the whereabouts of this place, and that cannot be permitted. Secrets. Secretsss. Sssecretssss…"

The words dissolved into meaningless sibilance, and my eyes closed, and cold blackness swamped my brain like the waters of a lake, and I knew nothing further.

CHAPTER TWENTY-FOUR

THE COMPROMISED STOCKBROKER

When I awoke, it was to a splitting headache and vision so badly blurred I could barely make out my hand in front of my face. My mouth felt as dry as a desert, my tongue like sandpaper, and as I attempted to rise from my supine position I was overcome by a nausea so intense, I only narrowly avoided vomiting. Every single one of my muscles ached, and most of my bones as well, a state of affairs not ameliorated by the hard wooden bench I was lying upon. Baron Cauchemar had drastically undersold the after-effects of his oneirogenic gas. "Some discomfort" my eye!

To add to my woes, a loud rapping sound started emanating from nearby, which seemed to pierce my brain like a hammered rail-spike. At the same time a gruff voice growled, "Get up. Get up, you lazy beggar. How dare you. These are private premises, not for the likes of you to use."

I blinked hard, and my focus sharpened to the extent that I could just make out another bench a few yards away. A man was stretched out on it, and a second man stood bent over him, hitting the back of the bench lustily with a walking stick.

This latter was a stranger, a rotund and extravagantly muttonchopped gent with a correspondingly tubby Cavalier King Charles spaniel at his feet on a lead. The subject of his angry attentions was Sherlock Holmes, who, like me, was gradually coming round from his gas-induced stupor. Holmes's face was pinched and grey, his eyes so bloodshot the whites were almost wholly red. He looked as wretched as I felt.

The man with the spaniel, unable to prompt more out of his victim than a groan, took to prodding him in the belly with the walking stick's ferrule.

"I pay a handsome subscription, as do all who live in this square, for exclusive access to these gardens," he said. "We expect to be able to stroll round them of a morning without bumping into riffraff like you and your friend over there. If you're going to sleep off a gin hangover, do it somewhere else – in the gutter, preferably. By the looks of you, the smell of your clothes in particular, that's where you belong."

Holmes had had enough. He sat bolt upright, parrying the walking stick aside.

"You do me a great insult, sir," he snapped. "I am here neither by choice nor of necessity. Poke me one more time and I shall not be held accountable for my actions."

The other man took umbrage. "You threaten me, you wastrel? As a trespasser on private property? I'll have you know I share a degree of affiliation with several of the most influential men in this city. I am not someone you cross lightly."

The spaniel elected to match its owner's bark by starting to yap incessantly. The dog's din could not have improved Holmes's delicate frame of mind; it certainly wasn't helping mine.

The man might yet have emerged from the altercation unscathed if he hadn't then taken one last vicious jab at Holmes with the walking stick. That was the final straw as far as my friend was concerned, and he went on the offensive.

"I realise how important you think you are," he said to the man. "But how would your wife take it if she found out that your overseas investments have failed and you are dangerously close to penury?"

The man looked shocked, utterly flummoxed. His mouth opened and shut like a goldfish's.

"Not only that," Holmes continued, "but you have sworn to her that you have abandoned your unseemly practice of accosting men in public places, soliciting them to join you in indecent acts, but it is a habit you have yet to break."

"I… I…" The man's thunderstruck discomfiture was almost painful to behold.

Holmes pressed on. "The United Grand Lodge would surely have something to say about *that* behaviour, not to mention about the funds of theirs which you have embezzled in order to cover your financial losses. My associate and I may appear to be riffraff, but you, sir, are proof that even the most respectable-looking of persons has his seamy side. Smart clothes and fine words cannot hide the true riffraff of this world."

The not-so-gentlemanly gent tottered backwards from Holmes and collapsed onto the lawn on the other side of the pathway. The spaniel whimpered up at him as he buried his head in his hands in horrified disbelief. Holmes had unravelled the man's entire life in a matter of seconds, ransacking closets to allow countless skeletons to come tumbling out.

Holmes, his work done, levered himself off the bench and helped me to my feet. Then together, the groggy pair of us, we stumbled to the gate which afforded egress from the gardens. In the street, we caught our breath and took our bearings. The garden square we found ourselves in was in Bloomsbury, one of London's more prestigious addresses. Cauchemar must have dropped us off here after gassing us into unconsciousness, no doubt deriving an ironic amusement from making us look like inebriated vagabonds dossing in a high-class part of town.

"I apologise, Watson," Holmes said.

"For the way you treated that man back there? Think nothing of it. He was unforgivably high-handed. He pushed you too far. He deserved what he got."

"Did he? Well, maybe. Actually, I was apologising for not anticipating that Cauchemar would move to incapacitate us the way he did. I should have seen it coming. The fact is, he impressed me to such a degree that I let my guard down. His prowess, his praise, his blandishments, all appealed to my vanity, and I allowed myself to relax when I should have stayed on my mettle. As for that fellow in the gardens, one can understand why he made the assumption about us that he did. You and I both look a mess, old chum, and do not smell of the freshest. Perhaps I could have been kinder to him. Yet I cannot abide a hypocrite."

"It was all true? Everything you said to him?"

"Every word. His precarious financial situation was easy to infer. One of the first things he mentioned was how much his subscription for use of the gardens was costing him. Money, clearly, has been preying on his mind. He happened to have a copy of the *Financial Times* folded under his arm, with the overseas investment statistics column uppermost. The newspaper was dog-eared and the ink on that page smudged. The same ink was smeared on his fingertips. All of which would signify that that section of the paper had been well pored over. Now, a successful investor would not dwell on a single portion of a financial journal obsessively. He would glance at it contentedly, then move on. An *un*successful investor, on the other hand..."

"What about his inclination towards his own gender?"

"He wore a wedding band but also a green carnation in his buttonhole. The latter is a secret emblem allowing those of his persuasion to recognise one another. The playwright Oscar Wilde famously sports one. He was out walking his dog, yet the animal was overweight, bordering on obese, which suggested it does not get as much exercise as it ought. Logically, therefore, when the dog should have been taking its constitutional with its master, it was in fact spending most of the time tethered to a bush or a set of railings while he was otherwise engaged. Now, I have nothing personally against such proclivities, especially if conducted with discretion, but they contravene the law of the land and, as far as this individual is concerned, make a mockery of his wedding vows."

"And the Freemasonry?"

"A ring on his right hand with the Square and Compasses made that perfectly apparent. Like the carnation, the badge of a clandestine brotherhood. He also employed a singular turn of phrase: 'I share a *degree of affiliation* with several of the most influential men in this city'. This perhaps was once a little in-joke of his that has since become a fixture of his everyday vocabulary, a 'degree' of course being an order of Freemasonry."

"But you claimed he was embezzling funds from them."

"That, I admit, was a stab in the dark, but it seemed one worth taking, and in the event proved a palpable hit. The *Financial Times* has not been around long but has already earned the sobriquet 'the stockbroker's Bible', which gives us a strong hint as to our friend's line of work. As a Freemason, might he not offer his services *pro bono*, managing his lodge's investment portfolio? And if his own finances were compromised, might he not be dipping his hand into someone else's pockets in order to make up the shortfall and continue funding his affluent lifestyle? Such an act would be in keeping with a man who is not continent in other areas of his personal conduct. And now, Watson," said Holmes, "I propose we make our way – gingerly – to Baker Street, where we shall prevail upon Mrs Hudson to brew us some strong tea and cook us a fortifying breakfast, so that we may recoup our strength and alleviate the effects of Cauchemar's damnable gas."

But this happy prospect was not to be realised, for as we began our trek westward, we discerned a raucous hue and cry echoing over the rooftops. It was reminiscent of the baying of wolves who have caught the scent of blood.

Fearing we were about to get embroiled in another riot, we took a detour away from the source of the noise, going southward. The hullabaloo, however, seemed to change direction as we moved, or else was coming from all directions at once. Whichever way we turned, it was ahead of us.

We rounded a corner, to find a small group of people hurrying towards us along the pavement with obvious purpose. I shrank away, retreating into a shop doorway, but Holmes did the opposite, stepping into their path. They veered around him, but he waylaid one of them, a baker's boy barely out of his teens, and rapidly interrogated him.

"What is all this? What is happening? Where are you running to?"

"Haven't you heard?" replied the panting youth. "They've only gone and got one."

"*Who* have only gone and got *what*?"

"One of the bombers. Peelers have nabbed him, caught him in the act, so it's said, and they're taking him to Scotland Yard. We want to have a look."

Holmes relinquished his hold on the youngster, who raced off to catch up with his comrades.

"Can it be true?" I said. "Can the nightmare finally be over?"

"Who knows? The police may be bringing in a suspect, but whether or not he's the culprit is entirely another matter. We must, I'm afraid, put our other plans on hold and go and see for ourselves, Watson. It's the only way."

CHAPTER TWENTY-FIVE

FEIGNING FENIANISM

Within quarter of an hour we had circumnavigated Covent Garden, crossed the Strand, and were travelling southward along the Victoria Embankment. Ahead rose the Palace of Westminster and its clock tower, home to Big Ben, and before that lay the Met's newly constructed headquarters, popularly known as New Scotland Yard even though it was no longer situated near the street, Great Scotland Yard, from which the name originally derived.

A tide of chattering, eager people hastened along the Embankment in tandem with us, moving faster than the incoming flow of the river. News of the arrest had spread like wildfire, and it seemed as though fully half the population of London had dropped whatever they were doing and headed out in order to catch a glimpse of the terrorist being brought in for questioning.

By the time we came within sight of the Yard itself, the building was surrounded by a turbulent sea of curiosity-seekers and gawkers. The throng surged against a cordon of uniformed constables who stood, arms linked, before the main entrance.

The mood of the crowd was turning restive and ugly. Teeth

were bared; fists pumped the air. The bomber, it transpired, was already on the premises, and there were calls to send him out, give him to the public, let them deal with him. It was, in short, a lynch mob in the making. Someone shinned up a tree with a length of rope in hand, giving some idea what sort of justice the crowd had in mind to mete out.

"There isn't a hope of us pushing through," I said to Holmes. "They're too tightly packed together."

"There is a way," he replied. "Watson, do you trust me?"

"I'm not sure I like the sound of this."

"Answer the question, yes or no?"

"Yes. Of course. Implicitly."

"Then bear with me. There will be some risk, but if you do exactly as I say, you should be safe."

"'Should be'?" I echoed querulously.

Holmes grabbed me by the scruff of the neck and yanked my arm up behind me in a half-Nelson. "Keep your head down. Move fast. Act Irish."

"Act…?"

"Coming through!" Holmes yelled out. "Make way! Undercover police officer, escorting another bombing suspect."

The crowd, incredibly, parted for us. Holmes had addressed them with commanding authority, not to mention a soupçon of Lestrade's nasal-inflected pomposity. He also mimicked the inspector's bustling comportment. No one doubted for a moment that he was what he pretended to be.

As he frogmarched me along, a localised hubbub grew around us.

"Another one. They've collared another one!"

"Copper's bringing a second one in."

"Look at the state of him. Bet he's been hiding out in someone's coal cellar."

"Oi, you lousy mick! You'll swing for what you've done."

Some kicks came my way, and the odd clumsy punch. Holmes deflected the worst of the blows and kept us moving, although what he couldn't prevent was a number of people showering me with spittle. I could scarcely believe my friend was taking such liberties with my welfare, but I showed willing and played my part, muttering the odd "begorrah" and "to be sure, to be sure" in order to reinforce my credentials as a son of Erin.

As soon as we reached the police cordon, Holmes went straight up to the first constable he recognised. His memory for individual officers' faces was remarkable. To me, they were all too often indistinguishable, one bobby in a dark blue tunic and conical helmet looking much like another.

"You," he said. "Mitchell, isn't it? You know me."

"That I do, Mr Holmes. I was there when you solved that murder at the Theatre Royal, the one where you worked out who poisoned the female lead in her dressing room by how many strawberries had been eaten from the bowl on the table and by the way the hem of her petticoat had been adjusted so as to –"

"Yes, quite. Let us through, this instant, or I fear Watson here may wind up dangling from a noose, and London will have lost one of its pre-eminent general practitioners and I my closest confidant and friend."

"Right you are, Mr Holmes," said Constable Mitchell, and within moments my companion and I were free from the buffeting, agitated crowd and were passing through the arched doorway of the Yard, that grand Gothic, castle-like structure which was both beautiful and imposing. The door closed behind us, shutting out the worst of the mob's ruckus, and Holmes at last let go of me.

"I would rather we never did that again," I said, mopping saliva from my face with a handkerchief. "Did I have to be an Irishman? Wasn't that tempting fate, given the antipathy of the people out there to all things Irish?"

"I needed to impart a sense of urgency," said Holmes. "If I had announced you as just some average criminal, we would never have made any headway. I calculated that, for all the hostility on display, more of the crowd would wish to see a Fenian bomber tried and convicted and then hanged, than simply hanged. Not only that but they would, by habit, not wish to impede a policeman in the performance of his duties, either out of deference or fear of getting arrested themselves. We were never in serious danger."

"*You* were never in serious danger," I grumbled. "What if they had become bold and wrested me from your grasp...?" I shuddered to think of the potential outcome.

"But they didn't, and now we are where we want to be. Let us go in search of a friendly face or, failing that, a familiar one."

New Scotland Yard still smelled of fresh paint and recently dressed stone. We weren't yet used to the layout of the place, having visited only a couple of times since its inauguration. It was a sign that the Metropolitan Police was thriving, this brand new headquarters. The force had outgrown its original premises on Whitehall Place and required somewhere modern and purpose-built to accommodate its expansion. The crime rate had risen commensurately at the same time, so one might argue that the police's increased prevalence and prosperity came at a cost to the general public.

As we traversed a seemingly endless succession of labyrinthine corridors, I recalled how Holmes and I had been summoned to the site while the building was under construction some two years earlier. Workmen had stumbled upon a female torso in a cellar they had recently completed. It was wrapped in black cloth, a sort of grisly parcel, and it was found to match an arm and shoulder which had turned up on the shore of the Thames at Pimlico a fortnight previously. Holmes had successfully linked this murder, which the newspapers dubbed "the Whitehall

Mystery", to the Jack the Ripper killings which were then in full spate. The woman was never identified, mainly because her head was never discovered, but she bore the marks of having been a prostitute like the Ripper's five known victims and her uterus had been excised, much in the same way that internal organs had been removed from most of the other murdered women. Holmes averred that the body parts had been placed at the building site in order to taunt the police. The Ripper, after all, was fond of sending letters that mocked the vain efforts of the Yard to catch him; one, mailed to George Lusk of the Whitechapel Vigilance Committee, even contained a half a human kidney. This was just another such jibe, on a larger, grislier scale.

Holmes spent a significant proportion of 1888 in pursuit of Jack the Ripper, taking on no other cases and devoting himself exclusively to ending this one brutal killing spree. He confided to me at the time that it was one of the most gruelling and exhilarating challenges he had ever been set. I have somewhere in one of the battered tin dispatch boxes that hold all my papers a full account of the hunt for the Ripper and how Holmes finally trapped and unmasked the villain, and perhaps someday the public will be permitted to learn the truth about his identity and why the whole affair was hushed up by the powers-that-be, with Holmes's connivance; but not yet, not yet. There are some revelations the world is just not ready for.

I digress, again. An old man's prerogative, and curse.

As luck would have it, Holmes and I ran into Inspector Lestrade, who informed us that he had just sat in on a conference with the commissioner Colonel Sir Edward Bradford, William Melville of Special Branch, and various other higher-ups in the Met, with regard to the bombing suspect. Melville, he said, was cock-a-hoop that there had been a breakthrough in the case and was pressing for the terrorist's immediate arraignment on charges.

"That's my news," Lestrade said. "You two evidently have a story to tell, judging by the state of you." His nose wrinkled. "And the smell of you. I dread to ask what you've been up to."

"Then don't," said Holmes. "Tell us what you can about the suspect. Where was he caught? What grounds did the arresting officer have for apprehending him?"

"The 'where' you will find hard to believe. The sheer nerve of it! On Grosvenor Place, just outside the grounds of Buckingham Palace. A stone's throw from the person of the Queen herself."

"No!" I ejaculated.

"Yes, Doctor. And to answer Mr Holmes's second question, we have recently doubled the number of patrols around the periphery of the palace, for obvious reasons. The suspect aroused the suspicion of a pair of constables by acting oddly, erratically, and was found to be carrying a canvas knapsack inside which was a bundle of dynamite fitted with a long, slow-burning fuse. Doubtless the knapsack was destined to be flung over the wall into the palace gardens."

"Put like that," I said, "one would be hard pressed to find a more open-and-shut case."

Lestrade nodded in agreement.

"The terrorists have grown audacious," said Holmes.

"Or reckless," said the policeman. "Either way, we have one of them in custody now, and before long names will have been named and we'll be rounding up the rest of the gang. There is just one thing, however." Lestrade's face turned sneeringly sly. It was evident that he knew more than he was letting on, and that he relished having the upper hand over Holmes, an event that occurred rarely.

"Out with it, then, Inspector," said Holmes. "What am I missing?"

"You said 'him' when referring to the suspect."

"Repeating what I heard the crowds outside say. Am I wrong on that front?"

"You are, and so are they. You're all assuming the suspect is male."

"He is not?"

"*She*," said Lestrade, "is anything but."

CHAPTER TWENTY-SIX

A Note of Shame

Holmes immediately sought permission to interview the prisoner. He was excited and intrigued. All the residual lethargy and soreness, the legacy of the events of the previous night and the sleepless days prior, had left him. He was fully reinvigorated, the sparkle back in his eyes, the colour in his cheeks.

Lestrade steadfastly refused his request. There were protocols to consider. The suspect was Special Branch's charge, not his. He did not have authority to take someone down to see her. Besides, the woman, at present, was not talking. Indeed, she had not uttered a word during her arrest or since. She refused to identify herself, despite repeated entreaties to do so. Nor had she shouted any slogans in support of her cause, or yelled any kind of defiance, or crowed about her and her fellow terrorists' accomplishments. She had remained mute the entire time, and docile, and in light of this, Melville's policy was to leave her alone in her cell, without food or water. In due course, having stewed in her own juices long enough, her will would be broken. She would be begging to speak to somebody, to tell all. It was only a matter of time.

Holmes persisted. "If anyone can get her to open up, it is surely I. You know my methods, Lestrade, my powers of insight. A few judiciously chosen words, and I can crack a person like an egg."

Remembering the man in the garden square, I knew how right he was.

"Mr Holmes, it is just not possible," said Lestrade. "I don't have the jurisdiction. Only Mr Melville can grant permission to visit her, and I can assure you he will say no. His mind is made up."

"In which case…" Holmes produced a notepad, scribbled a few sentences down, and tore out the page, which he folded in half and passed to Lestrade. "Would you be so kind as to take this to him. See that it is delivered direct to his hand."

"May I…?" Lestrade made to unfold the piece of paper, but Holmes stopped him.

"The note is for Melville's eyes only."

"I could always peek at it later, when I'm out of your sight."

"That you could, but it would be ill-advised," Holmes said sternly, and the look on his face brooked no dissent.

Lestrade strode off with a more than usually disgruntled air about him, muttering that he was a CID inspector, not an errand boy.

In years to come I would ask Holmes time and again what he wrote in that note, and he always refused to divulge. It was a personal matter relating to Melville, that much I could glean, and connected with the previous year's state visit by the Shah of Persia, for whose protection the head of Special Branch had been directly responsible. From hints Holmes dropped, and reading between the lines, I can only surmise that the married Melville had contracted a short-lived liaison with one of the eighty-four wives in Shah Nasseredin's harem during the visit, and that Holmes was cognisant of this fact. "I have many of these useful titbits of knowledge squirreled away for a rainy day," he once told me. "One might call them insurance policies." One might equally call them blackmail threats, although I am content to think that my friend would never resort to such an underhand tactic unless it was wholly necessary.

Regardless, it worked. Lestrade returned not ten minutes later, accompanied by a Special Branch officer. It was the intimidating-looking fellow we had encountered at Waterloo Station, Grimsdyke. Lestrade proceeded to make introductions, but Grimsdyke forestalled him with a curt, "We've met."

"Well, miracles do happen, Mr Holmes," Lestrade said. "Your request has been granted, although to say Melville was grudging about it would be an understatement. Whatever was in that note, it made him go white as a sheet. Makes me think I should never get on your wrong side. In fact, if you ever decided to turn to a life of crime, I think I should run for the hills. Grimsdyke is here to escort us, by the way."

The Special Branch man folded his hands together in such a way that his thick knuckles bulged.

"And to demonstrate that William Melville is not a man who responds kindly to being strong-armed," Holmes said in an aside to me as we made our way down to the basement, Grimsdyke in the lead.

Two rows of cells stretched on either side of a long gas-lit corridor. All were full, occupied by the various anarchists and Fenians who had been detained earlier in the week. Shouts of protest and complaint resounded from behind steel doors, echoing off the tiled walls. The atmosphere down there was rank with caged resentment and despair.

Grimsdyke unlocked the furthest door along, and Holmes, Lestrade and I trooped inside the cell.

There, seated on a bunk of the narrowest and meanest

proportions, was perhaps the last person I would have expected to see.

It was the Vicomte de Villegrand's maid, Aurélie.

CHAPTER TWENTY-SEVEN

THE BLOOD BENEATH THE FINGERNAILS

"The young lady is known to you?"

Lestrade had noted our reaction to the sight of Aurélie.

"She is," said Holmes.

"How?"

"That's not important right now."

"I think it is."

"Inspector, I doubt highly that this woman can be a terrorist."

"With all due respect, Mr Holmes, what rot. I've told you the circumstances under which she was arrested. There were countless eyewitnesses. There's no question but that the girl was making a direct attempt on the lives of the royal family."

"She could not have been responsible for the Waterloo bomb, at any rate."

"Says who?"

"Do I need to remind you that the dynamite was placed in the *gentlemen's* lavatory?"

"Yes, I thought of that," said Lestrade. "Could be she wore a disguise, dressing herself in men's clothing, passing herself off as a man. Some of the toms I've met do a very good job of it. You'd hardly know, to look at them. A bloke could be forgiven for mistaking them for members of his own gender."

"Or else," said Grimsdyke, "she did not personally plant that bomb; one of her associates did. Terrorists work in gangs, after all, never solo. She is part of the conspiracy, of that there can be no question."

"I think there can be question," said Holmes. He turned to Aurélie, who throughout the foregoing exchange had sat placid and unperturbed, her gaze fixed on the wall opposite her. It was as though she were still alone in the cell, we three a quartet of silent, invisible phantoms, not registering at all with her senses.

"Aurélie." Holmes squatted before her so that he and she were eye-level with each other. "Do you remember me? Dr Watson and I visited your master's home a few days ago. I fought your master in the back garden, perhaps you recall that. Fought him and won."

The girl's unnaturally blank face showed not a flicker of recognition. I recalled de Villegrand likening her to an automaton. She certainly seemed that way now. Without instruction, without someone to guide her actions, she was all but lifeless.

Holmes tried again, saying much the same thing as before, only this time in French. The sound of her native tongue stirred something in Aurélie. Briefly her expressionless features turned curious, as though she was hearing a strain of a song she knew well from long ago. But that was all.

Holmes continued in the same vein for several minutes, trying to coax a firmer response from her, using all the French at his command. Eventually he gave it up. He might as well have been addressing a shop-window mannequin.

Outside the cell, we conferred with Lestrade. Beetle-browed Grimsdyke looked on.

"The girl is, for want of a better word, feeble-minded," Holmes said. "It is not imposture or pretence. She is capable of simple menial duties, but no more than that. I find it hard to believe she could be involved in a sophisticated terrorist plot at any level."

"On the contrary," said Lestrade. "She sounds just the sort to be easily duped into carrying out the terrorists' bidding. She is compliant and suggestible. Simpletons often make the best foot soldiers. Tell them to do something, and they'll do it, unthinkingly, unquestioningly."

"I'll bow to your superior expertise on that front."

Lestrade preened, unaware that he had just been subtly slandered.

"Yet," Holmes continued, "with someone of Aurélie's low mental capacity, there is every chance she might misconstrue her instructions or perform them incorrectly, rendering her useless as a reliable puppet. Watson can back me up on this."

"She spilled sherry in my lap," I said. "A small accident, but it flustered her completely."

"She would only be reliable if something forced her to concentrate, if some incentive was given which allowed her no alternative but to rally her inner resources and comply. In short, if someone twisted her arm hard enough."

"She's not Irish, though," Grimsdyke said. "That didn't sound like Gaelic you were speaking to her."

"French," said Holmes.

"Which begs the question," said Lestrade, "how *did* you two meet her? Who's this 'master' of hers you referred to? What don't I know?"

Holmes would tell me afterwards that he was tempted to answer, "A lot." In the event, what he said was: "You noticed, of course, the dried blood encrusted beneath her fingernails."

"As a matter of fact, I did."

"But you said she has been quiet all this time. 'Docile' is, I believe, the word you used."

"She didn't resist arrest, I'm told. Came as meek as a lamb."

"So whence the blood? Has she scratched anyone in the interim?"

"Not that I'm aware of."

"There's no indication that she has scratched herself either. Which leaves no other logical conclusion than that she came by the blood prior to her abortive bombing attempt. Violent coercion has been used, not against Aurélie directly but against someone she cares for, to get her to attempt an act which her conscience rebels against. I would like to go back in and speak to her one more time."

Inside the cell, Holmes knelt before Aurélie again. He took her hands gently in his.

"Aurélie," he said. "*Regardez. Ce sang, auquel appartient-il? Est cela peut-être votre frère?*"

Slowly, almost with the leisureliness of a lizard, Aurélie blinked.

"Benoît?" she said faintly. It was scarcely even a whisper.

"Yes, Benoît," said Holmes.

All at once, Aurélie's face contorted and she let out a shrill, piercing scream. She clutched her cheeks, half covering her eyes. She was seeing something, some horror undetectable to the rest of us.

"Benoît!" she cried. "*Mon pauvre frère! Aidez-le, quelqu'un! S'il-vous-plaît, aidez-le!*"

Her screams turned to uncontrollable, inconsolable sobs. Her whole body was wracked in a paroxysm of anguish. Nothing would calm her or snap her out of this tormented state, not soft words from Holmes, not an artfully dispensed slap from me. The racket she was making disturbed the inmates of the other cells.

They started clamouring and howling in sympathy.

"Lestrade," I said, "is there another doctor in the building?"

"No."

"And I don't have my medical bag with me. Do you have a first aid kit of any kind? The woman is hysterical. She could cause herself harm. I must administer a sedative."

Lestrade sent Grimsdyke off in search of what medicinal supplies he could find. He returned shortly with a bottle of laudanum.

"One of the lads in my squad has a taste for the tincture," the Special Branch officer said. "Keeps it in his desk drawer. Stresses of the job and all that."

While Holmes did his best to restrain Aurélie, I tipped the laudanum down her throat. She spat out some of the concoction, but ingested enough of it that soon its soothing effect began to take hold. Her sobs subsided, her spasms eased, and she lapsed back onto the bunk, drugged into a daze.

Outside the cell again, Lestrade was not looking best pleased.

"Well, this is a fine to-do, isn't it?" he snapped. "You've only gone and upset our prize suspect, Mr Holmes, and now she's off away with the fairies for the next few hours and there's even less chance of getting anything useful out of her than before. Melville's not going to be happy when he hears about this."

"No, he is not," said Grimsdyke. "His nibs isn't a man to take bad tidings well. Trust me, I know."

"Well," said Holmes, "the two of you will just have to come up with a way of breaking the news gently, won't you?"

"Why not do it yourself, Mr Holmes?" said Lestrade. "Seems only fair. You're the one who set her off on her fit of the screaming abdabs, so you should be the one to carry the can for it. Some of us have our careers to consider. Melville can't sack or demote you the way he can me or Grimsdyke, you not being a copper."

"I'd be only too glad to help you out, Inspector. However, Watson and I are required elsewhere, and we need to be there in a hurry. This building has a back entrance, am I correct?"

"Up the stairs, bear left, second right," said Lestrade. "It's how we sneak in some of our arrestees, like we did with Sleeping Beauty there. But you're not getting off that easily. Melville first, then you can leave."

"Really, Lestrade, no time!" Holmes was already moving down the corridor, dragging me with him. "Apologise to Melville on my behalf. Say it's all my fault. I'm already low enough in his estimation that I doubt it will make much difference."

"Mr Holmes! Mr Holmes, come back here. That's an order."

"Sorry, Inspector. 'Not a copper', remember? You can't order me to do anything."

"I can jolly well arrest you, if I have to."

"Then do," said Holmes, breaking into a run. "But another time."

"Where are you off to anyway? Who is that girl? Who's this Benoît? You've still got questions to answer."

"Want me to go after them?" I heard Grimsdyke ask Lestrade, just as Holmes and I were almost out of earshot. "I can bring 'em back, no problem. Give 'em a bit of a sorting out while I'm about it."

Lestrade seemed tempted, but sighed, "No. Let them go. Sherlock Holmes may be a liability sometimes, and he never shares information if he can possibly avoid it, but damn him, when it matters he gets results."

CHAPTER TWENTY-EIGHT

In the Conservatory

A hansom ferried us north. Our destination: Hampstead.

De Villegrand's enviable, pristine villa sat silent in the morning sun. Holmes rapped on the front door several times, without answer. It seemed that no one was home.

"We'll try round the back, Watson. It should be easier to effect an entry, should we have to, via the conservatory."

"What did Aurélie mean about her brother – 'someone help him, please'?" I said as we stealthily circumvented the house.

"I don't know for sure. But I fear very much for Benoît's safety."

"Holmes, there's a lot you're not telling me."

"I am only just beginning to thread together the elements of this case into a coherent narrative, my friend. I feel I am grasping the outline of a monstrous scheme, something so enormous and potentially devastating that it could change our nation forever."

"The bombings…"

"…are only the start. The *hors d'oeuvres*, one might say. The *entrée* threatens to be even more ruinous. Wait!"

We had reached the far corner of the villa, the large, wrought-iron conservatory at the rear just coming into view. Holmes shoved me back. I fell into a crouch, and he did likewise. He peeked carefully out.

"Who did you see?" I hissed. "Is it de Villegrand?"

Holmes crept round the corner on all fours, beckoning me to follow. Arriving at the conservatory, he raised his face just high enough to peer through the glass. I did so too, and saw someone inside seated on a mahogany fiddleback chair. The person's head was bent forwards. Fast asleep? Or...?

Then I realised who it was, and perceived at the same time that he was fastened to the chair.

"Benoît," I said.

"Quick," said Holmes. "We must break in."

He snatched up a stone, part of the border of a flowerbed, and used it to smash out a pane in the conservatory door. He snaked an arm through the empty frame and turned the latch. We rushed inside.

I went straight to examine Benoît. The young manservant was bound to the chair by his wrists and ankles using window-sash cord, and had been most cruelly and sadistically beaten. His face was a pulpy mess of contusions and blood. More blood soaked his shirtfront and spattered the chessboard-pattern floor tiles around him. I felt for a pulse, not expecting to find one. Benoît was so motionless, he must surely be dead.

At my touch, his head snapped up. He drew in a raspy, lurching breath. I shouldn't have been startled, but I was, so much so that I nearly fell backwards.

"Aurélie!" he yelled.

"Benoît, *soyez calme*," said Holmes. "You are safe. Aurélie is also safe."

Holmes bent to the task of undoing the knots that secured Benoît to the chair. Together we bore the Frenchman across to a wicker settee which sat adjacent to the rear wall of the house. I made him as comfortable as possible and checked him over thoroughly.

I gave Holmes my prognosis in the form of a single, sombre look. Benoît was in a very bad way. His injuries were such that he had, I estimated, a few minutes left to live, if that. Nothing I or any other doctor could do would help him.

"Benoît," said Holmes. "Please, if you can, tell me all you know. What happened to you? Who did this?"

Benoît moaned, semi-delirious. The stuffed wolf and boar, de Villegrand's trophies, looked on with their dead glass eyes, pitiless. They had seen everything but could reveal nothing.

"Listen to me, Benoît. It is vital that you give me all the information you can. To judge by the fact that it is only the left-hand side of your face that has been hit, whoever hurt you favours his right hand when punching. Could it be that he had no left arm at all? Was it Abednego Torrance?"

"Torrance…" Benoît murmured. It sounded like confirmation.

"Torrance is an associate of your master, yes? He works for *le vicomte*?"

"*Oui.*" The word was barely more than an expelled breath. "Works for… *le maître*. He is… wicked man. *Méchant.*"

"He is," said Holmes. "*Très méchant.* He and de Villegrand forced Aurélie into taking a bomb to Buckingham Palace, didn't they? They made her carry it there and told her to throw it over the wall."

"Did… Did she…?"

"No, Benoît. Aurélie is a good girl. When it came to the crunch, she couldn't bring herself to go through with it."

"*Dieu de remerciement,*" said Benoît. "I knew… hoped… she would not. They made her watch. *Le maître*, he held her while Torrance, he…"

"He beat you, yes."

"Aurélie, she screamed. Begged them to stop. Said she would do as they ask. Without me she has nothing, so she would do anything to keep me safe. But Torrance, he only pretended to stop. After *le vicomte* let her embrace me then took her away, Torrance started again. He laughed. He enjoyed."

My fists clenched. I could well imagine the vicious Torrance deriving pleasure from pummelling a helpless captive.

"He said to me it was 'tying up loose ends'. He was killing me." Benoît coughed and choked. Blood frothed from his mouth, oozing down his chin and neck in a gory slick. "I think maybe he has succeeded."

"You'll be fine, Benoît," I lied.

"Benoît," said Holmes, "where are de Villegrand and Torrance now?"

"I do not know. I do not know. Gone. I think they will not be coming back."

"This isn't de Villegrand's own house, is it?"

"No. He… lends it?"

"Rents it?"

"Yes, rents. To look good. Look like true *vicomte*, with wealth."

"But you and Aurélie are genuinely his servants?"

"We are. We are all that is left of his father's household. His father – not a wise or prudent man. Cruel to his wife. *Le vicomte* is also cruel to women. I have seen… As a boy… There was a young woman, and her lover, and *le vicomte*, he destroyed them. Used them and destroyed them both. For his own amusement. That is how he is. Yet Aurélie and I, we must still be loyal to him. We owe him our service. But always I must watch out for Aurélie, take care of her, because he is dangerous. She is innocent and sweet and he is a, how you say, *prédateur*?"

"Predator."

"Yes. Of women. Especially young women. So I must care

for her, and we must work for him because he tells me, if we do not, he will have Aurélie, and ruin her. He pays us little money, he treats us like slaves, but I am scared to run away and so make him angry, because of my sister. We run away, perhaps he finds us, and I am not frightened for myself, but for poor Aurélie I am. She is my only family, my world. I must protect her, even if it means we live with a man who might at any time turn on us and do her harm and shame."

My fists clenched even tighter. Now it was de Villegrand I loathed, more than Torrance. No wonder Benoît had been so full of glee when he saw Holmes best the vicomte in combat. Holmes had done exactly what Benoît wished he himself could do, but was unable to. It must have been like Christmas come early for the beleaguered, downtrodden manservant.

"What is de Villegrand's next move?" Holmes asked. "Do you have any idea?"

But Benoît was fading fast. The effort of talking was accelerating his decline. Brave man, he realised it, too.

"I know... so little," he gasped. "*Le Duc Enfer*. I hear him say to Torrance about *le Duc Enfer*. I do not know what he means."

"The Duke of Hell? Benoît? Did I get that right? Is that what he said?"

Benoît burbled out a few more words, the only one of which I caught was his sister's name.

"Aurélie will be all right, you have my word on it," I told him. "Every conceivable measure will be taken to keep your sister safe from harm. And de Villegrand will never again menace her or anyone else, that I also swear."

My reassurances were falling on deaf ears, however. That is to say, *dead* ears. For Benoît had passed away. His head lolled to one side and his eyes stared sightlessly out between their swollen lids. A faint rattle in the back of his throat was the sound of the soul leaving his body, commencing on its journey to, as Shakespeare has it, "that undiscovered country from whose bourn no traveller returns".

CHAPTER TWENTY-NINE

GLASS GUILLOTINES

I straightened up, smoothing out the seams in my trousers. I was calm in my anger, the eye of my own personal storm.

"This cannot stand, Holmes," I said. "We must find de Villegrand and Torrance without delay. We may not know where they have gone, but they will surely have left behind clues."

"Why here, I wonder?" said Holmes, glancing round the conservatory.

"What do you mean?"

"Why drag Benoît into this room, of all places, in order to torture him? That is a dining-table chair he was tied to, not a conservatory chair. They hauled it, and him, out into the conservatory for a reason."

"So as not to get bloodstains on the dining-room carpet. You can scrub quarry tiles clean with a mop and bucket. A carpet is a much trickier proposition." I was being somewhat glib. In truth, I was none too bothered about the circumstances of Benoît's beating. I just wanted to lay my hands on the perpetrators. "Now come on, old fellow, we need to get cracking."

"The placing of Benoît here seems deliberate. We found him easily. Too easily. Almost as though we were meant to." He looked up, frowning. "There is something about the design… Those ceiling panes – there are an abnormally large number of them. And the mullions and transoms in between are unusually thick."

"You can admire the architecture another time. How about we go into the house itself and you scrutinise that instead? I don't doubt that you have your magnifying glass on you. There'll be something indoors that will put you on de Villegrand's trail, some stray fibre, some specimen of mud, a heap of tobacco ash…"

Holmes gave no indication that he was listening, or had even heard. Well, I thought, if he is unwilling to take action, I am not. I stepped between the wolf and the boar and grasped the handle of the door that connected to the main part of the house.

"Watson," Holmes said, "I wouldn't do that if I were you. Not until –"

But I had already depressed the handle.

The door did not budge.

But something else started moving.

There was a whirring, as of counterweights in action, and a clattering, as of chains running through ratchets. The entire conservatory thrummed loudly around us, coming to life.

Overhead, the ceiling panes began to turn.

It was weirdly, beautifully fascinating to watch. Each rectangle of glass rotated, independent of its fellows, spinning on its lateral axis. The panes, *en masse*, seemed to ripple in waves, as though some invisible giant hand were running fingers down them, stirring them to motion. The sunlight glanced off them at a multiplicity of angles, flashing prismatically in all directions. The entire glass room was filled with brilliant little rainbows darting this way and that.

As I said: weirdly, beautifully fascinating. I was mesmerised. I had no idea what the revolving of the panes portended.

Holmes, however, had some inkling.

"A trap," he said dully. "Of course. I have seriously underestimated the vicomte's deviousness."

"A trap?" I said. "How can it be? This is just some – some exotic method of ventilation. There will be a sound scientific principle behind it, a horticultural justification, perhaps to do with the propagation of tropical plant species which require cool breezes or shifting patterns of light in order to –"

Then one of the panes slipped from its mounting. It hit the floor with an ear-splitting crash.

"Or," said Holmes, "to reiterate, it's a trap."

"One pane coming loose does not mean –"

Three further panes fell, landing at various different spots. Holmes had to step smartly aside to avoid being struck by one of them.

"Yes," he said. "Quite definitively a trap. With us as the prey and Benoît as the bait."

The panes started dropping with insistent and increasing frequency. There was no appreciable pattern. The choice of which fell next seemed wholly random, a lethal lottery. It was impossible to predict when or where one was going to be released from its frame and descend.

The door to the garden was some half-dozen yards from where I stood but it might as well have been a mile. It would have been madness to attempt to reach it when at any moment a sheet of glass might plummet onto one.

I tried the door to the house again, but it was locked fast. The handle, it was obvious now, had served as a trigger device, springing the trap. Presumably it functioned normally except when the trap was set.

Shards were piling up on the floor. As if to demonstrate

how deadly the falling panes could be, one thudded into the late Benoît's throat. It buried itself as far as his spinal column, all but severing his head from his neck.

"Holmes!" I cried above the din of glass smashing and shattering. "There's no way out. I can't break down this door, and we daren't make a bid for the other door. Chances are we'll never get there."

Holmes, like me, had pressed himself flat against the side of the house. It was not safe doing even that, however. One of those glass guillotine blades narrowly missed my shoulder, and I heard Holmes give a hiss of pain as another landed so near to his leg that a sliver embedded itself in his calf.

Sooner or later the shower of panes would catch one or other of us, or both. They were thick, heavy and sharp-edged, fully capable of lopping off a limb or cleaving a skull. We were pinned in place, and it was only a matter of time before our luck ran out and the trap claimed us as its victims. If we were lucky, we might get away with cuts and lacerations. But if we were not...

Then Holmes said, "Watson, was it wolf then boar or boar then wolf?"

"Good Lord! What?"

"The order in which de Villegrand patted the stuffed animals' heads. Wolf then boar or boar then wolf?"

"How should I know? I don't remember. I wasn't paying attention. Does it matter?"

"Or was it both at once? No, there was definitely an order."

"Holmes, have you gone quite mad? We are about to die!"

"Not if my supposition is correct. Try wolf then boar, Watson. I think that was it."

"You mean... pat their heads?"

"Yes. You're right next to them. I can't reach them from here. Wolf then boar."

Convinced that my friend had taken leave of his senses, I stretched out a hand towards the wolf to my right. I feared that at any moment a pane would come whooshing down and remove my arm at the elbow.

"Wait! Boar then wolf," cried Holmes. "That was it."

I stretched out my other hand and patted the boar's head firmly. Then I did the same to the wolf's.

Abruptly the panes that remained in the ceiling stopped turning, coming to a halt. A last one plummeted, adding to the accumulation of sparkling débris on the floor. Then all was silent and still.

"A failsafe," Holmes said, limping over to me. "It decommissions the trap. Look."

He tilted the wolf back on its hind legs. The tile beneath its front paws was a false one, spring-loaded. A kind of pressure switch.

"There'll be another beneath the boar, the two connected to each other. Trip them in the correct sequence and the trap is neutralised. De Villegrand had to do this the other day when he led us outside. His 'talismans' indeed!"

CHAPTER THIRTY

THE FRENCH CONNECTION

Our brush with death made me less keen than before to enter the house proper. Who knew what other similarly lethal snares awaited within.

Holmes was of the same view, and so we picked our way carefully across the broken glass and exited the conservatory as we had entered. I aimed a last glance back at poor Benoît's body. It was spiked all over with a mass of glittering glass fragments, festooned with them like some ghastly festive ornament. The young Frenchman had been abnormally courageous. His death, I vowed, would not be in vain.

Outside, on the lawn, I examined Holmes's leg. He insisted that it was nothing, a mere scratch, but I wanted to ascertain for myself that no major damage had been done. Thank the Lord, it hadn't. I prised out the sliver of glass without much effort, leaving just a shallow flesh wound.

"I should like to swab that out with peroxide and iodine when I have the opportunity," I said, "to prevent infection."

"Yes, yes," said Holmes dismissively.

"And Holmes – I apologise. For setting off the trap. In my defence, I had no idea it was there."

"Yes," he said again, no less dismissively. "In many ways I blame myself. I should have been more circumspect. De Villegrand is proving even more formidable a foe than I expected. I had him pegged as a dilettante, shrewd and physically able but no great intellectual. However, if he is the one who devised and built that trap, then there is much more to him than I initially suspected."

"He and Torrance are the bombers, though? That's confirmed?"

Holmes gave a weary nod. "Torrance I had become certain was involved in the terror campaign. Being a gun-for-hire, he would not need a motive for committing acts of terrorism, beyond money. De Villegrand, on the other hand…"

"Could he not also be a gun-for-hire? Let's assume Fenians are employing him. He could be nursing a grudge against Great Britain. Many French still do. There's been nigh on a thousand years of rivalry and enmity between our two nations. Treaties may have been signed, we may both be drawing closer together politically because of a shared fear of German expansionism, but plenty of Frenchmen still regard Britain as a continuing threat. Over sherry, de Villegrand proposed a toast to the Entente Cordiale, but who knows if he really meant it."

"He did not," said Holmes. "He said many a fine word about our country which he does not, in truth, endorse wholeheartedly. You're right. Whatever Louis Philippe the First claimed about a 'cordial understanding' forty years ago, some French are still fighting the Napoleonic Wars in their hearts. Our two empires continue to spread and sprawl, our colonies and protectorates rubbing up against one another in Africa and South America, often sharing borders. That is bound to cause friction. De Villegrand is one of those who would like to see the atlas of the world covered in French blue rather than British red, and is willing to take drastic steps to see that goal become a reality, even perhaps to the extent of throwing in his lot with his enemy's enemy, the Fenians. However, consider the possibility that the Irish angle might be a red herring. Does the vicomte need to ally himself with anyone else? Why, when he's perfectly capable of doing the job unaided? Remove the Fenian issue from the equation, and it still balances. Cauchemar intimated as much last night."

"You're saying Home Rule has nothing whatsoever to do with it?"

"French Rule, on the other hand, has everything to do with it."

I pondered this information, then said, "Was it de Villegrand, I wonder, who shot at Cauchemar at the church?"

"An excellent deduction, Watson. The wolf and the boar in the conservatory are testimony to his being a good shot, on top of his being an accomplished martial artist. We must now add 'engineer of some distinction' to his list of attributes."

"Under fire, in the graveyard, it occurred to me that it could be one of two kinds of rifle being used against us, a Lee-Metford or a Lebel."

"The latter a French make of gun. Watson, you are redeeming yourself by the second. I'll wager that's exactly what de Villegrand had."

"What about the Abbess? How does her murder fit into all of this? De Villegrand too?"

"Yes. She gave us his name. I assumed when I told him we knew about his penchant for fallen ladies, especially very young ones, he would have no idea how we came by that information. At the least he would reckon it came from Torrance. But he must have put two and two together and, not best pleased by the Abbess's indiscretion, elected to punish her for it. I did not foresee that, and it is an error of judgement I will rue for the rest of my days."

I recalled Holmes's teeth-grinding yesterday afternoon, and

now knew the true source of his anger. He had been furious with himself as much as with de Villegrand.

"The fiend," I said. "Is there no end to his savagery?"

"No, nor to his vindictiveness and opportunistic cunning. He arranged a rendezvous with her in the back alley behind the brothel, then pounced. As he was a regular client of hers, she would not have suspected his true intent, not until the very last second."

"Hence the lack of signs of a struggle."

"One can picture de Villegrand emerging from the shadows during the storm. Perhaps he and the Abbess exchange a friendly word or two. Then he accuses her of betrayal. Perhaps she denies it, perhaps not. The vicomte presses her, forces her to own up. Then, without warning, he strikes."

"*Savate.* A kick to the chest."

"Delivered by an expert, it caused instantaneous death."

"Could Torrance not have done it on his behalf? He, after all, is an acquaintance of the Abbess too, so could have set up the meeting with her. And de Villegrand doesn't appear to like getting his hands dirty, not if there is an intermediary available."

"But could Torrance have made it look like something Baron Cauchemar would have done?" said Holmes. "There's the rub. De Villegrand's intent was not simply to exact vengeance on the Abbess but to frame Cauchemar for murder. A means of throwing the police onto the wrong scent. That's in the unlikely event that they would be on the vicomte's scent in the first place."

"You knew this all along?"

"I believed de Villegrand to be the Abbess's killer but had no way of proving it, and without proof, belief is nothing. All I could do was bide my time and hope that he would do something to incriminate himself. With Benoît, he has at last shown his hand. We now know him to be a cold-hearted desperado, and deadly dangerous too."

"He would not have left Benoît here, as he did, if he had not expected someone to discover him."

"Not 'expected', Watson. Wanted. And not just 'someone' – us. De Villegrand knows we are breathing down his neck. The conservatory trap was supposed to do away with us, or at any rate leave us in no fit state to continue to pursue him. But what killing Benoît and pressuring Aurélie into committing an act of terrorism tells us is that the dénouement of his plan is drawing nigh. De Villegrand is sacrificing a few last pawns, in order to set up the checkmate. He and his sidekick Torrance, wherever they are, are getting ready to deliver the final blow."

"Which is?"

"One final attack. An atrocity to make all its predecessors pale into insignificance. The spark that will ignite the powder keg our nation has become and cause it to tear itself apart."

"Briton at war with Briton," I said in chilled tones. "Anarchy reigning. Mob rule."

"A fire will burn that will reduce this country to ashes and leave our imperial dependencies vulnerable and ripe for takeover. France becomes the supreme global power. De Villegrand is victorious."

"Not if we stop him."

"And we shall," Holmes declared. "It all hinges on one question."

"Namely?"

"Who – or what – is the Duke of Hell?"

CHAPTER THIRTY-ONE

WHEELS IN MOTION

We arrived back at 221B Baker Street dirty, dishevelled, demoralised, footsore and hungry. Mrs Hudson took one look at us and clucked and fussed like a despairing mother hen.

"Honestly, two gents of your standing, out the whole night long and coming back all bedraggled, like something the cat brought in. I'm used to *your* shenanigans, Mr Holmes, but to see you dragging the nice Dr Watson down to your level – I don't know! Sometimes I wonder if it's a madhouse I'm running, not a lodgings. You'll be wanting a hot meal right away, I'll be bound. Neither of you's eaten since suppertime, by the looks of it."

"Food, Mrs Hudson, would be more than welcome," said Holmes. "And perhaps you can tell me how long my brother has been waiting upstairs?"

"How did you –?" Mrs Hudson shook her head. "I'm not going to go to the bother of finishing that sentence. You always seem to know everything."

"Not everything, my dear lady. But Mycroft wears a distinctive eau de cologne with, in my opinion, rather too much emphasis on the citrus notes. The scent of it continues to loiter in the hallway. From its strength I would estimate he passed through here roughly half an hour ago."

"More like three quarters!" boomed an angry voice from the floor above. "Where in God's name have you been, Sherlock?"

Holmes grimaced at me. "The mountain has come to Mohammed. Let us go kowtow on bended knee."

Mycroft was ensconced in Holmes's own armchair, and his expression was as choleric and distempered as I have ever seen it. His cheeks were bright red and there was a film of sweat on his brow, as though he had been exerting himself physically. I would have been surprised, however, if he had so much as stirred from his sedentary posture since assuming it. Rather, he had been sitting here all this time, quietly smouldering, outraged that he had left his precincts – Whitehall, Pall Mall, the Diogenes Club – and travelled halfway across town, only to find his brother out. It was like a circus elephant performing some unique, unprecedented stunt, with no audience to applaud the feat.

"I need not ask if it is important business which brings you to my door, brother," said Holmes. "Nothing but the gravest matter of state could compel Mycroft Holmes to make use of his legs and abandon his clubland Parnassus for the less rarefied climes of Marylebone."

"And I need not tell you, Sherlock," said Mycroft, "that impudence is no way of atoning for your absence. I ask again: where have you been? Nowhere I'd want to be, by the look of you."

"Forgive me for not realising that an event as rare as a solar eclipse was about to occur: a house call from Mycroft. I would never have had the temerity to venture out, had I had some foreknowledge. I would have waited here like a virgin anticipating a visit from her paramour."

"Virgin?" Mycroft spluttered. "Paramour? You really do –"

"We have been pursuing the case," I interposed. The Holmes brothers were building up to one of their sibling spats, and I wished to defuse it before things turned nasty. "We have turned up several major –"

"Yes, whatever," said Mycroft with a flap of a pudgy hand. "I came here to tell you in person, Sherlock, that while I initially chose to heed your recommendation, against my better judgement, I have since revised my position. In light of this morning's events, and on mature consideration, I have decided that I am right and you are wrong."

"Then you have done it?" said Holmes. "The Queen is to be dispatched to Balmoral? Even after I counselled in the strongest possible terms against that?"

"No."

"No?"

"Not 'to be'. Has been. The arrangements are in place. The wheels are in motion. The Royal Train has made its way to Euston Station, whence it will carry Her Majesty and various family members northwards. It is for the best. A bomb at Buckingham Palace itself? If that isn't a sign that the terrorist threat impinges directly on the monarchy, I don't know what is."

"This is not good." Holmes sank disconsolately into the other chair. "Not good at all."

"I rather think it is," said Mycroft. "I took the precaution of warning Her Majesty a few days back that she and her immediate family should be ready to depart at short notice, were the public situation to deteriorate substantially. This morning I was finally able to convince her that the hour had come. I'm glad to relate that she saw eye to eye with me on the matter. Her very words were, 'A ruler must know when to stand firm and when to show discretion, and must appreciate that the latter is in itself a kind of standing firm. I will do as you say, Mr Holmes, not for my own benefit and peace of mind but for the country's."

"She really is a magnificent woman," I avowed. "As wise as she is gracious."

"No, no, no," protested the younger Holmes to the older. "This is a disastrous course of action. Mycroft, you must put a stop to it."

"Wouldn't even if I could, Sherlock." Mycroft consulted the Vienna clock that hung not far from the bullet holes which Holmes had shot in the wall, their pattern forming the letters "VR" in tribute to our monarch. "As I said, the wheels are in motion. Literally. Her Majesty and family boarded the Royal Train some ten minutes ago. It will be pulling out of the station even as we speak. I simply don't understand your objection to any of this. Where could she be safer but at Balmoral?"

"How about at Buckingham Palace, where she already was, watched over by a contingent of guardsmen?" suggested Holmes acerbically. "Even so, it is not her being at Balmoral that troubles me. Once there, I am sure she will be well protected."

"Absolutely. A battalion of the Royal Scots Greys is already encamped in the grounds. They are patrolling the estate and manning the boundaries. A jackrabbit couldn't get past them, never mind a bomb-toting terrorist."

"But between here and there, she will be dangerously exposed."

"On the Royal Train? Balderdash! She and her offspring and retinue are being closely guarded by a dozen of Special Branch's finest. Not only that but the 'Iron Duke' class locomotive pulling the carriages is one of the fastest in the land, and the route has been fully cordoned off. All other scheduled LNWR and Caledonian Railways journeys that intersect with it have been either diverted or cancelled. The signals are all up and the points appropriately aligned. Save for stops to take on more coal or water, the Royal Train will not halt. It will hurtle through the night and, barring mishaps, will reach Perth well before sunrise, whereupon carriages will transport the royal party the remaining sixty miles to the castle. The whole operation has been planned meticulously down to the minutest detail. Nothing can go wrong."

Holmes remained sceptical. If his frown had been any deeper, I daresay his brow might have cracked in two.

"But don't you see, Mycroft? This is exactly what the terrorists want. This has been their intention all along."

"That we make the Queen safe?"

"No. That she is flushed out of Buckingham Palace and forced to go on the run. They have scared the fox from its burrow."

"I don't follow."

"Look at the facts. The first bomb exploded on Cheapside, the next at Regent's Park, the third at Waterloo, the fourth in St James's Park. The fifth would have blown up at the palace had the hapless bomber not had such a struggle with her conscience. She was a scapegoat, by the way, a sacrificial lamb, and acting under duress. I will be recommending to the police that she be released from custody at the earliest opportunity, once her personal security can be ensured, and that she be exonerated of all culpability."

"I am as aware of where the bombs were placed as you are, Sherlock. So what?"

"So," said Holmes, "do you not see the pattern?" He fetched a book of maps from the bureau and flicked through to a page detailing the layout of London's streets. Taking a pen, he marked each of the bombing locations in turn with an X. "The far end of Cheapside, where the restaurant that was bombed stands, is approximately four miles from Buckingham Palace, as the crow flies. Regent's Park is about three. Waterloo is two. The boathouse in St James's Park is less than one. It is like a countdown in distances, zero being the final, aborted bombing immediately outside the palace garden walls. This arrangement can be no accident. We are looking at a clear, deliberate progression."

Mycroft donned a pair of pince-nez spectacles and squinted through them at the map. "Why did you not point this out before?"

"I didn't think I needed to. I felt that, to someone of your perspicacity, it should be quite obvious."

"I have innumerable demands on my time and attention," Mycroft blustered. "I can't be expected to remark on every single tiny detail of every single subject that falls under my purview."

"But I could not have been more explicit in the telegram I sent you. I told you that under no circumstances should Her Majesty be moved."

"Had you laid out your rationalisation in full, perhaps I would have given the advice more credence. I heeded it anyway, until the fifth bombing made the prospect of the Queen staying put untenable."

"This is typical of you, brother," Holmes fulminated. "You act without properly digesting the data or considering the consequences. Normally you arrive at the right decisions, but this once, you have been foolhardy, and as a consequence the Queen's life is at risk. The terrorists have one last, heinous misdeed planned, and I am now firmly of the view that it is going to be an attack on the Royal Train. We, by which I mean you, have played right into their hands."

"Preposterous, Sherlock! How could they hope to attack it?"

"Why not with a bomb?" I said. "That has been their chosen *modus operandi* thus far. Why deviate from it now? A strategically placed bundle of dynamite somewhere along the train's route, attached to the piling of a bridge perhaps, would send it careering off the tracks. The accident at Staplehurst in Kent, the one in which Charles Dickens narrowly escaped death, showed us just how deadly such a derailment can be. The terrorists could easily replicate that tragedy."

"Knowing de Villegrand," said Holmes, "he has something

more sophisticated and theatrical lined up."

"De Villegrand?" said Mycroft. "Thibault, the Vicomte de Villegrand, you mean? He's behind all this?"

"You know him?"

"Know of him. Never met him. Vaguely connected to the French embassy, isn't he? Some kind of cultural liaison nabob. Ambassador Waddington does not think too highly of him, that I do know. His Excellency is a staunch defender of France's interests and the French way of life, which comes from being the son of English immigrants – keen to assimilate into his adoptive country, *too* keen some might say. There's none more devoted to his nation than the naturalised foreigner. However, even he thinks de Villegrand is a tad overzealous in his patriotism. It's rumoured that *le vicomte* has ties to a clandestine extremist group of reactionaries who seek to promote France as the ultimate world superpower. Les Hériteurs de Chauvin, they call themselves, after the mythical Napoleonic soldier, the epitome of Gallic manhood and sovereign loyalty."

Holmes nodded. This was not news to him, even if it was to me. "But if it is known amongst the authorities here that he belongs to these 'Chauvin's Heirs', how come he is allowed in Britain at all? Surely someone with links to such an organisation would be precluded from holding any kind of official position over here, or even any kind of residency permit."

"I said 'rumoured'," said Mycroft. "It's one of those things which you hear talk of but which can't be proven one way or the other. There are some in the Foreign Office who claim the Hériteurs de Chauvin are as apocryphal as Nicolas Chauvin himself, a fictional ideal, a figment of the collective French imagination, nothing more. Equally, it has been reported by our spies across the Channel that not only is this group real, it recruits only the brightest and best from among its countrymen. Its exclusivity is such that one must be a master of several disciplines simply in order to be *considered* for membership. Its tentacles reach into the topmost strata of French society, and it receives funding in the form of donations from the wealthiest individuals that nation has to offer."

"De Villegrand would certainly appear to be the perfect candidate for its ranks," Holmes said. "Moreover, my own recent enquiries indicate that not only does this secret society exist, but that the vicomte is a pre-eminent member of it."

I recalled the certainty with which, a short while earlier, Holmes had spoken of de Villegrand's yearning for "French Rule". "He continues to fall in my estimation – and he wasn't that high in the first place."

"You're quite sure about this, Sherlock?" said Mycroft.

"I delved into his background," my friend said. "The details are sketchy, conclusive evidence hard to come by, but I found enough to confirm to my satisfaction that the Hériteurs de Chauvin are no fiction and that de Villegrand plays a prominent role in their activities. He is over here posing as a cultural attaché when really he is an *agent provocateur*."

"A viper in our midst," I said, feeling that "*agent provocateur*" was altogether too grand and refined-sounding an appellation for de Villegrand.

"And," continued Holmes, "should he succeed in assassinating our Queen and the rest of the royals, it would decapitate this country, as surely as France's revolutionaries decapitated their aristocrats. It would leave us foundering, lost, our empire a shambles. All at once there would be a power vacuum in the world, which France would be more than happy to rush in and fill."

"You are quite positive, then, that the Royal Train is their ultimate target?" said Mycroft.

"Yes. Your very own words, but two minutes ago, triggered a

somewhat belated 'eureka' moment for me, dispelling every last shred of doubt."

"What did I say?"

"You referred to the locomotive which pulls the train as belonging to a certain class of such engines."

"What of it?"

"Benoît, de Villegrand's servant, mentioned with his dying breath the '*Duc Enfer*'. I misheard him. I thought he said '*Duc d'Enfer*', meaning 'Duke of Hell', whereas actually he was saying '*Duc En Fer*', three separate words."

"Duke In Iron," I said. "Iron Duke. My God…"

"That settles it." Mycroft rose ponderously to his feet, using the chair arms to assist him in craning up his great bulk. "I must go at once to Whitehall and send missives. The Royal Train must be intercepted and made to turn back."

"It may be too late for that to do any good," cautioned his brother.

"Nevertheless I must try."

Mycroft lumbered off down the stairs, which creaked piteously with every step he took. He passed Mrs Hudson on the landing as she brought up a tray with our lunch on it. The front door slammed as he departed.

Mrs Hudson set the food down before us and was about to withdraw, when Holmes sprang up and whispered in her ear for some while. When he was done, his landlady frowned at him, perplexed, but nodded assent. She left the room in haste, and moments later I heard the front door slam a second time.

The meal looked delicious: eel soup, lamb chops with onion custard, browned tomatoes and baked beets, and cocoa flummery for dessert. Holmes tucked in with gusto. I, on the other hand, found it hard to muster an appetite.

"How can you eat at a time like this?" I upbraided Holmes.

"Because I am famished. You should join me. There is no point in starving yourself just because you are anxious and upset. The more sensible course of action is to replenish one's depleted reserves while one can. We will soon be needing all the energy we can get."

"What for?" I was close to despair. "What's the use? De Villegrand has the Queen at his mercy. There's nothing we can do other than pray that Mycroft is successful and the Royal Train is halted before he strikes."

"Nothing we can do?" There was a glint in my friend's eye. "Hardly. I have, in fact, already done something very constructive."

"Oh yes? What?"

"Instructed Mrs Hudson to send a telegram," said Holmes.

"That's it? Send a telegram? Whom to? The man in the moon? Or perhaps our Maker, begging for divine intercession?"

"Neither. God will not save our Queen, old friend. But, with aid from a particular quarter, *we* yet might."

CHAPTER THIRTY-TWO

AN EARTHQUAKE ON BAKER STREET

I ate, in accordance with Holmes's recommendation, and we both cleaned ourselves up and donned a change of clothes.

I felt somewhat better for that, but remained in a state of ungovernable agitation. Unable to settle, I paced the floor. Holmes, meanwhile, sat puffing away at his pipe, Sphinx-like in his imperturbability. It drove me to near distraction.

"All right!" I exclaimed, when I had had my fill of his taciturnity and his seemingly unwarranted composure. "Tell me, since I cannot fathom it for myself. The telegram – who is the recipient?"

"His name," said Sherlock Holmes, "is Sherlock Holmes."

I halted mid-stride. "What? You sent it to yourself?"

"Yes," said my friend.

"What on earth is the use of that? Are you so conceited as to think that only you can be Her Majesty's rescuer?"

"Watson, you do me a disservice. Think, man, think. My purpose in sending myself a telegram cannot be to inform myself of anything. That would be ridiculous. However…"

"…it would get the telegram into the system," I finished. Light was dawning. "And if it's in the system…"

"…then it will be perused by a certain masked man of our acquaintance."

"Cauchemar. Good grief, Holmes." I slapped my forehead. "I have been a dunce."

"That's perhaps putting it a little strongly."

"What better way to summon his help in our hour of need?"

"Quite," said Holmes. "I cobbled together a message containing several of those 'key words' he spoke of – words that would catch his teleprinter's automated attention and cause it to flag the telegram up as urgent. 'Royal' was one, 'danger' another. My own name, of course. And two other names which are of special relevance to the baron. One is Torrance. The other: de Villegrand."

"The former needs no explanation, but why the latter?"

"You'll recall my saying that I intuited a connection between them – the genuine French nobleman and the vigilante with the assumed French aristocratic name."

"I do."

"Cauchemar knows de Villegrand. In fact, I'd go so far as to say that the two of them are, or once were, intimately acquainted."

"How?"

"That remains to be discovered, although Benoît provided what might be a clue. For now, we must sit tight and hope that the Bloody Black Baron intercepts the telegram and responds to it with alacrity."

"And if he does, are we to travel in that damnable *Subterrene* fandango again?"

"It would not get us far, definitely not as far as we need to go. However, my study of the blueprints in his workshop leads me to think that Cauchemar has developed another, altogether more impressive mode of transport, one which will much better suit our purposes."

I racked my brains trying to recall what had been on those blueprints, which I had viewed glancingly over Holmes's shoulder. Perhaps it was a consequence of Cauchemar's oneirogenic gas, but my memory of the night's events was hazy, a series of impressions glimpsed as though through fog. Now, these many years later, I have been able to piece them together for the benefit of this narrative and make them coherent, but that is with the luxury of considerable hindsight and, also, the application of a modicum of creative licence (many of my accounts of Holmes's adventures are the product of reminiscence bolstered by imagination). At the time everything was vague and nebulous in my exhausted mind, the blueprints in particular a blur.

"You will have to enlighten me," I said.

"I would not wish to raise your expectations unduly, in case I am mistaken. It's possible that Cauchemar hasn't yet constructed the vessel. However, there were bales of sailcloth in his workshop."

"There were?"

"You were too busy toying with his glue-firing gun to notice them. Likewise the offcuts of said sailcloth."

"A ship?"

"Be patient and we shall see." So saying, Holmes steepled his fingers and lapsed into a meditative trance.

I, in turn, resumed my floor pacing, wearing out both carpet and shoe leather as I circled the room. Every so often I paused to glance out of the window. Baker Street seemed more or less its usual self. I saw familiar sights: the newsvendor on the corner, the itinerant hawkers, the crossing sweeper, the errand boys, the chimney sweep doing his rounds, the pedestrians, the clattersome toing and froing of traffic. There was a perceptible sense that London was getting back to normal, or at least trying to, after the alarums and excursions of recent days. With an alleged terrorist in police custody, people were allowing themselves to believe that the crisis was past. Little did they suspect that worse lay in store. This period of tranquillity was merely a lull, not an ending; a comma rather than a full stop. The nation had been softened up for a killing blow it didn't even realise was coming.

As midday shaded into afternoon, all I could think about was the Royal Train puffing energetically northward. Where would it be by now? Peterborough? Grantham? As far as Doncaster? With every minute that passed, it became more and more likely that de Villegrand would have already committed his shocking, demoralising act of regicide. I could scarcely contain my inner torment. It felt as though the world was trembling around me, starting to fall apart.

Then I realised that the world *was* trembling around me. At least, the room was. Ornaments were shaking and dancing on their shelves. The windows were rattling in their frames. The floorboards were shivering underfoot. An immense vibration permeated the building's fabric, as though 221B were a bass pipe in a cathedral organ.

"Holmes! What is this? An earthquake? It's not possible."

"This," said my friend, "unless I am very much mistaken, is our transportation arriving."

I ran to the window. Out in the street, people were peering upwards, eyes wide and mouths agape. Twisting round, I followed their gazes but could not descry what they were looking at. The angle was wrong, too steep. Whatever was the source of their astonishment, it lay directly above the house, out of my line of sight.

Holmes took to the stairs, with me in hot pursuit. We ascended past his bedroom and my former bedroom, past the bathroom and the water closet, all the way up to the attic. Picking our way around linen hampers, packing cases, steamer trunks and odds and ends of discarded furniture, we reached the skylight. Holmes opened it and slithered nimbly out. He extended down a helping hand and I wriggled out after him.

Perched on the roof slates, we both looked up.

Hovering overhead was what appeared to be a cross between a blue whale and a hot air balloon.

"An airship," I said.

Yet it was unlike any airship whose photogravure picture I had seen in magazine or newspaper. It made the efforts of Tissandier, Renard, Krebs, Campbell and Wölfert seem clumsy and ungainly by comparison. Where their dirigibles were elaborate confections of rope, wood and canvas, this was sleek-contoured and to a large extent metallic. Where theirs looked awkward and fragile, this looked agile and tough. It had something of the Portuguese man o' war about it, or else the great white shark; some deadly sea creature at any rate.

Gigantic gimbal-mounted propellers churned, keeping the aircraft stationary and stable above the house, yet I had no doubt they could also impel it along at tremendous speed. Beneath the aerodynamic gas-filled envelope clung a torpedo-shaped gondola, and from a hatch in the base of this there now issued a rope ladder, along with an exhortation in the familiar booming tones of Baron Cauchemar.

"All aboard, gentlemen, quick as you can. Your carriage awaits. Where to?"

CHAPTER THIRTY-THREE

THE MAIDEN VOYAGE OF THE *DELPHINE'S REVENGE*

Our pilot was in his armour, helmet-less but with his padded under-mask on. He bade us make ourselves at home. There was at least somewhat more floor space available in the gondola's cabin than there had been in the *Subterrene*'s, so Holmes and I did not have to stand hugger-mugger, squashed shoulder to shoulder, as last time.

"Mr Holmes," Cauchemar said, "the contents of your telegram, which I can safely assume you intended me to read, alarmed me greatly. I am at your disposal. We are to go north?"

"North," my friend confirmed. "It would be simplest if you were to head for Euston Station, then follow the main line north towards the Scottish border. Don't you agree?"

"No sooner said than done." Cauchemar pushed sideways on the large brass steering column that was situated between his knees. The airship began to rotate around its vertical axis and its longitudinal axis simultaneously, a most unnerving sensation which had me reaching out to grab the nearest handhold for support. I had endured long ocean voyages and was well versed in the pitch and yaw of a ship on a sea swell. This, though, was different, a quality of motion I had not experienced hitherto, an uncanny rolling through space, with a sort of sickening greasiness about it.

Worse was to come as Cauchemar then thrust the steering column sharply forwards, at the same time toggling a lever to increase the power output to the propellers. The airship lurched upwards, its nose rising steeply. It felt as though my stomach were still anchored to the ground even as the rest of me gained height. Dizziness drizzled down through my head as the blood rushed to my feet.

"Watson?" Holmes enquired. "You have gone a ghastly shade of pale. Are you all right?"

"I have been better," I replied. "If this is flight, then it's for the birds."

"Ha!" laughed my friend. "You and your pawky sense of humour."

"I assure you, I was not trying to be funny. If I cracked a joke, it was purely by accident."

"You will soon get used to it," Cauchemar said. "I was told by a balloonist I once met that one finds one's 'air legs' far more readily than one does one's sea legs. It might help if you were to look outside. It will acclimatise you, harmonising the input from your eyes with the messages your inner ear is sending you. As sailors are wont to say, 'Keep your eyes on the horizon.'"

I peered out of a porthole set into the gondola's curved hull. Below, rooftops and chimney pots were diminishing fast. I could make out almost the entire length of Baker Street, from Regent's Park to Oxford Street. The grid arrangement of Marylebone became clear, thoroughfares broad and narrow intersecting neatly at right angles. The swarm of life in the roads down there seemed remote, something I was no longer entitled to be a part of. The higher the airship sailed, the more detached I became from the quotidian world. It was like entering a dream.

Having attained an altitude of, I would guess, six hundred feet, Cauchemar levelled the vessel out and poured on speed. We soared over the park, all green lawns, blue lake and autumn-gilded trees, like an illustration in a picture book. We crossed what I took to be Albany Street, and soon the huge glass dome that capped the Great Hall of Euston Station hove into view. Cauchemar pivoted the airship above the tracks which issued like multiple tongues from the terminus's mouth. Singling out the main line, he matched our bearing to its.

Then we were gliding faster, ever faster, above the city. Over Primrose Hill we went, and the densely packed rookeries of Camden and Kentish Town, the imposing brow of Parliament Hill, and onward across the suburbs of Hampstead, Highgate and Finchley, which gleamed in their newness.

From up here London looked improbably tranquil, a sprawl of splendour and ambition, truly the capital of the world. If only, I thought, everybody could see it from this perspective. Too often one became mired in the hubbub and squalor of urban life. I, as the companion of Sherlock Holmes, had been exposed to the seamy underbelly of London, the cupidity and murderous passions of its inhabitants, more than most. I had seen the place, too often, at its worst. Yet now, aboard Cauchemar's miraculous airborne conveyance, I was able to see it at its best.

I was able to see, too, that this city and all it represented were unquestionably worth saving.

Such was the aim of our urgent, desperate mission. We could not afford to fail.

The airship hurtled on, soon traversing open countryside. The railway track stretched ahead, a thin grey line like a thread connecting us to our destiny, winding through verdant livestock-dotted pastures and the furrowed brown rectangles of harvested fields. We were buffeted by winds that came sweeping in from the side, skewing the airship from true. Cauchemar, with deft counter-manoeuvres, kept us steady and on course. The railway might now and then veer beyond the limits of the viewing portals at the gondola's bow, but always he brought it back into sight.

We had been aloft for over half an hour when Holmes said, "This truly is a splendid creation, Cauchemar. Does it have a name?"

"Thank you. It does, as a matter of fact. I call her *Delphine's Revenge.*"

"And would I be right in thinking that she has never flown before?"

"You would."

"That would account for the absence of reported sightings. Something like this could not ply the skies above London, even after dark, without being noted and remarked upon."

"Until today she has been berthed at a warehouse which I rent privately," said Cauchemar. "I have been fine-tuning her, off and on, for seven months. I kept meaning to take her for a test flight and then procrastinating. Perhaps I feared the disaster that would ensue should some catastrophic mishap occur – a propeller working loose from its mounting or a leak in one or more of the helium cells. My concern was not for my own wellbeing, I hasten to add, but for that of innocent people below. I might conceivably have never taken her out for a spin, had the import of your telegraphic request not compelled me to, Mr Holmes. I am grateful to you for, as it were, pushing me out of the nest. Now I have proved that my 'wings' work."

"I wish someone had told me this was a maiden voyage," I said. "I might have thought twice before climbing aboard."

"Do ignore Watson," said Holmes to our pilot. "He is only to be taken seriously when he is *not* complaining. I suppose a logical question to ask is: who is Delphine?"

"I'm afraid that's personal," said Cauchemar.

"As is your relationship with the Vicomte de Villegrand?"

Cauchemar was momentarily lost for words. "That you say such a thing suggests you already know the answer."

"I shall tell you how much I know," said Holmes. "I know that all your vigilantism so far, all your crime-busting and altruistic acts of derring-do in the East End, these have all been in the way of a warm-up, a preamble, a dry run. You have been familiarising yourself with the use of your armour, practising, discovering its limitations and ironing out any snags. You have been field-testing it with a view to perfecting it, making it ready for some ultimate, all-or-nothing sortie."

"Go on. I'm not saying you're wide of the mark."

"I know also that, all along, de Villegrand has been in your sights. A long-held, simmering enmity exists between the two of you. He has crossed you, wounded you grievously in some way, and you wish to get even."

"Not get even. Utterly discredit and destroy him."

"Yes. That would make sense. So things have progressed to the stage where you are all set to do battle with him openly. You have identified him as being behind the bombing campaign but have refrained from going after him until now. Why? Because previously he was operating covertly, in the shadows, using intermediaries such as Abednego Torrance. He has not directly entered the field of play until now, and it is there that you wish to snag him."

"I should have guessed that you would burrow through to the truth in the end, Mr Holmes." Cauchemar sounded rueful but also resigned. "It was inevitable. Once your and my paths crossed, it was only a matter of time before my secrets were brought to light."

"They will be safe if you share them with us," said Holmes.

"You need not worry on that account. We are most avowedly on the same side, the three of us. Were that not so, I might find it hard to forgive you for gassing Dr Watson and myself."

"Again, I apologise for that. It was discourteous and speaks more about my own lack of self-confidence than my confidence in you. In retrospect, I realise I should have shown greater faith in your discretion, Mr Holmes, and yours, Dr Watson."

"It's nothing," said Holmes. "But now is the time, I think, to come clean. Tell me, how fast are we travelling?"

Cauchemar consulted the bank of instruments in front of him. "Our airspeed, according to the anemometer attached to the gondola's keel, is in excess of a hundred and ten knots. Allowing for the wind factor, which introduces a variance of plus or minus ten per cent, we're still travelling at a mean one hundred knots."

"The Royal Train will be averaging eighty miles an hour. It has a three-hour head start on us. Allowing for refuelling stops, we should catch up with it in, what, two hours?"

"Give or take."

"No quicker than that?" I said, despair and desperation vying within me for supremacy. "But what if de Villegrand launches his attack before we get there?"

"De Villegrand may be lying in wait for the Royal Train somewhere up the line. If that is so, then there is little we can do to stop him other than hope that we get there first. If, however, he too is pursuing the train just as we are, then there is a decent chance of us overtaking him. My money is on the latter."

"You can be so damnably calm at times, Holmes."

"I have learned, Watson, not to fret about matters over which I have little control. It is a waste of energy. In the meantime, since we have this opportunity, I can think of no more excellent or profitable way of passing the time than you telling us your history, Baron Cauchemar. Starting with your real name."

CHAPTER THIRTY-FOUR

BARON CAUCHEMAR COMMENCES HIS STORY

I am (said Cauchemar, after some initial reluctance) from good solid Home Counties middle-class stock, just as you gauged from my accent, Mr Holmes – no baron at all. There is some trace of aristocratic lineage on my mother's side, but it is so faint and etiolated as to be hardly worth the mention. My real name could not be more unassuming: Frederick Tilling. Just plain "Fred" to my friends. I am the son of a provincial barrister and a part-time milliner, born and raised in a small Sussex market town. My late father was moderately successful in his profession, enough to be able to afford a governess for his sole offspring and then later send that same child to boarding school, but my mother nonetheless was obliged to work at the hat shop in order to make ends meet and keep our heads firmly above water.

My boyhood was mostly happy. I was aware that our family financial situation, though comfortable by the standards of most, bore an underlying precariousness, and I was conscientious enough to try and not be an excessive burden on my parents. I pursued quiet, unobtrusive hobbies and pastimes. Foremost among these was a fondness for taking mechanical objects apart and fathoming how they worked. I did it with a clockwork train set of mine, and a wind-up tin soldier. I also did it, much to my parents' initial dismay, with the cuckoo clock in the hallway and my father's hunter-case pocket watch. The good news was that, having disassembled the items, I was able to put them back together, restoring them in such a way that they worked as well as, if not better than, before.

It became obvious that I possessed a natural facility for, I would even say affinity with, machinery. I was drawn to things such as railway engines while they waited at the platform at our local station, and the jiffy steamer and treadle-powered sewing machine at my mother's place of work – intrigued and fascinated by them. I could divine, almost at a glance, how their component parts fitted together, the physical principles that drove them, what made them "go". Where other children my age would be playing with conkers or aimlessly kicking a ball around, I would be tampering with a musical box so that it tinkled its tune in a minor rather than a major key, or crafting Japanese puzzle boxes out of wood that required fifty or more manipulations to open.

School was a wretched time for me. I had no leisure or opportunity to pursue my interest in matters mechanical. It was all rote learning of Latin verbs and long health-giving swims in a near-freezing lake; not to mention endless Bible study, for it was a High Church establishment. If there is one thing guaranteed to foster an abiding aversion to religion, it is the reading aloud of the "begat" sections of the Old Testament. To stave off boredom I would scrawl pictures in the margins of my King James Version *ad infinitum* – designs for an electric mousetrap, a motorised lawnmower, a carbon-arc clothes iron – until I was caught in the act one day and soundly beaten for my pains. From then on, that avenue of self-expression was closed to me for my remaining schooldays.

What saved me from a slow death by frustration and boredom was the discovery in the school library of several of the works of Jules Verne, in translation. I became lost in those books, engrossed in their depictions of science as a positive, transformative force in the world. My heroes became Captain Nemo, Professor Lidenbrock, Phileas Fogg, men for whom the application of knowledge and ingenuity is the solution to any and every problem. This type of novel has come to be known as the "scientific romance", and I cannot think of a more apt name. Verne inculcated in me a true love of science, and it was, for me, the blossoming of a lifelong romance.

After school I floundered somewhat. While I continued to dream up various projects and devices, some more harebrained than others and none that got any further than the drawing board, I drudged through a series of uninspiring jobs – accounts clerk, draper's assistant – finding scant satisfaction in any of them. In my spare time I hunted down and bought as many Verne novels as I could – and he is a prolific author! Often I could not wait for them to be published in English, so would purchase French editions by post from a dealer on the Left Bank in Paris. A ruinously expensive exercise, but such was my addiction to the great master's writings. Incidentally, I could not have been more flattered when you, Dr Watson, described my *Subterrene* as "a thing from a Jules Verne novel". To me there can be no higher accolade.

I had only the rudimentaries of the French language to begin with, so I struggled to read the books, but the effort was repaid in the pleasure they gave me. As a bonus, repeated exposure to Verne's prose and the use of a French-English dictionary meant I rapidly became more fluent, until eventually I could read the tongue as well as any native Frenchman, though not speak it with nearly the same facility.

It struck me that France was the place where scientific

innovation was at its boldest and most daring, where the greatest feats of engineering and the most radical technological breakthroughs were happening. This was the land of Eiffel and Pasteur, Poincaré and the Curies, Braille and the Montgolfier brothers. Not to denigrate our own fair nation and its pantheon of physicists, chemists, biologists, botanists, builders and explorers, pioneers all; but it seemed to me that at the level of sheer attainment and progress we simply could not compete. You can surely forgive my lack of patriotism. At the time I was a twenty-year-old in the grip of an infatuation, and there is nothing stronger nor more absolute in its convictions than youthful ardour.

I resolved that France was where my future lay, and not only that but the future of the world. I must go there and live and partake of its culture and its thrusting ambition. There my genius would be recognised and celebrated. My talent for invention and my mechanical expertise would bloom more fruitfully in French soil than in English.

I had little to leave behind. Two parents who had begun to despair of me ever making anything of myself. A string of jobs that were beneath me and provided nothing but an income, and a paltry one at that. I sold all I owned, apart from my precious collection of Vernes, and crossed the Channel by packet steamer to start anew in what I firmly believed was the country I had been born to belong to.

It is a decision I regret to this day, deeply.

Do I have to go on?

CHAPTER THIRTY-FIVE

Baron Cauchemar Continues His Story

Holmes insisted that Cauchemar, or rather Fred Tilling, must continue his narrative.

"You cannot," he said, "leave us in the lurch. You arrived in France, and then what?"

Then (said Cauchemar) I travelled straight to Paris, the city where most of the French intelligentsia were gathered, the hub of that nation's cerebral industry. I set myself up in a cheap atelier apartment in Montmartre – that *arrondissement* which is the haunt of artists, musicians, writers and other Bohemian types, an impoverished, absinthe-soaked demimonde – and I cast about, looking for suitable gainful employment, something to tide me over while I built up a list of useful contacts and made my way in the world.

Soon I found work with a manufacturer of clockwork automata. This is a field the French have long excelled in, its best-known exponent being the stage conjuror Jean Eugène Robert-Houdin, famous for his Marvellous Orange Tree illusion, in which a replica orange tree grew before the audience's eyes and sprouted real fruit, and his Mystery Clock, which ran perfectly and told the right time but had no apparent mechanism.

I was engaged in constructing altogether less dramatic devices: singing canaries in cages, monkeys that ride bicycles, and dolls – androids, as they are known in the trade – that can seemingly draw pictures, write poems or play chess or cards. We produced these as fairground attractions, props for illusionists, or toys for the rich. It was not terribly demanding work, at least not for someone with my aptitude, but I enjoyed it because of the miniaturist precision it required, the necessity for millimetre-perfect accuracy at all times. A single misaligned ratchet, a single faulty cog, a single eccentrically turning cam, and nothing would happen. One's creation would refuse to spring into action or grind to a screeching halt.

But oh, when it did work, when a machine functioned as though the very breath of life infused it – that thrill never palled.

I began to offer my employer, Monsieur Pelletier, suggestions for improvements. I told him how we could make our automata yet more complex, more uncannily realistic still. At his encouragement, I devised a system whereby an android could be given the power of mimicking speech. A rubber voicebox, with puffs of air pushed through it pneumatically and piston rods to manipulate it, could replicate vowel sounds. Combine that with a malleable rubber "tongue" which could modulate those sounds and introduce plosives, fricatives and glottal stops, and you had a fairly authentic reproduction of human vocal patterns. Individual phonemes could be triggered by keystrokes. Put them in sequence and you had actual words, or a reasonable facsimile thereof, close enough to the actuality to deceive the human ear.

The trouble with this was that it was a step too far. An automaton which could point to letters on a blackboard or tell someone's "fortune" by dealing out tarot cards, that was one thing; that was acceptable. One which seemed actually to be conversing with you? The reactions to that were almost invariably shock, disgust, horripilation, cringing dread. I saw people recoil from the doll much as though it were a farmyard pig that had suddenly opened its mouth and started talking. One woman to whom I demonstrated my *androïde qui parle* swooned away in a dead faint. Another person, a highly respected actor who was later appointed a Chevalier of the Légion d'Honneur, made the sign of the cross and ran shrieking from the workshop.

There was, I realised, such a thing as a too-lifelike machine. Mine offended people's sense of themselves as divinely favoured beings. If a doll could talk – and most who saw my creation were firmly convinced it could, in spite of my protestations to the contrary – then what did that mean for those of us on whom God had bestowed the supposedly exclusive gift of a soul?

There was one man who did not regard my talking android as an affront against religion and nature. Rather, he was impressed and captivated by it and insisted I reveal to him its mysteries. He was a charismatic fellow, high-born and urbane, ever ready with a quip and a neat turn of phrase. He seemed to me, naïve and inexperienced as I was, to be the epitome of class and sophistication.

I am talking, of course, about the Vicomte de Villegrand.

I did not know him then for what he is. At the time, I could not have been more delighted that this nobleman, of seemingly impeccable credentials, who had apparently dropped by the workshop on an idle whim, was taking such a keen interest in my work. He professed himself an engineer too, although not, he said, of my calibre – not in the same league. An amateur, he called himself modestly, a tinkerer. Not a genius, like me. That was the word he used: genius.

Naturally, all this flattery turned my head. Thereafter, de Villegrand became a regular visitor at Pelletier's, always keen to admire my handiwork, though never to buy anything, much to my employer's chagrin. We discussed engineering-related topics for hours on end, he and I, and soon we were meeting up in the evenings. He would take me to glamorous night spots, Paris's finest watering holes, the best cafés and brasseries, even the notorious Moulin Rouge, and there introduce me to various of his friends. All of them appeared as high-ranking as himself, and those of them who weren't affected airs and graces as though they were.

He was a roué and a reprobate, that much was obvious. He enjoyed a drink and had an eye for the ladies. Indeed, I lost count of the number of times he and I parted company at the end of an evening's carousing and I would watch him stagger homeward in the company of some lively mademoiselle, about whom, when we next met, he would have many a racy, lascivious tale to tell. He was ten years my senior, he was a handsome rake, he appeared not to have a care in the world – he was everything that I wished to be, and better still, he was my friend.

I recall this one occasion when we were both in our cups and wandering along the banks of the Seine. It was a gorgeously warm, clear spring night, the city alive and buzzing all around us, and de Villegrand began describing his ambitions for the promotion and advancement of *la belle France* across the entire world. He bemoaned the current administration's desire for rapprochement with England in the face of the aggressive rhetoric coming France's way from von Bismarck and Kaiser Wilhelm. He was firmly of the view that France could stand on its own two legs against any enemy and that no alliance with "*les rosbifs*" was necessary.

I jokingly said that, as a *rosbif* myself, I ought to take offence, but could not bring myself to, being such a devoted Francophile.

De Villegrand's response was to wrap an arm around my shoulders and call me, not merely a Francophile, but an honorary Frenchman. I all but melted at the compliment.

"I must confess, *mon ami*," he said, "it was no accident that we met. I came to Pelletier's not by chance, as I claimed, but because I had heard rumours of this marvellous doll with the power of speech and I wished to make the acquaintance of the Englishman who had built it. He sounded to me as though he must be a man of brilliance. And he is! And that is why I am asking you now to come and work with me. Leave Pelletier and his trinket factory. Together, you and I could achieve such things, Fred, such wonderful, incredible things. Join me in building a better, stronger France and a brighter future for all."

There were two reasons why I didn't accede to his request on the spot, why I asked for time to consider. The first was that I liked my job. Pelletier was a decent man and, although my talking android had proved something of a fiasco, he remained open to new ideas from me. He claimed he was proud to have me as an employee, and I was proud to call him my boss.

The other reason was Pelletier's daughter. I haven't mentioned her until now because… Well, it is difficult. It is difficult for me even to think about her, let alone talk about her.

Her name was Delphine. She was seventeen. She was the loveliest creature in all of Paris, and that is saying something in a city whose women are generally held to be the most beautiful anywhere. She was sublimely pretty, with perfect lips, tip-tilted nose, and auburn hair that tumbled about her face in glossy ringlets. She moved with the utmost gracefulness, and her conversation was by turns witty and intelligent. She was a very paragon of femininity. All who met her fell instantly in love with her, and I'm not ashamed to say I was one of the smitten.

We were introduced for the first time when Pelletier invited me to dinner at his townhouse on the Rue des Rosiers in the Marais. I have to say I was dumbstruck throughout the entire meal. My grasp of French appeared to have deserted me, along with my senses. All I could do was gaze across the table at this vision, this angel dressed in the latest Parisian fashions, while Monsieur and Madame Pelletier tried in vain to extract some sort of meaningful conversation from their English guest. It was "*le coup de foudre*", in the French parlance. The thunderbolt. Love at first sight.

I must have come across to Delphine as a complete nincompoop. I certainly was behaving like one. Yet she had the politeness not to laugh out loud at me, nor to be offended by my helpless staring. I imagine she was accustomed to it. There can't have been a man alive who didn't become her adoring, tongue-tied thrall the moment he laid eyes on her.

Thereafter Delphine started coming down to the workshop, which by all accounts she had never done beforehand. She would even try to talk to me, lobbing questions to which I would offer fumbling replies. She would listen patiently as I launched into long, technical explanations about whatever piece I was working on, and she never showed signs of boredom, however much I rambled.

Ignoramus that I was, I had no idea that Delphine Pelletier had taken a shine to humble Fred Tilling. I could never have believed such a thing possible. She was Aphrodite, I was lowly Hephaestus, but unlike in the myths, no divine edict could surely bring two opposites such as us into union. As far as I was concerned, I was barely worthy to be in the same room as her.

Monsieur Pelletier, however, knew his daughter's mind and perceived what was going on. He took me aside one day and dropped hints so broad, so unsubtle, that even I could not misconstrue them. The penny dropped. I was beside myself with joy. Could it be true? Delphine was showing a romantic interest in *me*?

Being a father, Pelletier was at pains to warn me not to take advantage of his girl or abuse her feelings in any way. I vowed to him that I would not. I would behave as honourably towards her as it was in my capacity to do. He need have no fears on that front, I told him.

Consequently, I was permitted to squire Delphine on walks in the park, with her mother or one of the family maidservants acting as chaperone. I understood Pelletier's caution. His daughter was such a rare pearl, so great a prize, he could not afford to let her go out with any man unescorted. I did not mind. An hour spent with Delphine all to myself, even though we were never truly alone, was an hour in heaven.

What we spoke of during those walks, I scarcely remember. Nor does it matter. It was everything and nothing, the sweet nonsense of young lovers. Amid all the billing and cooing, however, there was a clear sense that she and I were coming to an understanding. I could foresee the direction my life was taking, and Delphine was a part of it. No. She *was* it.

You can see, therefore, why I was so reluctant to jeopardise my situation with Pelletier. If I quit my job, might I also not ruin my chances with Delphine?

In the end, I told de Villegrand I would be available to him at evenings and weekends. It was my best offer, and he, though he obviously would have preferred more, consented.

So I found myself, a few days later, calling round at de Villegrand's apartment in the district of Saint-Germain-des-Prés. Occupying the whole of the second floor of the building, it was a nice set-up, perhaps not as grand as I might have expected for a man of his background and breeding, but relatively opulent and spacious. He kept two servants, a brother and sister, both young: Benoît, who was my age and acted as general factotum, and Aurélie, who was barely a girl and acted as scullery maid. I had little interaction with either of them. Aurélie was clearly a simpleton, while Benoît seemed to me unusually surly and resentful of his master. This inclined me to look down on him, for who on earth could dislike the magnificent Vicomte de Villegrand? Of course, I know now that Benoît was fully justified in his antipathy, and I regret how contemptuously and dismissively I treated him.

The apartment had a studio, where de Villegrand had been busy drawing up plans. He showed me portfolios full of sketches and diagrams of inventions he wished to build, and scale models of some of the same. He invited me to offer my input on his ideas and suggest ways of refining them.

What did he propose to create?

I'll tell you.

War machines.

Astounding, frightful war machines.

Things to make the ordinary infantryman redundant and render rifle and cannon as primitively ineffectual as a Stone Age man's club.

I can barely convey the bizarreness and awesome ingenuity of what he was dreaming up. You think my armour and weaponry remarkable? My *Subterrene* and this airship extraordinary? They are nothing next to de Villegrand's designs. They are mere toys compared with the massive, artful engines of destruction he hoped to assemble.

Some of his creations I could tell at a glance would never make it beyond the draft stage. They were too big, too unwieldy, too *impossible*. Gigantic crab-like troop transporters, for instance, that would stride across the landscape on eight articulated legs, each leg the size of a column in a Roman temple. A huge mobile platform suspended aloft by helical rotor blades, much like those of da Vinci's ornithopter, from which airborne shock troops might descend on enemy lines from on high, swooping down with silk-and-balsa glider wings attached to their backs. Seagoing vessels shaped like manta rays which could both skim the wavetops and submerge and travel underwater in the manner of Nemo's *Nautilus*.

One cannot fault de Villegrand's imaginative powers or ambition, but there are limits to what can be accomplished even with the latest materials and engineering techniques. Some of his designs were on such a colossal scale they were simply unfeasible. Their own weight and dimensions would prevent them getting off the ground, both figuratively and literally.

On the other hand, some of his less hubristic ideas were, I could see, readily achievable. Complex, to be sure, fantastically intricate, and they might take years to complete – but they could be made nonetheless. I told him so. He was pleased.

Would I assist him, he asked, in ushering them from the page to reality? Midwiving his brainchildren?

I, to my eternal shame, said I would.

It would be for the greater glory of France, he said, in order to give his homeland an unassailable military edge over its rivals.

I, the "honorary Frenchman", had few qualms about that.

We sealed the deal over a fine bottle of Margaux, and I returned to my rooms in Montmartre feeling heady, not only from the wine, but from excitement. I had agreed to co-operate on a project that was truly exceptional and that had the potential to alter the course of history. If all went as planned, France would ascend to become the sole, dominant global power. Once de Villegrand's designs were realised and put into mass production, the might of the French military would be unstoppable. And then…

Worldwide peace.

That could be the only possible outcome. So de Villegrand claimed, and so I, in all my juvenile idealism, believed. No more would there be empire versus empire, vying to gain the upper hand. No more would the larger powers gobble up the smaller ones like sweetmeats on a salver. No more would there be rapacious exploitation of one country's resources by another. France would rule over every continent, from east to west, from pole to pole, a benevolent, world-spanning dictatorship.

In de Villegrand's words: "What Bonaparte failed to achieve, our brave new France will. Its sovereignty will know no bounds. Today, Fred, you and I have laid the foundations for a new reign of concord and prosperity for all, a Third Republic that will endure a thousand years."

I can feel a pair of stern gazes boring into the back of my neck. You reckon me a fool at best, gentlemen, and at worst a traitor. You might be right on both counts.

My only defence is that I was under de Villegrand's spell. He wove fine words, couching his vision in such a way that I was swept up in it, taken in fully. With hindsight, these several years on, I can see that what he was proposing was nothing short of worldwide conquest, the subjugation of all. And I realise that no dictatorship rules peaceably. It crushes opposition with cruelty and brutal suppression. It buys its continued existence with the blood of rebels and insurgents. But I knew no better back then. I wanted only to please my newfound friend, and if that meant helping him develop a new and terrible generation of war machines, so be it.

As the work began, I discovered that many in de Villegrand's social circle were more than they seemed. They started showing an increased interest in me, not as a person but as his collaborator. They quizzed me almost daily about how the work was proceeding. It was as though I had been inducted, without my knowing, into some secret brotherhood.

Which, in a way, I had been. One evening, de Villegrand and I went for dinner at the mansion of a friend of his on the outskirts of Paris. It started out like some salon occasion, full of lively and good-tempered debate. Then the mealtime conversation turned to politics. Our host, the Marquis of somewhere or other, recalled with disgust the débâcle of the Franco-Prussian War, the short-lived German occupation of Paris in 1871, and the subsequent two months during which the Commune held sway over the city, until the army wrested back control, bloodily. The Marquis lamented how Parisian had been pitted against Parisian, which could be blamed, he said, on a weak government that could not marshal its own people and had forfeited their trust through incompetence and a series of disastrous policies. The French had lost their self-respect. France as a nation had lost its way. It should remember the example of Nicolas Chauvin – enlisted soldier, wounded seventeen times under Napolcon, maimed, mutilated, yet even at Waterloo, while serving in the Old Guard, this seasoned campaigner fought on long after the other troops had surrendered, defiant in the face of defeat. "If only more of our countrymen," the Marquis said, "could be like Chauvin, tirelessly devoted to their homeland, always putting France before themselves."

The Marquis then proposed a toast: "To Chauvin, who has shown us the way! And to us, his heirs!"

I joined in the toast, raising my glass high and shouting the oath as loudly and joyously as anyone in that room. I did not want to be left out. On the contrary, I wanted to demonstrate how "in" I was.

And so, half without realising it, but willingly nonetheless, I joined Les Hériteurs de Chauvin, a society of nationalist zealots dedicated to the exaltation of France as a country above all others.

That was one of the greatest mistakes I made.

But a greater was to come, a mistake that would prove, in every sense, fatal.

CHAPTER THIRTY-SIX

Baron Cauchemar Concludes His Story

Again, Cauchemar had to be coaxed into carrying on.

My error (he said) lay in inviting de Villegrand round to the Pelletiers'. I admit I wanted to show him off to Delphine. I wanted her to meet him, so that she could see that her Frédérique – how I adored the way she pronounced my name in the French manner, "Frédérique", like a phrase of song – was getting ahead. I wanted her to be impressed by de Villegrand's title and *noblesse*. I hoped the glow of his glory would reflect onto me and make me shine brighter still in her esteem.

As soon as de Villegrand walked into the house and laid eyes on her, he was bewitched. How could he not have been? His bow to her was low. His kiss on her hand lingered. His gaze, throughout the visit, seldom strayed from her. Delphine gave him no encouragement. She was her usual demure self. She remained a model of womanly self-restraint even when, in her presence, he delivered an encomium to her beauty which lasted several minutes. He professed himself infinitely jealous of me for having laid claim to her. Were it not for that, he said, he would even now be making love to her for all he was worth.

In the days that followed, all de Villegrand could talk about was Delphine. He interrogated me on her habits, her likes, her dislikes, what books she read, what foodstuffs she preferred, which shops she favoured. We seldom had a conversation that did not at some point touch on the subject of Delphine. I found nothing troubling in his fascination with her. Rather, I was delighted that my friend was so enamoured of the girl whom I intended to be my betrothed. I regarded it as a positive reflection on my achievement in securing such a rare, radiant creature for my own. If de Villegrand so admired her, it meant I had chosen well. What he liked, I liked. That was how badly I wanted to please him and earn his approval.

Our work continued, sporadically. What we were designing between us… Well, I'm afraid you're likely to see for yourselves soon, gentlemen, the nature of the war machine that we devised. It is a source of gut-wrenching misery to me that de Villegrand is even now pursuing our Queen in something I helped to create. Her death will be in no small part on my hands, should we not succeed in stopping him. I do not bear that guilt lightly.

But now we come to the nub of my tale.

I received a note from de Villegrand one day, enjoining me to attend a soirée at the Marquis's residence. He specified that I was to bring Delphine along. It sounded like it would be a grand occasion. I begged Pelletier to allow his daughter out with me, just this once, unchaperoned. It would only be for a few hours. De Villegrand would be there, along with other representatives of polite society. Delphine and I would be in company at all times. Nothing could go awry, surely.

Pelletier was persuaded, against his better judgement. He harboured a few reservations about de Villegrand, he told me. He had heard a few unsettling rumours about the man. But he was aware of the high regard in which I held my friend and he had no wish to impinge on the happiness or prospects of his future son-in-law. He instructed me to bring Delphine home by eleven o'clock at the very latest, a stipulation I could live with.

It promised to be a wonderful, magical, unforgettable evening.

It certainly proved unforgettable, and how I wish that that were not so.

No sooner had Delphine and I walked through the front door of the Marquis's mansion, than I sensed something was amiss. The only other guests were select members of the Hériteurs de Chauvin. Most had brought along female company, but the married ones had eschewed their wives in favour of their mistresses while the rest were with women such as actresses, dance hall performers, and exponents of an even lower profession.

Champagne was served. Delphine and I took a few sips, I more trepidatiously than she. The atmosphere felt wrong in a way that I could not quite define. For all the smiles and banter around us, I could not help feeling that we were out of place here. We were too much the centre of attention. Everyone else seemed over-keen to chat with us.

The phrase "sacrificial lambs" springs to mind.

Then we guests were ushered through to the dining room. Even as my nerves were becoming increasingly skittish, my thoughts were becoming increasingly clouded. I could not seem to string a meaningful sentence together any more. I sought out de Villegrand, my one true ally here. He, out of all the male partygoers, was the only one to have come solo. The great womaniser for once had no woman. I wished to ask him about this strange state of affairs. I desired to know, too, what sort of champagne we were drinking that was leaving me so light-headed, making my legs feel so leaden, my speech so slurred.

De Villegrand merely laughed and shook his head in a pitying way. "Can't take your drink, eh, Fred?" he jeered, and helped me to a chaise longue in the corner. "You lie down there. Have a nap if you need to. Don't worry, I'll take care of Delphine. She won't want for masculine attention while I'm around."

My champagne had been drugged, of course. A soporific of some sort. I could barely keep my eyes open. I fought to stay awake. I must not abandon Delphine! I must not let her out of my sight! But sleep bore down on me with the force of a tidal wave.

I came to at brief intervals during the evening. Now and then I would be conscious enough to catch a glimpse of what was going on.

The horror of it.

The soirée, if that was what it had ever been, swiftly degenerated into an orgy. That is the only description for it: orgy. The Hériteurs de Chauvin stripped off their clothes, their political posturing, and their decency and decorum, and became a herd of grunting, rutting animals. It was debauchery on a scale that would make the Hellfire Club blush. I cannot begin to tell you the sights I saw during those intermittent snatches of lucidity – the couplings, the unnatural conjoinings, the troilism. The room had become a jungle of limbs akimbo and leering faces. The women, sad to relate, were no better than the men. Some even committed unmentionable acts of tribadism. If it shocks you to hear such things, Mr Holmes, Dr Watson, imagine how much more shocking it was to witness them at first hand. Every time my eyelids parted I was confronted with some fresh spectacle yet more obscene than the last. And I was powerless to move. I had been so strongly sedated that I could not raise my body from the chaise longue any more than I could lift a five-ton elephant.

And what of Delphine? Doubtless that's the question you're asking yourselves. It was the one I was asking *myself*, that's for sure. I could not see her anywhere in the room. Nor, for that matter, could I see de Villegrand. Their absence both heartened

and disturbed me. I hoped – how I hoped – that de Villegrand
had whisked her off to safety the moment the bacchanalian revels
broke out. I feared, however, that he had not. I continued to
nurture a belief in my friend's fidelity and goodness, yet this faint
flame was waning fast.

Around midnight I awoke and was finally able to stir my limbs
to motion. The candles in the chandelier had burned down to
stubs. The dining room was filled with sleeping bodies in various
states of undress. The smells of spilled liquids – alcohol, vomit,
bodily fluids – were nauseating. I picked my way stumblingly
over the snoring figures, careful not to tread on them or slip in a
puddle of something awful. I searched through the house, calling
Delphine's name softly. I prayed to a God I didn't believe in that
she wasn't here, that she was even now back at home, unharmed,
intact, that de Villegrand had behaved with chivalrous integrity. I
doubted she would ever consent to see me again, given what I had
inadvertently exposed her to, but I could live with that, as long as
she was not ruined.

Upstairs, a voice responded to my enquiries, quavering out
"Frédérique?" from behind a bedroom door. I opened the door,
trembling with anguish. I found Delphine curled in a sobbing heap
on the four-poster bed, with de Villegrand beside her, the latter
deep in slumber. I helped her up. Poor Delphine, my dearest darling
Delphine, was bleeding profusely and so weak she could scarcely
walk. We staggered together out of that hellish mansion. My heart
had shrivelled to a black coal of anger and despair. Rain was falling.
I cursed the night sky. I cursed God. I cursed the day I had ever set
foot in Paris. Above all I cursed the betrayer of my trust and the
agent of Delphine's downfall, the Vicomte de Villegrand.

Had Delphine been in better physical condition, I might have
turned round on the spot, re-entered the house, and dashed de
Villegrand's brains out while he slept. But Delphine needed a

doctor. That was my first and foremost priority. Saving her took precedence over avenging the wrong done to her.

I got her back to her parents' house, I don't remember how. Monsieur Pelletier refused to listen to my explanations, my excuses, my entreaties. He called me every vile name under the sun. He beat me with his bare fists. He threw me out. I did not object or retaliate. I deserved every bit of his ill-treatment, and more.

The doctor came. I waited outside in the pouring rain, as dejected as it is humanly possible to be. He emerged an hour later, and his expression told me all I needed to know.

Delphine…

Delphine had died from internal injuries. Such was the brutality with which de Villegrand had used her. Abused her. That… that *monster* had taken the very best, the purest thing in all this world, and destroyed it.

In breaking her, he broke me.

I returned to the Marquis's mansion, resolved to have it out with de Villegrand. I was a seething cauldron of rage and hatred, a veritable Fury. I found Delphine's despoiler sitting with his cronies, enjoying a breakfast of cold cuts and leftover champagne. They were recounting the previous night's exploits and laughing uproariously. I bearded de Villegrand. I rebuked him for his grotesque, savage behaviour. I called him a rapist and murderer.

"Rapist?" said he. "That's a matter of opinion. From a woman's perspective, what begins as rape does not always end up that way. But murderer?"

I told him that Delphine was dead. He had as good as killed her with his lusts.

He at least had the decency to look startled, albeit only for a moment.

"Well, if she wasn't woman enough to handle me…" he said, and sniggered.

That snigger did it. I snatched up a table knife and lunged at him, fully intending to cut out his heart.

I had no idea that he was a martial artist of some proficiency. It seemed there was much I didn't know about the Vicomte de Villegrand, much I had been blinkered to.

In a single swift action he wrenched the knife out of my hand and laid me low on the floor. His reflexes were astounding. I scarcely saw him move. I tried to rise but he kicked me back down with one foot. He stamped on my chest, pressing me in place. I squirmed but could not free myself.

"You did not deserve her, *rosbif*," he sneered. "There are some girls who are made to know the touch only of a real man – a real French man. Anything else is a waste of their time, especially a limp, feeble *Anglais*." He leaned closer. "Delphine loved it. You should have heard her cry out. She could not get enough. Once she had succumbed to me, once her resistance was broken, I repeatedly had to pleasure her, to meet her insatiable demands. If I am to be the only lover she ever had, then she has truly died content."

I screamed at him then, until my lips were coated in a froth of spittle. What I said, I cannot exactly recall, but by the end of it I had exhausted my fund of French expletives and most of my English ones too. I had threatened to kill de Villegrand in a myriad inventive ways. I had vowed not to rest until he and all his coterie of insane nationalists were either behind bars or swinging from the gallows.

De Villegrand was unperturbed. He asked the others what should be done with me. The suggestions ranged from "lock him up in the cellar until he calms down" to "slit his throat and toss the body in the Seine". The consensus tended towards getting rid of me permanently, so that I wouldn't be a pest. In a surge of desperation, I burst forth with: "I challenge you to a duel!"

This elicited gales of laughter.

"I mean it," I said. "If I am to die, at least let it be with honour. And if it also affords me an opportunity to gain reparation for the atrocious insult done to Delphine and her family, so much the better."

The idea took de Villegrand's fancy. "How terribly quaint you are, Fred. Yet, if it's a duel you want, why not? Swords or pistols?"

I had never fired a shot in my life, nor for that matter wielded a sword. However, of the two options, the latter was the more appealing. There is little one can do about a bullet if it is aimed true. At least with a sword one stands a sporting chance.

When I informed de Villegrand of my decision, I realised I had chosen wrongly. He, it turned out, was an excellent shot but his swordsmanship was even more notable. "With a gun you might have got lucky," he said. "With a sabre, not a chance."

The date was set – a week hence.

"In the meantime," de Villegrand said, "do not go to the police. I say this not as a warning but as a piece of practical advice. It will not be worth your while. My friend the Marquis here, do you know who his brother is? The Director-General of the Sûreté, no less. Any claims you make against me and my friends will be ignored. You may even be incarcerated at La Santé for slander and defamation of character."

I did not waste a minute of that week. I found myself the best fencing master I could, spending every last franc I had on him. I block-booked lessons for the entire day, every day, and I learned and I trained, and when I wasn't learning or training I practised in my own time. I barely ate or slept. I was a man obsessed. I would beat de Villegrand, whatever it took. Failing that, I would not make it an easy fight for him. He would pay dearly for his victory.

The fateful day came round. Dawn saw us at the Jardin du Luxembourg. A low mist hung between the elms and shrouded the hard earth. The sun was a faint disk, struggling to rise above the rooftops. Paris was sombre and silent. It would be a good morning to die.

Several of the Hériteurs de Chauvin had turned out as spectators. I had no second, so the Marquis volunteered to fulfil that role. He pronounced himself unimpressed with the sword I had brought, but it was the best I could afford. I had sold my collection of Verne first editions in order to pay for it. He also advised me to offer no opposition, simply to surrender to the inevitable. It would be quicker that way, he said. Less painful.

De Villegrand and I faced off. He saluted me, sabre to nose.

"Let's see how a *rosbif* fights," he said. "*En garde!*"

To his surprise, and mine, I acquitted myself well, at least to begin with. My fencing master had taught me some sneaky tricks which might give me an advantage, such as the *appel*, stamping one's foot in order to distract one's opponent, and the *flèche*, bringing the rear leg before the front leg and sprinting past one's opponent to strike him from the side. These put de Villegrand temporarily off-kilter and allowed me to deliver attacks that almost – almost – penetrated his defences.

Yet always he managed to deflect and riposte, so that I was forced to fall back on the repertoire of parries. Only once did I land anything like a convincing blow, when I lunged towards him using a *disengage* feint. He answered with a *coup d'arrêt*, but I anticipated this and switched to a second-intention *moulinet*, a circular cut. It caught him unawares, and the tip of my sabre slashed his cheek.

"Touché," he said, dabbing off the blood with the back of his hand.

Up until that point he had not been taking me, or the duel, particularly seriously. He had danced around, playing to the crowd, showboating with flamboyant bits of footwork such as the *balestra* and the *patinando*. I had seemed more a nuisance to him than a serious threat.

That changed with the drawing of first blood. De Villegrand set about me in earnest. Flurries of thrusts and stabs came my way, his blade flashing like a dragonfly's wing in the strengthening sunlight. My primary and secondary parries became less and less effectual, until in the end I was flapping my sword frenziedly around, blocking his attacks without elegance or precision, simply trying to survive. Delphine was still in my thoughts, but predominantly I was a man enduring a vicious, relentless onslaught, doing his level best not to get hurt.

He pressed me backwards, raining blows on me like a whirling dervish: *glissade*, *coupé*, *remise*, and some I had no names for. Eventually we ended up in an *engagement*, face to face, blade to blade, our bodies pushed together.

"You have no refinement," he said to me, "no *élan*. What basic skills you have learned, you have mastered, I'll give you that. But you lack a command of the higher techniques that make one exceptional. You will die here today, *mon ami*, defending the honour of a woman who is past caring. It is so sad. We could have done so much together, Fred. We could have gone so far. Your name would have echoed down through history, alongside mine. And you have thrown it away, all over some silly, simpering female."

My blood boiled. How dare he talk about Delphine in that way! I brought my knee up sharply between his legs and heard with deep satisfaction his grunt of agony. He shoved me away with both hands, uttering a stream of profanity.

"A dirty trick," he wheezed. "No Frenchman would ever stoop so low. For that, I will not kill you after all. I will instead leave you wishing you were dead."

He fell upon me once more. I, by now exhausted, tried a simple extension attack, but de Villegrand dexterously flicked my sabre sideways, then disarmed me with a *prise de fer*, using his blade to twist mine out of my grasp.

Now utterly without means of defending myself, I was at his mercy.

What he did next...

You have seen my bare face, gentlemen, somewhat disguised. Those scars were stage makeup, for the most part. However, had you seen me without the fake burns, you would have beheld an ugly, permanent truth.

De Villegrand tripped me up, laid me out flat on my back, and proceeded to work on me all over with his sabre, paying particular attention to my face. There is almost no part of my body that does not still bear the marks of his blade. I am crisscrossed with cuts. Naked, I look as though I have been taken apart by a surgeon and put back together, reassembled much like one of the toys I dismantled as a child, or like Dr Frankenstein's patchwork monster in the novel. One side of my face is so hideously marred that no one can look at it, even me in the mirror, without wincing. No woman, certainly, could ever deem me attractive again. De Villegrand has ensured that. Even if I could have found someone who could be a worthy successor to Delphine, someone who could come close to her in terms of beauty and luminosity, she would not give me a second glance. She would cross the street to avoid me.

De Villegrand left me there, lacerated, shredded, in the Jardin du Luxembourg. He and his Hériteur chums swanned off, and I might have bled to death had not a park keeper come by on his early rounds and hurried to fetch assistance. I was patched up at the Hôtel-Dieu Hospital, and a month later I was on my way back to England, still swathed in bandages like some ambulatory Egyptian mummy.

I stepped off the boat at Dover on a chilly, blustery autumn day. But I did not feel the bite of the wind. A fire was burning inside me, a fire that has kept me warm ever since, even on the coldest nights.

My mother's brother – whom I had met but once, and that when I was a mere stripling – died shortly after I returned to England, and I became, unexpectedly, a man of independent means. My uncle bequeathed me, his only close male kin, his extensive plantations in the West Indies. My parents were all in favour of me going out to the Caribbean and running them. It might help me recuperate, they felt, from the terrible ordeals I had suffered in France, about which I refused to talk. I might even win myself a bride out there, where eligible white men were few and far between and therefore the standards for what constituted handsomeness were lower. But instead I sold off my uncle's holdings and ploughed the money into a series of specialised engineering projects – into becoming Baron Cauchemar.

For I knew this: that de Villegrand would continue his scheme to build war machines, even without me. The Hériteurs de Chauvin would continue to bankroll him. They would not abandon their dream of a worldwide French hegemony. Someone would have to stop them. And that someone would be me.

CHAPTER THIRTY-SEVEN

Two Iron Dukes

In the wake of Cauchemar's sorry tale, silence reigned in the gondola, the only sound the rumbling churn of the airship's propellers. Outside, the sky was paling, the afternoon dissolving into evening.

Eventually Holmes said, "You have my sincerest condolences, Mr Tilling."

"And mine," I said.

"Thank you, but you should save your sympathies for de Villegrand." Cauchemar's voice was brittle. "When I am done with him, he will be fit for nothing but exhibition at a freak show, like Treves's Elephant Man."

"You will not kill him?"

"No, Mr Holmes. He spared my life – just – when it was his to take. I shall extend him the same courtesy, and let him spend the rest of his days as disfigured and loathsome as he left me."

"I am still unclear why you have left it so late to confront him," I said. "If you have known all along that it is de Villegrand who has been terrorising London, why not go after him sooner? His home address is no secret. Lives could have been saved."

"But, Doctor, I did *not* know all along. Mr Holmes's earlier surmises were not quite on the mark. The fact is, I didn't begin to suspect de Villegrand might be behind the attacks until after the third bomb, the one at Waterloo. I was already closing in on Torrance at the time. I knew him to be an associate of de Villegrand's, but I did not know how thick the two of them were with each other, to what extent they were in cahoots, if they were at all. Torrance could quite easily have been working independently of the vicomte where the bombings were concerned. At the back of my mind there lurked the strong possibility that de Villegrand himself *was* involved, but he is wily as a fox and left no clear trail, doing nothing to incriminate himself, not even sending any telegrams that might implicate him. Only after someone shot at me in the graveyard were my suspicions about him confirmed, the accuracy of the bullets compelling me to the conclusion that my old enemy was the one pulling the trigger and that the trail of information which led me to that church had been laid to lure me there. Thereafter, everything fell into place. In hindsight, there was one glaringly obvious clue that the bombings were the Hériteurs de Chauvin finally making their long-awaited move."

"And that clue was…?"

"The choice of location for the third bomb. Waterloo Station. A deliberate provocation. The venue has significance for the Hériteurs, deriving its name as it does from Nicolas Chauvin's final battle and England's last great victory over the French. That was when I realised that the bombers might have a different agenda, that this might after all be the handiwork of Frenchmen not Irishmen."

"De Villegrand has been in the country some while, though," said Holmes. "You have had ample opportunity to exact your vengeance on him before now, bombings or not."

"I was not ready. My armour was not ready. And his downfall

must be public, his every offence laid bare, so that the world will see right through his smiling façade to his rotten core. He must be brought down in such a way that his crimes will be known to all and sundry, the spotlight of infamy will be shone upon him, the man's reputation will be shattered along with the man himself. His humiliation must be total, and he must live to see it. It is not enough that he faces justice. He must lose everything he holds dear, everything that makes him a man: his reputation, his dignity, his standing. The name de Villegrand must forever after be associated with ignobility and depravity."

"Yet confronting him earlier would have spared a lot of people a great deal of suffering and hardship, Watson and myself included. Prevented deaths, what's more."

"What can I tell you? I am not perfect. I have put my own interests before those of others. I can only hope that the good deeds I have done in the East End outweigh my shortcomings elsewhere. If there is such a thing as a set of cosmic scales for each man's soul, then I trust that mine are balanced in my favour."

"Besides, you are hardly in a position to criticise," I said to Holmes. "There have been times when you have turned down clients whose cases you should, all things being equal, have accepted. You have left the police to deal with affairs which you could have cleared up in no time, but which you chose to disregard because they didn't sufficiently pique your interest. 'Let he who is without sin...' et cetera."

"Watson," said Holmes, "as ever you prick the bubble of my self-absorption and keep me grounded. I thank you for doing so. What would I be without you?"

It may have sounded like a fulsome tribute and apology, but my friend was quiet for some time afterwards and I could tell he was disgruntled. He did not like having his deficiencies pointed out to him. Who does?

We raced on. Dusk laced long mauve shadows across the countryside. We were, to the best of my judgement, well into the Midlands by now. The landscape had flattened out into a series of plains, with ribbons of low-lying hills running between, and here and there, like a splotch of manmade lichen, the grey expanse of a mining town or industrial city. We had yet to see a sign of the Royal Train, but we knew we were on the right track, as it were, since we had discerned no other trains travelling the rails below us. Mycroft's edict banning all scheduled journeys along the Royal Train's route was still in force.

The more time that passed, the better adjusted I became to being in the *Delphine's Revenge*. What had started out as stomach-churning and miraculous had become, within a couple of hours, tolerable and even in a way monotonous. We were aboard an airborne vehicle. So what? Mankind's great dream, to be able to fly like a bird, was here made real. But in becoming real it had become, perforce, mundane. I am writing this in an era when the great silver cloud of a Zeppelin is a common enough sight and people think nothing of boarding a passenger plane to travel abroad. Men have fought a world war partly in the skies and crossed entire oceans using aircraft. Any novelty, even one as remarkable as aviation, soon wears off. We are such a restless, never-satisfied species. It is our tragedy and our saving grace.

At any rate, I was beginning to drift off into a bored doze, as I might have done on any lengthy journey, especially on top of such a long, gruelling day and after so little sleep. Then Cauchemar announced that he spied something ahead. It was a plume of smoke, glimmering in the twilight haze.

But not a single plume.

There were two.

"It's as I thought," he said. "De Villegrand has his own locomotive, one to whose design I contributed, back when it was just a rough sketch on paper. The *Duc En Fer*, an Iron Duke to rival the fastest British engine of that name. Rival it and surpass it in so many ways."

De Villegrand's *Duc En Fer* was a sturdy black beast, big around the belly, with three huge driving wheels and two sets of bogies, fore and aft. It chugged hard along the rails, pistons pounding. Embers poured from its funnel along with the smoke, their glow lending the locomotive's coachwork an infernal orange lustre. Behind trailed a single carriage that was enclosed on all sides and windowless, like a freight wagon.

A mile or so up the track, the Royal Train was also making good speed. Its rolling stock comprised four carriages and a brake van. I pictured the royal family within one of the carriages, seated in sumptuous saloon accommodation. Their mood would be apprehensive, perhaps, but they could little realise how imminent the danger was, how an implacable foe of Britain was even now snapping at their heels.

The *Duc En Fer* was gradually gaining on the Royal Train, eating up the remaining distance between them.

"But where did he build the thing?" I said. "And, more to the point, how did he manage to get it onto the track? Didn't Mycroft see to it that no other trains were allowed on this route but the Queen's?"

"Here, I fear, is where we may detect the malign influence of Professor Moriarty exerting itself," said Holmes. "He implied to me that he has some stake in the bombing campaign and its ultimate outcome. In order to further his own ends, he has been helping the Hériteurs de Chauvin from the sidelines. I wouldn't put it beyond his abilities to bribe or threaten railway officials to look the other way while de Villegrand's train takes to the rails and to switch points so that it would have a clear run. As for building it, de Villegrand must have done so somewhere in England. He could hardly have exported an entire completed locomotive across the Channel, not without arousing attention. On the other hand, a rail shed somewhere, perhaps one owned by Moriarty, part of an extensive property portfolio… It's the most plausible explanation. Do you not agree, Mr Tilling?"

"I don't know as much as you do about this Moriarty," said our pilot, "but I have heard whispers, and if he is half the scheming genius people say he is, then he and de Villegrand are a match made in heaven. Or rather, hell."

"A finger in every pie, has Moriarty," Holmes muttered, "and the pies all laced with arsenic."

Cauchemar poured on acceleration, and at the same time pumped air into the ballonets so that the *Delphine's Revenge*'s neutral buoyancy was reduced and the airship began swiftly to descend.

"What is our plan, Mr Tilling?" my friend demanded. "I defer to you because you know more about the *Duc En Fer* than I do. I imagine you have some means of putting it out of action."

"The *Delphine's Revenge* is equipped with a pair of modified self-powered recoil-operated Maxim guns, firing point-four-five-inch rounds at a rate of six hundred a minute. Simply put, I intend to disable de Villegrand's locomotive by blasting away at it until it cannot go on. And," he added, picking up his helmet and fastening it on his head, "it is not 'Mr Tilling' any more – it is Baron Cauchemar."

"Very well," said Holmes, rapping his knuckles on that metal cranium, which still bore the dent from one of de Villegrand's bullets. "Then aim true, my good man."

The *Delphine's Revenge* levelled out. Cauchemar brought us in right at the rear of the *Duc En Fer*. He flicked a couple of switches, and the stocky barrels of the Maxim guns eased out in front of the viewing portals. A lens with crosshairs descended from the ceiling on the end of a telescopic arm. Cauchemar put his helmet's demonic face to it, sighting on the train. We were close enough now that I could just make out a pair of figures in the cab of the locomotive: one at the throttle, driving; the other shovelling coal for all he was worth. Both were silhouetted against the glare of flames from the open firebox flap, so that their faces were lost in shadow, but I nonetheless recognised them by their physiques and profiles. They were Torrance's associates from the Stepney graveyard, Gedge and Kaylock.

The absence of de Villegrand and Torrance on the locomotive gave me pause. If they were not immediately visible, then where were they?

I was about to give voice to my puzzlement when it happened.

The covered carriage opened up, roof and sides drawing back like the mouth of a snake when baring its fangs. Hinged metal plate folded against hinged metal plate, concertina-fashion.

"Oh," said Cauchemar. "That's new."

In the space of a few seconds, we were no longer looking at a freight wagon. Rather, it had become a flatbed truck on which was mounted one of the largest pieces of field artillery I had ever seen. The retracted plates which had been concealing this now formed a housing, within which two men, a loader and a gunner, stood alongside a stack of shells.

Torrance and de Villegrand.

The artillery piece's barrel angled upwards until it was pointing straight at the *Delphine's Revenge*. The three of us in the gondola stared into the rifled aperture as though into some pitiless Cyclopean eye.

De Villegrand had the nerve to offer us a wave – bidding us adieu, I'll be bound.

Then he yanked the lanyard and the big gun fired.

CHAPTER THIRTY-EIGHT

A Whale Harpooned

"Brace yourselves!" Cauchemar cried, and he thrust the steering column to the side as far as it would go. The airship canted steeply to starboard –

– an immense ripping sound –

– a rumble as of thunder –

– a terrible splintering and shuddering –

– and then the *Delphine's Revenge* was spiralling helplessly through space, like some airborne whirligig. Holmes and I were tossed about inside the gondola, battering ourselves on hard surfaces and bruising each other with our elbows and knees. The world through the viewing portals was a smear of green and grey, land and sky careening madly around us.

Cauchemar fought to regain control of the aircraft. He steered against the rotation of our spin, directing the rudders and elevators to counteract it and powering up the propellers to apply a braking force. With much shaking and straining, the *Delphine's Revenge* gradually stabilised. He brought us about to face the *Duc En Fer* again.

"A glancing blow," he said. "She's still airworthy."

"Not for much longer if you don't take evasive action." Holmes pointed. "Look. De Villegrand is busy finding our current range."

The artillery piece was revolving. Torrance hoisted a fresh shell, one-handed, into the breech. De Villegrand cranked the barrel higher, taking aim.

Cauchemar raised the airship's nose sharply. I heard the shell launch and come screaming towards us. I felt a huge pressure bearing down on me as our pilot throttled up and we shot skywards. There was no impact this time. The shell passed harmlessly below us.

"Enough of the ducking and scurrying," Cauchemar said. "Now we take the offensive."

The *Delphine's Revenge* switched from climb to dive in a single lurching manoeuvre, twisting and plummeting at once. My stomach ended up somewhere near my mouth. For a few disagreeable seconds I felt all but weightless.

Cauchemar lined up the Maxim guns on the artillery piece and opened fire. Parallel jets of bullets raked the flatbed truck, the wheels, the big gun itself, and the housing within which de Villegrand and Torrance sheltered. The two men were safe behind several thicknesses of metal plate. As for the artillery piece, it was of sturdy construction. The bullets bounced off, ricocheting in all directions, leaving dents and scratches but inflicting no serious damage.

"Damn it, I need to get closer," said Cauchemar.

"Are you sure that's wise?" Holmes said, but the enquiry fell on deaf ears. Cauchemar seemed to have forgotten about his passengers. He was focused exclusively on de Villegrand.

"First I shall cripple your gun, Thibault," he said. "Then you." His amplified voice sounded eerily uninflected and detached, as though once he had his full armour on he ceased to be wholly human.

The *Delphine's Revenge* zeroed in on the speeding train. Cauchemar swerved right and left in order to throw off the vicomte's aim. The nearer we got to the big gun, however, the larger a target we presented.

He let loose with the Maxims again, strafing the truck from end to end. De Villegrand, with something like nonchalance, continued adjusting the artillery piece's direction and elevation. All at once a third shell was sailing our way, and this one hit dead-on.

I don't think I shall ever hear a noise as heart-stopping and stomach-turning as the sound of that projectile tearing through the balloon envelope of the *Delphine's Revenge*. I picture it like a harpoon penetrating the blubbery hide of a whale. The rending of sailcloth and steel strut was akin to a scream of pain.

The entire airship recoiled, like a man when punched. Rivets popped from the gondola's seams. A reinforcing brace by my shoulder buckled.

"She's fine," Cauchemar maintained, but the *Delphine's Revenge* was not fine. Even a novice aeronaut like me could tell that. Cauchemar struggled with the controls, but for all his valiant efforts with the throttle and steering column he was getting little in the way of a result. We were aloft but adrift. I could feel the airship sagging, losing altitude.

"Set us down," Holmes urged. "It's the only way."

"No," said Cauchemar. "No, I can regain mastery…"

"You cannot! Don't be an idiot, man. The vessel is doomed. Find somewhere to land safely while you can, before the option is taken out of your hands and we crash."

Cauchemar relented, accepting the sense of Holmes's argument. "But if we just put down any old where, we will lose de Villegrand. We will never be able to catch up with him again in time. The Queen is as good as dead."

"What if we bail out onto the *Duc En Fer*?" Even as the words passed my lips, I could scarcely believe I was uttering them. Was I mad?

The avid glint in Holmes's eye told me that I was, but that he himself had run through all the possible scenarios and the one I had hit on was the only viable solution to our dilemma.

"Cauchemar," he said, "do you still have sufficient command of this thing that you can pilot us over the train and we can climb out?"

"Probably not," came the reply. Cauchemar consulted the dials and meters in front of him. "The envelope is compromised. Helium is escaping. The balloon is deflating rapidly. We have a couple of minutes' buoyancy left, if that. Once it's gone, I might as well be flying Westminster Cathedral. But," he said with bright resolve, "I shall do my damnedest, Mr Holmes. For England's sake."

He addressed himself to the controls once more. I heard him talking in a faint voice, murmuring to the stricken airship as though it were a sentient thing. "Come on. I built you well. Stay alive just a little longer. You can do that for me, I know you can."

The *Delphine's Revenge* sluggishly responded to his manual ministrations, if not to his verbal cajoling. He managed to eke out enough speed from the airship to match that of the *Duc En Fer*. In moments, we had drawn alongside the locomotive, and then we were directly above it, and though I feared another salvo from de Villegrand's artillery piece, it turned out that being in such immediate proximity to him was our salvation.

"He doesn't dare take a shot at us," said Holmes. "We're so low that hitting us means we might come down on top of him. Point-blank, and his gun is useless. Ha!"

"But I can't hold us in position for long," Cauchemar warned. As if to underscore his statement, the *Delphine's Revenge* jerked violently sideways. He counter-steered and succeeded in bringing us back to where we had just been. "So I would abandon ship now if I were you."

I didn't need to be told twice. I was already turning the locking wheel on the hatch in the gondola's belly. No sooner did I have it open than I tipped the rolled-up rope ladder out. It unfurled, lashing and flailing.

"What about you?" Holmes said to Cauchemar.

"I have to play pilot. If I don't keep the *Delphine's Revenge* steady and on course, you and Dr Watson don't stand a chance."

"How will you follow us out, then?"

"I shall find a way. I'm armoured, after all. I can survive what you could not. Now stop nannying me and go!"

I must say I didn't fancy essaying that ladder, so I was glad that Holmes seized the initiative and clambered down first. His body weight did much to quell its midair whipping and twisting. When I added mine, the ladder became more or less rigid.

Nonetheless we were barrelling along at something in the region of eighty miles an hour. Sheer speed drove the ladder back at an acute angle, and the hurricane-like force of motion did its best to blow Holmes and me off our perches. Every handhold and foothold had to be established with the utmost care. Our descent was as precarious as it was painstaking.

And all in order to climb atop a locomotive travelling at full pelt! I have surely performed crazier daredevil stunts in my time, but if so, I am hard pressed to think of one.

Then, to add to our woes, shots rang out. Torrance had hoisted himself on top of the artillery piece's housing and was firing a revolver at Holmes and myself. We would have been the proverbial sitting ducks but, fortunately, the rope ladder was still swaying to and fro somewhat, and the flatbed truck was juddering along the rails, and the two things conspired to foil Torrance's aim. His bullets whined past us but, thank God, all missed.

Holmes alighted on the *Duc En Fer*'s sand dome and grabbed hold of one of the valve rods that ran along its upper surface, securing himself.

I spidered my way down the last few rungs, ready to join him.

It was a drop of a yard or so onto the locomotive. Before taking the plunge, I paused to glance up at the *Delphine's Revenge*.

No longer was it a sleek leviathan of the skies. The punctured envelope was puckered and sagging. There was a tattered hole where the shell had entered, with spars of twisted steel projecting outward like broken ribs. One propeller was almost entirely gone, its blades sheared off by de Villegrand's first shot. The whole aircraft looked as though it was about to collapse at any moment, imploding in on itself. Cauchemar's creation was in its death throes, yet still it forged dauntlessly on, nursed and spurred by its pilot.

I should not have hesitated, for as I watched, the *Delphine's Revenge* shuddered horribly and its envelope suffered a sudden, catastrophic loss of integrity. It had had enough and could take no more. The balloon crumpled, as though a gigantic unseen hand were crushing it, and the gondola became just so much dead weight, with only momentum keeping it in the air.

The shock transmitted itself along the rope ladder, which seemed to convulse under me. I lost my grip.

Then I was falling, and all I could think, as I fell, was that this was a deuced stupid way to die, but at least it would be quick and I probably would not feel a thing.

CHAPTER THIRTY-NINE

HUMAN JETSAM

What I did feel, in the event, was a hand clamping about my wrist, a set of fingers digging into my flesh with considerable wiry strength.

Then I swung and slammed chest-first against the locomotive's flank. The wind was knocked out of me.

"Watson!" cried Holmes. "I have you, but I cannot hold you for long."

I dangled there, suspended from Holmes's grasp, heaving for breath. The *Duc En Fer*'s pistons pounded back and forth beside my shins, like the arms of some mighty metal boxer. The cinder path raced by below, mere inches from my toecaps.

"Watson!" Holmes yelled, louder than before. "If you do not help me, I will drop you. For God's sake, focus, man!"

A bullet zinged past my ear, so close that I swear I felt the shockwave of its passage.

Nothing galvanises a fellow quite like having his brains nearly blown out. I reached for the valve rod, which was just within my grasp, and by dint of my own efforts and Holmes's, I managed to scramble onto the boiler's summit. I knelt, breathless, the hammering of my heart louder than the clatter of wheels on rails.

"Thought you were a goner there, old chap," said Holmes.

"So did I," I gasped.

"Now, you get your breath back. I've an appointment with a train driver about an emergency stop."

He set off in the direction of the cab, crouching low, arms outstretched against the locomotive's rackety sway. Torrance, meanwhile, was squatting on the coal tender. He was reloading his revolver, a tricky business if you have only one arm. He gripped the gun between his knees, using them like a vice while he fed bullets into the cylinder one after another.

I decided to give him a taste of his own medicine. I drew my revolver and cocked the hammer.

At that moment, the *Delphine's Revenge* emitted one last dire groan overhead and came crashing down.

It landed, whether by luck or calculation on Cauchemar's part, atop the artillery piece. Airship and gun became entangled with an ear-shredding shriek of metal twisting against metal. Under the sudden imposition of additional weight, the entire train shook tumultuously. I feared a derailment was about to occur and every one of us was about to meet a horrible, mangled demise. I clung on for dear life, as did Holmes.

The screeching and rending continued. The gondola's aft end was impaled on the gun barrel. The other end swung out and down, until the hull of the thing was dragging on the ground. We were travelling along a raised section of track that cut through farmland, and the gondola ploughed the earth of the embankment, kicking up great churning waves of sod and soil. The deflated balloon was coming to pieces at the same time, individual ballonets bursting and ripping. The *Delphine's Revenge* was being dismantled before my very eyes, shaken to pieces, flayed. Bits of it went sailing off down the track and bounding across the fields.

With the airship acting as a kind of anchor, the flatbed truck began to slew, then all at once it jumped the track and was jolting crazily along behind the locomotive at an angle. It leapt and bucked as the wheels on one side of it rode the sleepers while those on the other side sheared through cinders and earth. I could feel the *Duc En Fer* being pulled backwards and sideways, struggling to stay on the rails itself. Holmes and I were completely helpless, like ticks riding the back of a runaway horse, with no choice but to pray it didn't slip and roll over.

Then an immense lurch. The *Duc En Fer* broke free of its stricken item of rolling stock and went rocketing forwards, more or less smoothly again. The locomotive and the truck had become uncoupled, I assumed thanks to the latter's torquing, skewing action.

Together, airship and truck plunged headlong down the embankment and collided with a solitary oak. The huge, venerable tree exploded into a million fragments, reduced in an instant to so much tinder. The *Delphine's Revenge* and the artillery piece did not fare much better, both disintegrating on impact. Débris fanned in all directions, and there was an almighty *whump* as the cache of shells detonated. A fireball the size of a five-storey house billowed up into the sky, its brightness momentarily eclipsing the red flare of the setting sun.

Baron Cauchemar. Had he still been aboard the airship? If so, armoured or not, I could not see him surviving such a fiery apocalypse.

We had just lost our strongest ally, our one uncontestable advantage over our enemies.

However, in the credit column, to offset that debit, we had destroyed the artillery piece, which de Villegrand had surely been meaning to use to bombard the Royal Train. His scheme, therefore, had been thwarted. And de Villegrand himself? Was it too much to hope that he had still been on the flatbed truck when it came off the track? Could he have been incinerated along with Cauchemar, the two antagonists fatally consumed in the same conflagration?

The answer, regrettably, was no. At the rear of the coal tender, de Villegrand's head popped up. He hauled himself up, joining Torrance on the piled coal. He looked unkempt, ruffled, murderously aggrieved. I realised he must have performed the uncoupling himself, saving the locomotive by sacrificing the truck.

Now it was him, Torrance and the two other accomplices, versus Holmes and myself.

I did not like those odds.

De Villegrand snatched Torrance's revolver and bullets from him, not happy how long it was taking the one-armed man to load the gun. He finished the job swiftly, and snapped the cylinder into place with a flick of the wrist.

Holmes, by this time, was at the cab, clambering down the side of it in order to get in. His plan, I took it, was to assume control of the locomotive and bring it to a halt. That meant overpowering Gedge and Kaylock, but I reckoned that in a fair fight, with his *baritsu* skills, he was up to the task.

De Villegrand did not wish it to be a fair fight, though, and took aim at my friend. I, in turn, levelled my revolver at the Frenchman and fired off what I am going to call, with pardonable modesty, the shot of a lifetime. Given that I was on a speeding locomotive, I would have been lucky to place my bullet anywhere near its target. That I managed to blast the revolver out of de Villegrand's grasp was little short of incredible. It is a feat I doubt I could repeat ever again, yet on this occasion providence, some might even say a higher power, smiled on me.

His gun gone, lost over the side of the tender, de Villegrand reared up with a growl of fury. He gesticulated at Torrance, instructing him to take care of me. Over the clamour of the engine I just made out the words "Kill that wretched —!" accompanied by a highly degrading epithet. Torrance obediently lumbered towards me, leaping up off the tender onto the cab roof. De Villegrand himself went after Holmes, scuttling across the heap of coal and down into the cab interior.

I could not leave my friend to fend for himself against *three* ruffians, especially when one of them was the vicious, *savate*-savvy vicomte. I headed rearward. Torrance moved to waylay me. With a grimace of resignation, I aimed my revolver at him and pulled the trigger – only to hear the dispiriting click of a misfire.

I pocketed the gun, knowing Torrance would never allow me the luxury of checking the firing pin or the mainspring or fishing some tiny foreign object out from between the hammer and the frame. The same higher power that had smiled on me a moment ago had abruptly and capriciously turned its face away.

He stood erect on the roof of the cab, fist clenched, legs splayed to brace himself. Through his beard, his grin was coldly gleeful.

"Gun failed, eh?" he crowed. "How unlucky for you. I shall make this quick. Wouldn't want you to suffer any, would I? Then history will celebrate me doubly, first as the man who aided in the death of an entire royal house, but also as the man who did away with the companion of the poxy meddler Sherlock Holmes."

"Better men than you have tried," I said. "Men with a full complement of limbs."

"Oh, I've never let a small thing like a dismemberment stand in my way, Dr Watson. Look at me. I've more vigour in my right arm than most men have in both."

I could not deny that. I had seen the evidence with my own eyes a number of times, and indeed felt it when he throttled me nearly to death at the docks in Shadwell. Yet I maintained my pose of grim bravado, hoping I sounded more courageous than I felt.

"I am an ex-soldier," I said. "You will find me more of a challenge than, say, a drugged Chinese girl."

"I didn't the last time," Torrance said. "Let us put it to the test again, shall we?"

And so we grappled, that great barbarous hulk of a man and I, as the *Duc En Fer* hurtled onward. We threw ourselves into a clinch, and as his hand sought my throat in order to obtain a stranglehold we both knew I would be unable to break, I fended off his arm with both of mine. His strength was just as appalling as I remembered. He bore down on me, and it was all I could do to keep him at bay.

We shuffled in circles on the cab as we wrestled, and I was acutely aware that I was being pushed inexorably outward, closer and closer to the roof's edge. Torrance, with sadistic fire in his eyes, was giving himself the alternative of shoving me off, if for some reason he could not throttle me. I fought back but it was like battling a grizzly bear. I had the terrible sensation, not of simply being outclassed, but of being toyed with. My foe, this one-armed Goliath, was revelling in his superiority.

Yet, if I could not match him physically, could I not outwit him?

"Is it worth what de Villegrand's paying you, Torrance?" I said through clenched teeth.

"Every penny – and there are plenty of them, believe you me. Money may not matter so much to a glossy-coated swell such as yourself, but for a bloke like me, coming from where I come from, it's all that counts. It's the difference between being somebody and nobody. I'm not fitted to scrabble around in the dirt all my life like some shoreline mudlark. I was made for better things."

"But to conspire against your own country…!"

"England's done nothing for me," Torrance spat. "I don't care if the whole damned place sinks into the mire, and every bloody Englishman drowns. Why should I? Long as I'm all right."

We were now in such a position that Torrance had his back to the direction the locomotive was travelling in. I glanced ahead, gasped in alarm, and then dropped straight onto my belly, pressing myself flat onto the cab roof, hands over my head. Torrance didn't even look over his shoulder but copied me without delay. It was pure instinct. If I was ducking in anticipation of an oncoming tunnel, then so must he.

I sprang to my feet in a trice, for there was no tunnel. Torrance rose too, realising he had been duped, but he was a split second behind me. As he hoisted himself upright, I kicked his arm out from under him. He collapsed awkwardly. His chin struck the coachwork, stunning him, and he sprawled. His legs swung out over space, and his own considerable body weight dragged him half off the cab roof. He groped with his arm, trying to gain purchase on the smooth metal. His expression was pure panic.

"Please!" he cried. "Please help me! You're a doctor! Your oath!"

I moved to grab him. Perhaps I could have been a mite faster, I don't know. Moments earlier this man had been hell bent on killing me, which would account for my hesitation. My incentive to go to his rescue was not great, especially as he would not have done the same for me had our roles been reversed.

At any rate, I did not reach him in time. His clawing hand slithered across the roof, and then it clutched empty air, and Abednego Torrance was gone, tumbling down the embankment at high speed like some piece of ghastly human jetsam. I saw him strike a wooden fencepost at the bottom, crown first, and lie still. It didn't take a knowledge of medicine to tell that he had suffered the kind of injuries one does not recover from. His body was twisted and bent around itself, his head canted against his neck in a deeply unnatural manner.

There was no time to feel either relief or remorse. I could hear a commotion below me, the thump of blows, grunts of pain – Holmes in a frantic physical altercation with Gedge, Kaylock and de Villegrand. Abruptly the *Duc En Fer* braked. I was thrown off my feet. Locked driving wheels squealed across the rails, showering out sparks. I tottered backwards off the cab and managed somehow to land in the coal tender rather than on the ground. I lay there on that heap of fuel, dazed. The locomotive juddered like a stutterer's tongue. I caught a glimpse inside the cab. Holmes was hauling back on the brake handle, pulling it fully round, while at the same time clutching Kaylock with an arm around his neck, using him as a human shield to ward off de Villegrand. Gedge lay unconscious on the footplate, half slumped against the water and steam injector levers.

The *Duc En Fer* grudgingly, grindingly came to a standstill, hissing like some monstrous serpent venting its frustration.

De Villegrand, the moment we halted, let out a similar infuriated hiss. As everyone recovered their equilibrium, he hurled himself at Holmes. Holmes thrust Kaylock to the fore. De Villegrand, without even pausing, drove his fists into his henchman.

"Out of my way!" he yelled, subjecting the hapless lackey to a tempest of blows. "Incompetent! *Débile*! You're no good to me any more, and I'm damned if you'll be any good to him."

Kaylock caved in under the furious onslaught, protesting and mewling. A brutal, bone-crunching *savate* kick to the skull left him just so much inert weight, more than Holmes could usefully support with one arm, so my friend was obliged to drop him.

Now it was just Holmes facing de Villegrand in the stationary locomotive, with me looking on from the tender.

"You haven't won, *monsieur le détective privé*," said the vicomte.

"It rather looks to me as though I have," came the reply. "There are two of us and one of you, and Watson and I will prevent you from restarting this locomotive even if it kills us."

"Hear, hear," I said. "So give up now, de Villegrand. It'll go hard for you otherwise."

"Who said anything about restarting it?" said the Frenchman. "How little you know. The *Duc En Fer* may look like an ordinary railway engine, but trust me, it is not. It has, shall we say, hidden depths. Behold. *Voilà!*"

De Villegrand reached for a control device I did not recognise. I cannot confess to being any kind of expert on steam locomotives, but this particular large red lever, situated up among the valve stopcocks, served no obvious function that I could see.

No sooner was it pulled, however, than the *Duc En Fer* began to vibrate and shake from stem to stern. *Something* was happening, that was for sure.

Holmes, whether or not he had any clearer idea than me what de Villegrand had initiated, looked alarmed. "Watson, I recommend we get off this thing – now!"

De Villegrand chortled. "Yes," he crowed. "Get off. Go. Shoo, *rosbifs*! Go and stand helplessly by as the future takes shape before you."

I scrambled off the tender, dropping onto the trackside. Holmes joined me there, leaping down from the cab. We backed away from the locomotive, which was now, as far as I could judge, starting to break apart. Segments of the boiler were separating from one another. The pistons were parting company with the wheels and sweeping outwards.

Had de Villegrand triggered some sort of self-destruct mechanism with that lever?

No. I swiftly realised he had not.

In fact, the very opposite.

CHAPTER FORTY

A Manmade Titan

Even today, I can feel the incredulity I felt then as the *Duc En Fer* somehow disassembled itself and put itself back together in a new form. Individual sections of the locomotive articulated outwards, folded, shifted, dovetailed, slotted into fresh positions. Jointed shafts extended and contracted. Cogs whirred and meshed. Bits of the engine's innards were briefly exposed then hidden again. The *Duc En Fer* underwent a kind of auto dissection, jumbling up all its parts and re-gathering them in a wholly different configuration.

"What in the world…?" said Holmes. It was rare to hear him so astonished, to see him so clearly awestruck. His customary diffidence had deserted him. He, like me, could only look on at the locomotive's metamorphosis and marvel and quail.

Up it rose, from prone to erect. The driving wheels and chassis became legs. The boiler became a torso. The cab surmounted the whole thing like a head. The coal tender tipped up, emptying its contents down a chute and becoming a back and shoulders. The pistons shot down to serve as arms. Each was tipped with one of the bogie frames, which had broken down into a set of finger-like rods, the little wheels serving as knuckles.

In all, it stood some thirty feet tall, a humanoid giant which had a minute ago been, to all appearances, a simple steam locomotive. The alteration from one state to another was complete, and now, with an eerie creaking and clanking, this fearsome, transformed *Duc En Fer* turned towards Holmes and myself.

De Villegrand leaned out from the cab and yelled down, "Do you see? This is what I had up my sleeve. How pathetically small you both look. And how emasculated. French knowhow! French genius! This is why my country will always be superior to yours. This is why the world deserves to belong to France and France alone."

"I am impressed, I admit," Holmes shouted back. "It just seems a shame to me that your ambitions are so limited."

"Limited? What are you saying? Absurd! How can ruling the entire world be a 'limited' ambition?"

"Think of what else you could achieve with this brilliance of yours, *monsieur le vicomte*. The benefits you could bring to all of mankind. You have the wherewithal to usher in a technological golden age, an age of wonders, single-handedly. But no, all you think of is domination and conquest. Petty aims for one so gifted."

"Holmes," I said out of the corner of my mouth, "he's sitting in a massive walking automaton that looks like it could make mincemeat out of us. Best not to bait him, eh?"

"I'm not baiting him, Watson, merely trying to talk some sense into him."

"I think he's gone beyond sense."

"But what else have we got? He's unassailable up there."

"It *will* be a golden age, Monsieur Holmes," de Villegrand insisted. "That is surely what is coming. But it will be an *age d'or*, a uniquely French golden age. There is no nation better suited to run the world. We boast the finest poets, philosophers, artists, scientists and, yes, inventors. All that piffle I told you about the greatness of Great Britain – pah! Nothing your race has to offer is the equal of anything mine has to offer. You will learn that. Once your Queen is dispatched, your country will be in disarray and ripe for takeover. French troops will swarm across *La Manche* and occupy. It will be touted as the decent thing to do, the act of a Good Samaritan coming to his neighbour's rescue. You will welcome us with open arms – anything to quell the anarchy you will have descended into. The Tricolore will be hoisted above Buckingham Palace and Westminster, and soon the pattern will be repeated elsewhere. America, Russia, even the prodigious Germany will succumb, especially with weapons of my devising at our military's disposal. This is just the beginning."

"You'd better hurry, then," said Holmes. "The Royal Train is out of sight. You've some ground to make up."

"This evolved *Duc En Fer* is faster than its other incarnation. I put the feet on the track like so…" The giant automaton's wheel-feet went from flat, like snowshoes, to vertical, like ice skates, as de Villegrand lodged one on each rail. "I run." The legs scissored back and forth, and the entire body moved a few yards. Steam purled from the funnel, which was now protruding from the thing's back. "I can achieve a good hundred miles an hour when I get up to full speed. I move like a skier, gliding along." He reversed, drawing level with Holmes and me again. "So I am not worried about the Royal Train, no. I can afford to let it travel a little bit further ahead. I have time."

"Time to do what?" asked Holmes, and we both wished he hadn't.

"To kill the two of you, *naturellement*," said de Villegrand. "You have been remarkably persistent opponents, and remarkably annoying ones. My conservatory anti-burglar mechanism failed to put an end to your snooping. I shall rectify that now. I cannot let you live to plague me again in the future. You have been pestilential like flies, and so, like flies, I shall swat you."

One vast metal hand rose into the air, furling into a fist.

"Holmes?" I said in a faint voice. "Should we run?"

"Watson, I believe that would be a capital idea."

We about-turned and ran. The *Duc En Fer*'s fist came down behind us like the hammer of God. It missed, but the impact knocked us clean off our feet. We fell prostrate on the ground but were up and running again in a flash.

De Villegrand's automaton stepped off the track, its wheel-feet reverting back to horizontal. It charged after us, each footfall sounding like Judgement Day.

"I will stamp on you!" the vicomte screamed. "I will crush you like cockroaches!"

All Holmes and I could do was keep running for our lives. We were in a cow pasture. There was little cover available, just the odd hawthorn bush or stunted tree. However, we could see an isolated wooden barn ahead on the far side of the field. Taking shelter there might save us, assuming we could outpace the metal behemoth pursuing us.

Closer the barn came, but closer, too, came the *Duc En Fer*.

"He's gaining!" I cried.

"No need to state the obvious," said Holmes. "Save your breath."

We had perhaps one hundred yards of open ground left to cross. We were sprinting flat out. My lungs heaved and burned. My leg muscles ached searingly. Twenty seconds to go, and the thunderous stomping of de Villegrand's manmade titan was ringing in my ears, filling my entire world.

We weren't going to make it.

Then I heard another kind of stomping, matched by a familiar *psssh-pah*, *psssh-pah*.

I dared to look sidelong, and there, coming at us from right angles on a course to intercept, was Baron Cauchemar.

He bounded across the landscape with his lolloping, piston-heeled gait, and he scooped Holmes up in one arm and me up in the other just as the *Duc En Fer* sent a fist down to pound us into the earth.

Cauchemar tucked round us, somersaulted, and rolled to a halt. He released us and straightened up.

"In the nick of time," said Holmes, smoothing out a lapel.

"You're welcome," said Cauchemar.

His armour looked half wrecked. It was scorched in several places, dented in several others.

"I'm very glad you survived that explosion," I said.

"It was touch and go, but this suit's built to withstand plenty of punishment. Digging my way out of the wreckage took some time, though. Now, if you'll excuse me, gentlemen…"

He swung round to confront the *Duc En Fer*.

"Ah-ha," said de Villegrand, bringing his automaton ponderously about. "Baron Cauchemar, I presume. Finally we meet in person."

"Meet again, you mean, Thibault," said Cauchemar.

"Yes, Fred, meet again. Such a stickler for detail. You always were. I used to admire that about you, as an engineer, an inventor. You had an amazing capacity to consider the little things. The trouble was, it hindered you from thinking big."

"Size isn't everything."

"It is when one of us dwarfs, in every sense, the other. How have you been doing, *mon ami*? I trust life has been treating you well since I – how to put this? – changed the way people look at you. But I suspect it has not."

"You did me a favour when you disfigured me, actually, Thibault."

"I did? How?"

"You stripped away from me any illusions I had about people. I saw the world for the false, superficial place it is. I understood about charlatans and liars and fanatics and corrupt evildoers, and I realised it was my duty to oppose them whenever and wherever they rear their heads. I have you to thank for that. In ruining me, you opened my eyes. You gave me a true purpose. You made me the man I have become."

"How touching," sneered de Villegrand. "Someone, I suppose, had to rid you of your loathsome dewy-eyed innocence, just as someone had to relieve your sainted Delphine of her virginity. Why not me?"

At the mention of Delphine, Cauchemar visibly bristled inside his armour. De Villegrand's words had penetrated Fred Tilling's metal carapace in a way that his rifle shots at the graveyard had failed to.

"You do not speak her name again," said Cauchemar with cold fury. "You are not worthy. Goodness like hers does not belong on the tongue of a blackguard such as you."

"My tongue and Delphine's goodness were more than intimately acquainted. And as for *her* tongue… *Ooh-la-la!*"

"Enough!" snapped Cauchemar. "This dream of yours ends today, Thibault. You and your fellow Hériteurs – your aspirations for a worldwide Third Republic will never be made real."

"Will you stop me, *mon pauvre petit* Fred? When I am five times larger, five times as mighty?"

Baron Cauchemar planted his feet, his armour's micro-furnace pulsing with fire and power.

"It's not the machine that counts," he said, "it's the man inside. And I *will* stop you, yes, or die trying."

"Then die!" declared de Villegrand, and battle was joined.

CHAPTER FORTY-ONE

DUELLING MACHINES

It was a rerun of their duel in the Jardin du Luxembourg, only this time, in place of a sabre, each man was equipped with a sophisticated, steam-driven vehicle.

This time, too, it would be a fairer fight, for Cauchemar was not young, inexperienced Fred Tilling any more with just a week's worth of fencing lessons to his name. He had full mastery of his armour and an array of weaponry to call upon.

And yet, the *Duc En Fer* was five times his size, constructed from a locomotive weighing several tons. Before de Villegrand's towering android, Cauchemar looked like a pygmy.

Cauchemar launched himself upwards by means of his leg pistons. He struck a blow to the *Duc En Fer*'s midriff, staggering the iron giant, then fell back to earth.

De Villegrand retaliated with a side-swipe kick that sent Cauchemar flying.

Cauchemar rolled, recovered and went for the *Duc En Fer*'s foot. He grabbed it in a bear hug and strained. He was trying to lift the entire leg in order to throw de Villegrand's creation over.

An immense arm shot down from above, a clenched fist striking Cauchemar on the head with a resounding *clang*. Cauchemar crumpled. Another blow flattened him all the way to the ground. A third came down, but the supine Cauchemar caught the fist with both hands and resisted. De Villegrand applied greater pressure. Cauchemar fought back, his micro-furnace roaring.

"Watson, we must find some way of helping him," Holmes said.

"I agree, but how? In case you've failed to notice, both of them are piloting powerful machines. You and I are not. Even my revolver won't make a jot of difference."

"I am not prepared to stand idly by and let Cauchemar face de Villegrand alone. There is surely something round here we can use."

I looked about. Nothing but bare farmland in all directions.

"It's hopeless," I said.

"It's never hopeless. This way!"

Holmes set off in the direction of the barn. I followed.

The barn doors were secured by a loose length of chain which had enough slack in it that Holmes was able to prise them apart and create a gap we could squeeze through. The interior was musty and dark. I found and lit a lantern, and as our eyes adapted to its dimly flickering glow, Holmes let out a grunt of satisfaction.

"See, Watson? All is not lost."

Before us lay a traction engine. It was rusty and mud-spattered, bearing all the hallmarks of heavy agricultural usage, but appeared to be in good working order. Its farmer owner would haul heavy wagonloads with it and set it up in fields with various attachments for threshing and sawing.

"No time to waste," said Holmes. "Let us get it started."

He alighted on the driver's platform and opened up the firebox door.

"All laid with dry tinder and coal, just as I thought. It is harvest season, so the farmer needs the engine ready to go at a moment's notice. Now, where are my matches?"

Outside, the clash between Cauchemar and de Villegrand continued, an earth-shaking ruckus. Inside, Holmes and I worked furiously to stoke a fire in the traction engine. Soon, water was boiling, a head of steam building, and Holmes set to familiarising himself with the controls.

"Should be straightforward enough," he murmured. "If a horny-handed son of the soil can drive one of these things, I surely can. That lever looks to be the throttle. That must be the clutch, yes. The steering wheel steers, obviously. Pressure gauge, steam regulating valve, handbrake, gear selector…"

The barn wall erupted inwards. Cauchemar hurtled through with a snap and crunch of planks, crashing into an empty stable below the hayloft. He picked himself up, shrugging flinders of wood from his shoulders.

"I need to bring it down," he said. "Once it's down, there is a weak spot, I know it. Out of my reach unless…"

It was hard to tell whether he was talking to us or himself.

"We will help!" Holmes cried. "Just buy us a little more time."

Cauchemar gave no sign of having heard. Head lowered like a bull's, he charged back outside to resume the fight.

Now the traction engine was thrumming with power. I joined Holmes on the driver's platform as he intrepidly engaged the clutch. A large flywheel began to spin and the traction engine gave a lurch. Holmes applied the throttle and the vehicle eased forward, its chunky wheels churning the earthen floor.

Holmes nosed the traction engine towards the doors.

"We can't afford to be graceful about this," he said, increasing speed.

The doors bowed outwards. The chain snapped. The doors

burst apart. The traction engine trundled through.

Cauchemar was again assaulting the *Duc En Fer*'s legs, at the same time darting around trying to avoid those two huge swinging fists. His armour was in bad shape. One arm hung limp. Whether it was Fred Tilling's arm that was broken or the armour's, I could not tell. Either way, the limb was out of action. The rest of his metal shell was a mass of fractures and concavities, as cratered as the moon. He battled on regardless.

Holmes guided the traction engine out onto the field, shifting up through the gears. A slight downward gradient added to our rate of acceleration. He was steering us on course for a head-on collision with the *Duc En Fer*.

"When I say 'jump', Watson…"

"Have no fear, Holmes, I am more than ready."

De Villegrand, up in his lofty perch, did not see us coming. He was too preoccupied with Cauchemar.

The traction engine rolled closer, wheels furrowing the turf. The roar of its boiler was tremendous. The driver's platform was vibrating so hard beneath my feet, I had to cling to its framework to stay put.

"Jump now, Holmes?"

"Nearly. Nearly."

"How about now?"

"We can't afford to miss. There'll be no second chance."

"Now?"

"A moment more."

The *Duc En Fer*'s left leg loomed immediately before us.

"Now!" said Holmes, and we both leapt off.

The traction engine was going flat out, which meant about as fast as a man can run. It rammed the leg with all of its considerable mass behind it.

The *Duc En Fer* staggered.

The traction engine's boiler burst on impact. Metal shards flew like shrapnel.

The *Duc En Fer* teetered.

Cauchemar came in from the side, rugby-tackling the other leg, applying a counter force.

The *Duc En Fer* began to topple.

Holmes and I scrambled out of the way as the manmade titan descended like a redwood felled by the lumberjack's axe.

The *Duc En Fer* slammed to earth.

Cauchemar sprang on top of it, raised a gauntleted fist, and drove it hard into the behemoth's chest.

Its furnace.

Its heart.

The weak spot he had spoken of.

There was a sound, an explosion so enormous, so all-consuming, it overloaded my every sense. The world went bright, then dark.

CHAPTER FORTY-TWO

THE VARNISHED TRUTH

For a time afterwards I could only lie still on the cold, clean ground, face pressed to the grass, and wonder that I was not dead.

When I finally managed to raise my head, I blinked dirt out of my eyes and stared at what was left of de Villegrand's machine.

It wasn't much, just a skeleton of burning, tormented metal sprawled on a quarter-acre of charred turf. Dark smoke poured up from it into the twilight sky, thinning and dispersing into the atmosphere.

Holmes, beside me, sat with his elbows on his knees, surveying the carnage. His aquiline profile was limned by the blaze, his eyes reflecting the leap and flicker of the flames.

"De Villegrand?" I said.

My friend shook his head. He gestured to a blackened corpse lying half in, half out of what was left of the cab. Enough of its face remained uncharred for it to be clearly identifiable as the vicomte's.

I scanned around. "And Cauchemar?"

"I do not see him," Holmes said, squinting.

"Do you think he…?" I said bleakly.

"It is possible he did not survive. Equally, he may be fine. His armour…"

We heard voices nearby, a clamour of alarm and curiosity. Locals, roused by the explosion, were making their way across the fields towards us.

"So what do we tell everyone?" I asked.

"The truth," Holmes replied. "Varnished. With certain careful omissions. A terrorist conspiracy has been foiled. The royal family is unhurt."

"Nothing about Cauchemar?"

"Assuming he is alive, he has fled the scene, and if he has done that, it is not without reason. He wishes to remain anonymous, to retain from others the secrets he has shared with us. We should respect that. He has gained recompense for the wrongs inflicted on him by the vicomte. Delphine Pelletier has been avenged. De Villegrand may not have had to suffer the shame and opprobrium he was due, but we can make sure that, posthumously, he gets everything he deserves."

Holmes rose and helped me to my feet. We dusted ourselves down and smartened ourselves up as best we could. Dim figures moved in the gloaming.

A man called out in a thick rustic burr, "Hoy there, what be all this malarkey then? Train crash?"

Holmes flashed a sly grin at me. "Smile, Watson. Wits about you. Bring your novelist's skill to bear. We have some highly selective explaining to do."

CHAPTER FORTY-THREE

A Departure

Two days later, I called at Baker Street, where I found Holmes snug in his armchair with the *Times* open in front of him.

"Ah, Watson, here you are! I take it you've already seen this?" He brandished the newspaper.

The front-page headline said it all:

TERRORIST PLOT AGAINST ROYALS THWARTED

Mastermind Named – Queen Safe – A Nation Breathes Again – Prime Minister Composes Official Letter of Complaint to French Ambassador

"I have read it," I said. "No mention of Cauchemar, of course. Nor," I added, "of us."

"Yes," said my friend. "I decided that Special Branch should take the credit for the victory, rather than you and me."

"Not that I mind, but any particular reason why?"

"First of all, it helps restore people's faith in the forces of law and order, which after recent events is sorely needed. Mycroft concurs, and Melville, of course, is only too happy for his department to be covered in glory, even though his men did nothing. Secondly, I would prefer it if certain elements in France were unaware of my involvement."

"Certain elements? You're referring to the Hériteurs de Chauvin."

"Indeed. You saw, I presume, the packed valise in the hallway."

"I did. You are going on a trip?"

"Nothing gets past you, eh, Watson?" said Holmes. "Yes, I am proposing to take an impromptu holiday on the Continent. My first destination is Paris, and from there, who knows? France is a large country, with much natural beauty to recommend it, not to mention fine food and wine. I know of a pleasant auberge in the Dordogne region where I stayed during my travels after graduating. It would be nice to go back there, revisit old haunts. Perhaps I shall venture even further south."

"Should I –?"

He held up a hand, forestalling my question.

"No. Don't offer to accompany me. It is generous of you, and no less than I would expect, but I do not know how long I am going to be away, and your patients need you and, more importantly, so does Mrs Watson. Your obligation to her as a husband, especially in her convalescence, outweighs your obligation to me. Besides, I travel lighter and faster alone."

"Very well," I conceded reluctantly. "But please take care. To judge by Cauchemar's experiences, the Hériteurs are a dangerous bunch, the more so because they are well connected."

"I have the full backing of the French embassy. Ambassador Waddington is most embarrassed by de Villegrand's devilry. A home-grown terrorist, right under his nose! He is also most grateful that you and I averted disaster, so that he is now dealing with an uncomfortable diplomatic incident rather than a full-blown crisis or worse. I am going to France with his and his government's blessing. His Excellency has urged me to use all my powers to 'root out the evil lurking in my nation's bosom', and I have assured him I will."

"I am confident you will, too."

"Thank you. By the way, you may like to know that Aurélie has been released without charge and without a stain on her reputation, as per my recommendation to Lestrade. At least one victim of de Villegrand has emerged more or less unscathed."

"Poor girl. Bereft of her brother, how will she live?"

"Waddington has found her a placement in his own household. His wife has promised to care for her as though she were their own daughter. Aurélie, given her mental condition, will find life difficult on her own, but I am optimistic for her. She will cope."

"Let's hope so."

"I have also vouchsafed to Lestrade that de Villegrand was the slayer of the Abbess, and he has accepted my rationalisation for it. Baron Cauchemar is in the clear for that crime. Speaking of whom, the police, sifting through the wreckage of the *Duc En Fer*, discovered only the three bodies – de Villegrand's and those of Torrance's two cronies."

"So will we be hearing from the Bloody Black Baron again, do you think?"

"Who can say? With his nemesis gone, so is much of his *raison d'être*. Then again, the East End – all of London, for that matter – is still riddled with criminals and crime. I wouldn't be sad to know that Cauchemar is out there, patrolling. I, for one, would sleep slightly easier at night."

"Well then." I extended a hand. "I shan't be seeing you for a while, so – best of British."

We shook hands warmly, and I left the house, wondering

when next Holmes and I would be called to action.

The memory of our recent hair's-breadth escapes and close brushes with death was still fresh in my mind. I bore a fair assortment of cuts, scrapes and bruises. I ought to have been dreaming of quiet nights in, a warm fireside, a well-upholstered chair, a good book, a glass of wine, the company of Mary, all the comforts of home and hearth. I should not have been contemplating how soon it would be before I sallied forth again into the cold, cruel world at Holmes's side to confront evil and risk my neck doing so.

Yet, for all that, I hoped it would not be long.

Afterword

In the opening passages of "The Final Problem" I wrote that Sherlock Holmes was "engaged by the French government upon a matter of supreme importance" in the winter of 1890 and the spring of '91, and that during this period I received from him two notes postmarked Narbonne and Nîmes, updating me on his progress.

What those notes said, in fact, was that Holmes had "denied some would-be heirs of their hoped-for inheritance" and that "a Marquis has learned that a commoner may be the equal, if not the better, of an aristocrat". These cryptic references pertain to his struggles against the Héritcurs de Chauvin, the full nature of which I may reveal in a further memoir, if I am so inclined.

For now, the time has come to set down my pen and add this manuscript to the many others currently being held for safekeeping by Cox & Co. Bank at Charing Cross, to whose vaults I entrust all of my never-to-be-published works.

The story of our involvement with Baron Cauchemar may yet see the light of day, should the executors of my literary estate see fit. I shall stipulate that this can occur only several decades hence, after

I am long gone and so is Fred Tilling. That should spare him, and any offspring and immediate relatives he may have, from reprisals. The criminal fraternity possess long memories, but not that long. Their grudges usually fade once a generation or so has passed.

What will the world be like then, I wonder, in the dawning days of the next century. Will technological marvels of the kind the Vicomte de Villegrand and Fred Tilling purveyed be commonplace? Perhaps civilisation will have altered beyond all recognition, the march of Progress sweeping all before it like a relentless tide. Perhaps the imaginings of writers like Jules Verne and our own Mr Wells will have come true, their wildest prognostications made manifest. Perhaps mankind, aided by science, will have advanced to a blessed state of social perfection.

Or perhaps technology will be the downfall of us all, with war machines becoming ever more prevalent, ever more terrible, ever more destructive of human life. The hostilities in Europe are not long over. There, indeed, was a conflict in which science played a chilling role, turning conflict into mass slaughter, battlefield into abattoir.

Could that "great" war simply have been a foretaste of yet worse to come? And could there, even now, be another de Villegrand waiting in the wings, a brilliant madman dreaming of global conquest, of a world remade in his nation's image?

I cannot say. I do not wish to speculate on the matter.

I am an old man and have no desire to spend my final years fearing for the future. I shall think only of the present and, of course, the past. Yes, the past. Always the past.

J.H.W.

Acknowledgements

This book owes its existence to the hard work and generosity of two people.

George Mann was the middleman who made the introductions and helped get me onto Team Titan. He also gave me the opportunity to have a trial run at a Sherlock Holmes story in his anthology *Encounters of Sherlock Holmes*.

Editor Cath Trechman is the one who decided to take a punt on a Holmes novel from an author better known for his science fiction and untried in the detective mystery genre. She shepherded *The Stuff of Nightmares* from outline to final draft with immense patience, skill and care, offering brilliant solutions to knotty plot problems and making me work harder than I ever have before on a book.

I was eleven when I first started reading about the exploits of Conan Doyle's great hero. It has been my dream, in the thirty-odd years since I fell under the spell of the character and his world, to write a Holmes tale myself. Thanks to the above two people, that dream has been made a reality, and I couldn't be happier or more grateful.

J.M.H.L.

ABOUT THE AUTHOR

James Lovegrove is *The New York Times* best-selling author of *The Age of Odin*, the third novel in his critically acclaimed *Pantheon* military SF series. He was short-listed for the Arthur C. Clarke Award in 1998 for his novel *Days* and for the John W. Campbell Memorial Award in 2004 for his novel *Untied Kingdom*. He also reviews fiction for the *Financial Times*.

SHERLOCK HOLMES

THE BREATH OF GOD
Guy Adams

A body is found crushed to death in the London snow. There are no footprints anywhere near it. It is almost as if the man was killed by the air itself.

Sherlock Holmes and Dr Watson travel to Scotland to meet with the one person they have been told can help: Aleister Crowley. As dark powers encircle them, Holmes's rationalist beliefs begin to be questioned. The unbelievable and unholy are on their trail as they gather a group of the most accomplished occult minds in the country… But will they be enough? As the century draws to a close it seems London is ready to fall and the infernal abyss is growing wide enough to swallow us all.

A brand-new original novel, detailing a thrilling new case for the acclaimed detective Sherlock Holmes.

TITANBOOKS.COM

SHERLOCK HOLMES

THE ARMY OF DR MOREAU
Guy Adams

Dead bodies are found on the streets of London with wounds that can only be explained as the work of ferocious creatures not native to the city.

Sherlock Holmes is visited by his brother, Mycroft, who is only too aware that the bodies are the calling card of Dr Moreau, a vivisectionist who was working for the British government, following in the footsteps of Charles Darwin, before his experiments attracted negative attention and the work was halted. Mycroft believes that Moreau's experiments continue and he charges his brother with tracking the rogue scientist down before matters escalate any further.

A brand-new original novel, detailing a thrilling new case for the acclaimed detective Sherlock Holmes.

TITANBOOKS.COM

PROFESSOR MORIARTY

THE HOUND OF THE D'URBERVILLES
Kim Newman

Imagine the twisted evil twins of Holmes and Watson and you have the dangerous duo of Professor James Moriarty—wily, snake-like, fiercely intelligent, terrifyingly unpredictable—and Colonel Sebastian "Basher" Moran—violent, politically incorrect, debauched. Together they run London crime, owning police and criminals alike. When a certain Irene Adler turns up on their doorstep with a proposition, neither man is able to resist.

"Compulsory reading… glorious." Neil Gaiman

"Newman's prose is a delight." *Time Out*

"A *tour de force* which succeeds brilliantly." *The Times*

TITANBOOKS.COM

ANNO DRACULA

Kim Newman

It is 1888 and Queen Victoria has remarried, taking as her new consort Vlad Tepes, the Wallachian Prince infamously known as Count Dracula. His polluted bloodline spreads through London as its citizens increasingly choose to become vampires.
In the grim backstreets of Whitechapel, a killer known as "Silver Knife" is cutting down vampire girls. The eternally young vampire Geneviève Dieudonné and Charles Beauregard of the Diogenes Club are drawn together as they both hunt the sadistic killer, bringing them ever closer to Britain's most bloodthirsty ruler yet.

"*Anno Dracula* is the definitive account of that post-modern species, the self-obsessed undead." *The New York Times*

"*Anno Dracula* will leave you breathless... one of the most creative novels of the year." *Seattle Times*

"Powerful... compelling entertainment... a fiendishly clever banquet of dark treats." *San Francisco Chronicle*

TITANBOOKS.COM

ANNO DRACULA

THE BLOODY RED BARON
Kim Newman

It is 1918 and Dracula is commander-in-chief of the armies of Germany and Austria-Hungary. The war of the great powers in Europe is also a war between the living and the dead.
As ever the Diogenes Club is at the heart of British Intelligence and Charles Beauregard and his protégé Edwin Winthrop go head-to-head with the lethal vampire flying machine that is the Bloody Red Baron…

"…stunning follow-up to his inventive alternate-world fantasy, *Anno Dracula*." *Publishers Weekly*

"Gripping… superbly researched… Newman's rich novel rises above genre… A superior sequel to *Anno Dracula*, itself a benchmark for vampire fiction." *Kirkus Reviews*

"A delicious mixture of wild invention, scholarship, lateral thinking and sly jokes… Unmissable." *Guardian*

TITANBOOKS.COM

ANNO DRACULA

DRACULA CHA CHA CHA
Kim Newman

Rome 1959 and Count Dracula is about to marry the Moldavian Princess Asa Vajda. Journalist Kate Reed flies into the city to visit the ailing Charles Beauregard and his vampire companion Geneviève. She finds herself caught up in the mystery of the Crimson Executioner who is bloodily dispatching vampire elders in the city. She is on his trail, as is the un-dead British secret agent Bond.

"He writes with sparkling verve and peppers the text with cinematic and literary references. *Dracula Cha Cha Cha* has full rations of gore, shocks and sly laughs." *The Times*

"Newman's latest monster mash is the third in a series of fiendishly clever novels… this novel is a rich and fulfilling confection." *Publishers Weekly*

TITANBOOKS.COM